DEATH AT THE SPRING PLANT SALE

Books by Ann Ripley

HARVEST OF MURDER

THE CHRISTMAS GARDEN AFFAIR

DEATH AT THE SPRING PLANT SALE

Published by Kensington Publishing Corporation

A GARDENING MYSTERY

DEATH AT THE SPRING PLANT SALE

ANN RIPLEY

KENSINGTON BOOKS
http://www.kensingtonbooks.com

KENSINGTON BOOKS are published by

Kensington Publishing Corp.
850 Third Avenue
New York, NY 10022

Library of Congress Card Catalogue Number: 2003103721
ISBN 1-57566-779-7

First Printing: October 2003
10   9   8   7   6   5   4   3   2   1

Printed in the United States of America

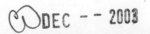
DEC - - 2003

To Tony

ACKNOWLEDGMENTS

Three old friends from Bethesda, Betty Bartky, Irene Sinclair, and Jessie Lew Mahoney, provided great help and encouragement with this story, which is laid in their Bethesda backyard. Detective Michael Turner of the Major Crimes Division of the Montgomery County (Maryland) Police and Sergeant Dan Barber of the Boulder County (Colorado) Sheriff's Department gave me expert advice on guns and police procedures. Kirsten Renehan did the sketches of the funeral bouquet. Pat Schimminger and horticulturalist Gwynne Owens were additional sources of useful information. Karen Gilleland, Margaret Coel, Sybil Downing, and Bev Carrigan reviewed the manuscript. I appreciate their suggestions. Additional thanks to my editor at Kensington Publishing, John Scognamiglio.

1

December

Sophie Chalois stared at the ominous, snowy world outside her window and decided it was time to pop a little yellow pill in her mouth. Then the doorbell rang. She pulled in a breath, regretting this intrusion into her sacred bubble of privacy. She'd expected to swallow the oxycodone and sink onto the bed and sleep without the nuisance of dreams. Instead, she'd have to continue to deal with life and people, whatever life and people lurked outside her front door.

She pulled aside the drawn bedroom drapes, looked down into her very private front entrance, and saw the unmistakable knot of auburn hair. Meg Durrance. She doubted Meg would be as good as a twenty-milligram pill, but knew her friend would continue to ring until Sophie answered. Meg would even peek in her garage, if necessary, to see if Sophie's BMW was there, and seeing that it was, wouldn't give up.

Sophie went into her dressing room and ran a brush through her hair, renewed her rust-colored lip blush, then ran down the stairs before the chiming doorbell drove her mad.

By the time she'd reached the last stair she'd convinced herself that it would be good to see Meg; never did she feel so alone in her flawless house as when the weather was changing. Usually, Lini, her domestic, was there to keep her company. Even when Sophie was blacked out in sleep, she liked Lini's daytime company. But the woman had pleaded mercy when the sky turned black at two, and Sophie had let her go home.

Snowstorms made her feel the worst. In Washington, D.C., snow was strange and unwelcome, out of place in the scheme of things. The snowflakes themselves were alien, big and wet, and clung like leeches. The storm had rushed in and enclosed her, turning her home into a prison. Here she was, beautiful and blond, still sensuous and strong at fifty-five. Yet she felt like an aged Rapunzel, fated to live alone in her castle. Sometimes visited by a phantom lover, that was true, but in daylight relegated to the role of woman abandoned.

In Sophie's small circle of friends, Meg was the closest—and also the crudest. But since she had to be awake, any company was better than none. By the time she reached her massive front door, she was full of anticipation. She unlocked and opened it and smiled at the big woman in the doorway.

Meg cried, "Quick, quick, let me in. In a minute I'll be a snowman. I'm chilled to the bone just walking from the car! And my hair is a mess. . . ."

Sophie helped Meg off with her wet coat, above which her magnificent hair had strayed from its bun and was cascading around her shoulders. With a quick movement, Meg twisted it up and pinned it in place.

"What a horrible day," said Sophie. "I'm so glad you came. I was about to give up on it and take a nap."

Meg gave her a knowing look. "You and your naps. And I suppose you let Lini go home: good thing I came over. So show your gratitude by pouring me a big drink." She plopped onto the brocade couch.

"Wonderful idea," said Sophie, glancing out the front

windows, where the unwelcome storm pelted as if in a demand to come in. "A drink is just the thing." She went over to the sound system and pressed a button, and Bacharach's music filled the air. She poured them both a Chivas, adding water to hers and soda to Meg's.

"Now, can I smoke in here today—or is your usual ban on?"

"Because it's such a foul day, I'll let you, Meg. And tuck that wool throw about your knees. You're shivering like an aspen leaf." Meg complied by pulling a mauve mohair throw around her legs.

"So," said Sophie, "I guess there's no bridge game today." Like Sophie, Meg had no family nearby, and lived in a big house alone. But unlike Sophie, Meg played bridge with several groups, and this soaked up lots of her free time.

Meg lit up and said, in her overly loud voice, "Nothing today. No bridge games. No lectures." Her eyes were serious when she asked, "And how about you? I worry about you sometimes, Sophie. You don't do enough. You're almost sixty—"

Sophie bent her curly blond head and stared in mock dismay at her friend. What kind of a head trip was she trying to do on her? "Not *that* old, dear. Try 'a little over fifty.' "

"Hey, I'm not putting you down, Sophie. You look great—kind of like Meg Ryan—in that hairdo of yours. And whatever age you are, exactly, I don't know, but you look forty. You're talented—you could do anything if you were in business. *You* have a mind like a steel trap, and you do numbers as well as an accountant. Unlike me. Remember that boutique I wanted to open in friendly downtown Bethesda? Well, I was too chicken to go ahead with it. But *you*, with your brains—"

"What is this, a reality show? You didn't come over to ask me fundamental questions like, *Where is your life go-*

ing—or did you?" She took a swallow of whisky. "Or did you?"

Meg shrugged her wide shoulders and said, "I didn't come over for that reason—but when I find you so down in the mouth, I have to say something." She cast a big-eyed gaze at her companion and said, "I could almost believe you were on drugs."

Sophie made a graceful gesture with her free hand. "Let me bum one of those cigarettes. I need one today." As Meg leaned forward to give her a light, Sophie said, "I'm only taking what everyone else is taking, my dear—a few pills." She drew in deeply and exhaled. "Really, I'm fine. You needn't worry about me." Inside Sophie, resentment rose, and she knew just how to get back at this woman for her presumption. "What you *should* worry about is what happens in this year's flower-arranging contest. Because I intend to get in there and try to beat the pants off you, Meg, darling."

Her friend grimaced, but it turned out it was all in play. Meg's response was far different from what Sophie expected. "Go ahead, make my day, Sophie. I'd a hundred times rather lose to you than *you know who.*"

You know who was the Mighty One, Catherine Freeman, the pompous president of the garden club to which they both belonged. Meg had jokingly invented the name the "Mighty One" because of Catherine's power and longevity as head of the club.

The matter of Catherine and her power and success stuck in Meg's craw, and for a reason. Meg Durrance had regularly come in second to Catherine in flower arranging, until garden club members now joked that she was like Susan Lucci, the TV soap star who, though nominated endless times, had never won an Emmy until a few years ago.

But suddenly Meg went from jokes to tears. The reminder of her constant failure overcame her, and not for the first time. She told Sophie, "You know what I've done: wherever I've traveled, wherever I've gone, I've picked up delightful, odd-shaped bowls with a character like no other—clay creations by crude potters no one's heard of. And twisted pieces of wood, rusty wire, corroded steel, stagnant moss and fungus, seedpods of all sizes and shapes. . . ."

Sophie thought Meg sounded as if she were an archeologist talking about her search for traces of ancient civilization.

Her friend's lament continued: "And I've used these precious objects, plus dried leaves, grasses, berries, big mushrooms, lush grapes, apples, pears mixed with the flowers . . . why, talent *drips* from my fingers." She put down her drink and let her graceful, big hands hang in the air, as if to illustrate this. "But where has it gotten me? I am *always* second to Catherine." Retrieving her drink, she took a big swallow, and Sophie noted with alarm that Meg's brown eyes were flashing with anger. But after a moment, she pulled out of it and managed a little laugh. "Believe me, Sophie, when I say I won't mind competition with you at all."

They settled into a companionable silence for a few minutes, united in their dislike of Catherine Freeman, and made further inroads on their drinks. Meanwhile, the storm outside grew heavier, but the whisky and the Bacharach helped them not to notice.

"I'm remembering ten years ago," said Meg. "That's when I moved from Chicago to Bethesda and first met you."

Sophie tried to laugh, but it came out as a small croak from an uncertain frog. Two failed affairs in ten years, followed by a huge loss in self-confidence. The only worse time in Sophie's life was a decade before that, twenty years ago, when she was thirty-five and living in Princeton, New Jersey, and in the prime of her golden-haired beauty. A literature professor's wife, in an elite college environment, but living with a private sorrow: the fact that she couldn't bear children. She'd discovered her professor husband cheating on her with his mousy little assistant—in *their* home, in *their* bed. Her face grew crimson as she remembered what she'd done *then*.

She'd moved away from Princeton and made a new life in the Ledgebrook neighborhood of Bethesda. A few unfortunate mis-tries at romance, but finally, along came the dashing and important Walter Freeman. Walter's star was rising, and he was afraid of nothing, especially a blond divorcée who'd proven she was tied strongly to the community. But Walter didn't last, either. . . .

Sophie's eyes glazed over, as the memories released morbid feelings that she had carefully bottled up. Suddenly, she cried out, "Ow!" as her neglected cigarette burned her fingers. She flipped it into the ashtray and stamped it out, as her friend commiserated. To Meg she said only, "I could hardly forget what happened with Walter."

Meg had to recount her version of events anyway. "You were dating him thick and fast, in public, and in private— I heard about that scuba trip you two took to the Caribbean. I thought for sure you were going to be married—just like I thought after I moved to Bethesda that I'd win that dratted state flower-arranging competition, like I used to when I lived in Winnetka."

Sophie gave Meg a sideways glance. All this talk of Walter made her nervous, for she had a secret: she'd recently let the man back into her bed. She only hoped Meg hadn't learned about it.

"Both of us were, if you'll pardon the expression, *screwed,*" said Sophie. She had meant the words to be casual, but they came out in a snarl. She smoothed things over with a little laugh, a pleasant laugh that floated over the room like a comforting balm. She turned a sincere, blue-eyed gaze on her friend. "I don't mean to be a bitch.

We must deal gracefully with the fact that I *didn't* marry Walter, and you never *have* won the state flower-arranging contest. But your time is coming, Meg. I truly believe you'll win this year."

Meg laughed, a harsh sound. She stretched her arms out, as if this movement would strengthen her for the competition ahead. The flower-arranging contest took few muscles, but lots of creative talent. Then she leaned back on the sofa and fell into her usual pessimistic mode: "I don't know why you think I can win this year when I've never won before."

Sophie sent her a sly glance. "Maybe something can be done about it."

"What, bribe the judges?"

She laughed. "That would be the easiest way, wouldn't it?"

"Did you ever realize," said Meg, "how many lives are ruined by Catherine Freeman?"

"Only too well," said Sophie. "She took Walter away from me with a method as clever as a Mafia boss. It's as if she'd murdered me to get him to be her husband. Those innuendos about me that were floated around town—I know she was responsible for them. The way she constantly showed off her Fortnum family wealth. Hell, *that* much was true: she's always been a lot richer than I am. Walter's sitting pretty. And, frankly, I think he liked the prestige of marrying into the Fortnums."

"That may have been true," said the wise Meg, "but it's too bad that we can't turn the clock back on that romance. Because you and I both know that the choice he made ten years ago was the wrong one."

Damn, thought Sophie. She wished her friend hadn't put her very thoughts in words. She turned to her drink and took several quick swallows. "But he chose her, and that's that."

Meg drawled, "Honey, we both know that *isn't* that. I was not born yesterday—I know you have a thing going with Walter."

Sophie's hand that supported her drink froze in midair. "How would you know that?"

Meg's glance wheeled over to Sophie. Mercifully, there was no scorn in her eyes, only a kind of patient acceptance. "Suppose I'm up and prowling about the neighborhood in my Caddy one night, and I happen to see him sneak in here."

Sophie straightened up a little. Quietly she said, "Keep it to yourself, will you?"

Meg shrugged. "What are friends for? Of course I will. But let me tell you, honey, adultery's one thing Catherine Freeman would never stand for, if she knew. Once a frozen Presbyterian, always a frozen Presbyterian. Why, Walter'd be out on his ear, living in a downtown bachelor pad."

"It was just a one-time—"

"Yeah, yeah," scoffed Meg. "Don't worry: I'm all sympathy. I say, *go,* girl!"

Sophie chuckled, not sure the chuckles wouldn't turn into sobs. "All I can say, Meg, is that it's a shame that genteel women like us can't do anything to control events."

Meg uncharacteristically giggled. "Not when we're being rolled over by a *blunderbuss.*" Sophie saw that the Scotch was getting through to Meg. "Is that what I mean? What in hell is a blunderbuss?"

Sophie gracefully shrugged, her humor somehow restored by hearing her friend innocently slaughter the language. She guessed the Scotch was getting to her, as well. "You don't mean that, because a blunderbuss was a weapon that Scots used to hit other Scots over the head with. What you mean is a *juggernaut.* Juggernauts were giant ships that—"

Meg waved away her words, as if she were waving away a gnat. "Never mind impressing me with your book knowledge, Sophie. You're talking to a woman who only went one year to a community college. So are we just going to sit here and bitch as usual, or are we going to *do* something, to at least slow the progress of the juggernaut?"

Sophie leaned forward in her chair, her blue eyes looking intently into those of her friend. "Would you really help me?"

"Help *us,*" amended Meg, pointing a finger at her own chest. "Remember me? I'm the one who loses all those contests. You're the one who had the guy stolen right from under your nose, and who now warehouses him in the wee hours of the morning. So the answer's yes, I'd help you. The question is, what could we do?"

Sophie had a dreamy look in her eye. "What could we do . . . and when would be the best time to do it?"

"You want to hit her when she's—"

"When she's experiencing one of those moments of queenly success that she loves so much."

"But c'mon, Sophie, we're just kidding ourselves. Two gals like us are in no position to stop Catherine."

Sophie reached forward for the Scotch bottle, and replenished their glasses. "Don't be discouraged so easily. Maybe two gals like us can think of something."

2

Walter Freeman was having a brandy at his club with a few movers and shakers, some of them locals, some national figures. It was one of his regularly scheduled "casual" get-togethers with people outside the financial world where he spent so much of his time. A valuable pursuit, this sort of friendly meeting, though as he looked out the leaded-glass windows, he saw it came on a bad day. An aberrant December storm had blown in from the Atlantic and turned Washington, D.C., into a sloppy Winter Wonderland. He trusted it would not make going home this afternoon an impossible task. But worrying would not improve things, so he turned to his companions and relaxed. These meetings kept him in touch with ordinary men's affairs, questions beyond, "Whither goest the Dow?" "Will the Asian market crash redound on the American market?" or the eternally asked one: "Do we need to lower rates?"

There were two groups he especially sought to keep in touch with: law enforcement and academia. Politicians, of course, were no trouble; he could hardly get away from them. They filled many of his hours during the day, got in his face at social events, and called him late at night with wild scenarios: "My God, Walt, don't you know the world will cave in unless the Fed lowers the rate tomorrow?"

His rejoinders were legendary: "The country, in order

to remain strong, needs a ferment of economic activity."
Sometimes he warned that there wasn't a sufficient "ferment," that "underlying trends guiding the future are
marked with uncertainty." After such remarks, the Dow
usually plunged at least half a percentage point. Walter
never flinched, for that was his job. Since the Fed Reserve
chairman was publicly reclusive, Walter had become the
nation's economic oracle—and often its Cassandra.

But as a man he had to have some relief. Here at these
little meetings, he had the opportunity to figuratively, if
not actually, loosen the knot in his tie, kick back, and
relax. His companions almost forgot that Walter Freeman
was the single man in America who was thought capable
of saving the country's future.

The head of the FBI and the director of the CIA had
dropped by, of course, since they were invited. They'd say
little, because they were never that comfortable with each
other, or with these other men who represented such a di-
verse group of professions. *Who in the hell are all these folks?*
they'd think to themselves, being as insular as, for instance,
Foreign Service people abroad hovering with their own but
never really mixing with the natives. But these two top-secu-
rity bosses came, as an homage to Walter. Walter would return the honor, introducing them first, then saying, "And
now, gentlemen, we locals would like to hear about the state
of things in the country, and in the world. . . ."

It was the local fellows he enjoyed most: the chiefs of
police of the District and surrounding jurisdictions, the
local college presidents, a few businessmen. They gave
him a taste of reality. "How do we find things, gentlemen,
in the nation's capital?" Walter had never lost sight of the
fact that you had to know your own home ground before
you could add many sharp insights to what was going on
in the country at large.

The chiefs were engaged in war stories—crimes that be-

fuddled their professional staffs. The Fairfax County chief
was holding forth about something that had happened
over there in northern Virginia. Walter didn't know
Randy Fremont well, but he had heard the veteran officer
had a fine record, especially with homicides. "We were
having a helluva confusing time with the murder of that
old science prof with the fountain-of-youth plant discov-
ery," said Chief Fremont. "There must have been half a
dozen suspects, and we were getting nowhere."

"Didn't some woman step into the situation and nearly
get killed for her trouble?"

"Yep. Without that, I don't think we ever would have
caught the guy."

Walter wasn't listening closely. He was otherwise engaged, the CIA chief leaning over in his chair to confide
some late-breaking international news that quite frankly
didn't sound good at all. Still, it titillated him to hear the
top cops talking shop. Walter, like a lot of other red-
blooded Americans, craved his mystery story, *liked* to hear
about intriguing crime cases.

The District chief, Joe Hathaway, was a big, confident-
looking black man. He sat forward now, opening his large
hands as if disclosing a top secret. "For God's sake, don't
quote me to any woman, but sometimes I think female suspects make the most trouble for us."

Maryland's chief, Philip Van Bouten, nodded his white
head, his blue eyes further signaling approval of Hathaway's remark. "Hear, hear."

"This sure happened in a case that came up nine years
ago," said Hathaway, directing a look at Walter Freeman.
"You may remember it, Walter, because the man involved
was very big in financial circles—a good-looking fellow, to
boot—I'm talking about a *fine catch*. The case was a real
puzzle. He was dating the same woman for a long time.
She moved into his fancy old Cleveland Park mansion

with him and stayed for a dozen years or so. Common-law marriage rules began to apply, of course. Then the man's eye wandered, and he had a fling with a blond mystery woman, some divorcée . . ."

"Oh, I remember that one," said Walter. "It didn't end well."

"No it didn't. Lo and behold, *he* turned up dead one morning, naked in bed, a hole in his forehead. The live-in girlfriend was out of town on a high-powered business trip. She puts her claim in for his estate, which does not, of course, reduce our suspicions of her."

The men laughed.

"Now, his new squeeze stays well off the radar screen, but the story was that she thought she was gonna marry the guy, but he suddenly threw her over and reverted to his old love. This blonde—apparently she used to be married to some high-muckety-muck Princeton prof—didn't have a good alibi, but so what? There was no physical evidence left around. And of course, it was impossible to shake the *first* girlfriend's story, maybe because she'd hired a very efficient hit man. . . ."

Laughter again. When he'd finished his story, Philip Van Bouten spoke up. "I think I can outdo you—and my case involved a female suspect, too. It happened about twenty-five years ago. A couple who resides in Ledgebrook is having marital trouble, and the man wants out of the marriage. Their pastor persuades the man and his wife to get counseling and work toward a reconciliation, since they have a son in common. Since it's duck-hunting season and they both like to hunt, the husband suggests that they go on a sporting trip together to the Eastern shore— for some *duck* hunting!"

Everyone laughed again. District Chief Hathaway said, "Not a good move—or as Walter here might elegantly phrase it, '*Such a drastic shift in movement is not indicated.*' "

Convulsions of laughter, as they recognized Walter's familiar idioms. Someone piped up, "I bet there was a little accident, and he got his head blown off."

All side conversations had ceased, as people listened.

"See," said Van Bouten, "you all were able to figure out what happened in this story. But it has a twist. Yeah, the husband's head is blown open—"

"—during their sporting experience," said the mirthful Hathaway.

"And lo and behold, someone steps up to pin it on the wife. Guess who?"

People murmured, speculating.

"You'll never guess."

"The son?" said Walter.

"Yes. Clever of you to guess."

"It's Shakespearean, to have a child accuse his parent."

Van Bouten laughed. "But a lot of good it did us. This was a teenage kid, maybe sixteen—a sly character. He laid it all out to us, chapter and verse, how his mother planned to blow his father away, because she knew the divorce would leave her a semi-pauper. Divorced women a quarter-century ago didn't make out as well as they do today in a divorce. As we were about to build a case, however, the kid reneged—said he'd manufactured the story because he got mad at his mother over a disagreement on curfew hours. Who the hell knows what's true? There was no evidence of her guilt, so the woman got off, of course. What that tells us is that if you're careful not to leave clues around, you can get away with murder."

"What happened to the kid?"

"He continued to live with his mother. The two of them acted as if the thing had never happened. We decided the kid was just jawboning for parental attention."

Walter's attention drifted. He'd forgotten that story

about the woman who'd "accidentally" blown her husband's head off. It sounded like what had happened to a friend of his wife's. And the account of the mystery divorcée: the woman's name may have been kept out of the papers at the time, but she resembled someone he knew very well.

3

"Thank God," muttered Laura Alice Shea. She couldn't believe her luck, to have run into someone who lived in Bethesda on the night her car broke down—which just happened to be the most miserable night of the winter. This afternoon, a nor'easter had unexpectedly veered south and dumped five inches of snow on Washington, D.C., enough to stop the city in its tracks. When she left her office in the Treasury Building, the Honda wouldn't start, and was now limping its way to a downtown garage. She was sure she'd pay top price for the repairs, but she'd had no other choice. It served her right for not taking the Metro every day. That was why they'd put in the damned system in the first place, so bureaucrats like her would use it instead of polluting the air with their selfish, one-passenger daily drives to and from the suburbs.

To make things worse, she'd dressed for fashion this morning, since she was meeting with a German foreign trade delegation. After all, temperatures yesterday in Washington, D.C., had been in the fifties, with only vague storm warnings. Though her outfit made the impact she expected when they went out to lunch, it hardly seemed worth it now. Cold snow had infiltrated through the sides of her skimpy black St. John three-inch-high leather sling pumps, and damp winds cut through her wide-woven designer wool coat as effortlessly as wind through a screen.

She'd stood there like an ice statue, watching the lights of the tow truck recede after the driver dumped her at the Metro stop. Just as she was about to see if her frozen feet could carry her down the subway stairs, she heard someone yell at her.

"Going north, Laura Alice?"

It was a woman, calling to her out of the half-open window of her Lexus wagon.

She propelled her numbed legs to the curb and bent to see who the driver was. "Reese?" She barely knew the woman, having met her only twice.

"Yes, Reese Janning. Get in."

Laura Alice opened the passenger door and slid into the warm vehicle. Shuddering, she looked over at her companion, gushed her thanks, and then told the sad story of her car troubles. "So, to put it mildly, Reese, I've never been happier to see anyone in my life."

Reese laughed, and this gave her thin face some warmth. It was a long face, with a big, intrusive nose that dominated all the other features. Her hair was caught back in a severe bun. Not one of the most attractive people Laura Alice had ever met, but obviously one with a head on her shoulders. She wore a sensible, puffy down coat with a high, fur collar, and low-heeled shoes, though even she'd been caught off guard by the weather and hadn't worn boots.

Reese was a very important person in the Capitol, because of the man for whom she worked. Every time Laura Alice had seen her in action, the woman had resembled one of those indispensable Washington aides who gave the illusion of being a work machine, not a human. "Wait," said Laura Alice, "didn't I see you today at Correlli's?"

"You did," said Reese. "I was with the chief"—the "chief" was Walter Freeman, the very important man for whom Reese was administrative assistant—"and a couple of the bosses: that's what I call members of Congress. If they're committee heads, I refer to them as the *godfathers.*"

Laura Alice laughed; she hadn't known this woman had a sense of humor. "I don't eat out that much myself. Usually I catch a salad in the cafeteria. But today was special: I entertained a foreign contingent. That's why I'm dressed so inadequately."

Reese smiled. "*Love* your shoes—they're *fabulous.* But not a wise selection for a day like today, are they?"

"No," said Laura Alice, "they surely aren't." It was a mild reply. Laura Alice had no idea whether or not this woman was as smug as she sounded; she'd met her once in the line of her work, and car-pooled home to Bethesda with her another time. Smug or not, Laura Alice didn't care tonight: it was thoughtful for the woman to pick her up when she could have whizzed right by in her big wagon. "So, do you still live in the condo near Bradley Boulevard?"

With another big smile, Reese said, "Yes, but I'm moving. I've bought a place."

"Wow, that's great."

"And let me tell you, I can't wait. Not to disparage Bethesda: I know you and your husband have a house there. But this will make life so much easier for me. I've signed a contract on a condo on the edge of Georgetown."

"All *right,*" said Laura Alice. "How'd you find it?"

"Oh, *I* didn't find it: I have a dynamite Realtor: she's done it all. She's handling all the details, and doing a fantastic job."

"I can believe it. I suppose you wouldn't have a lot of spare time for house hunting." As she was talking, it was all sinking in. This young woman was doing very well for herself. Reese couldn't be more than thirty-five, if that, and she was upgrading from a rental in Bethesda to her own condo in Georgetown. She owned, or leased, a fifty-thousand-dollar car. And Laura Alice recognized that puffy coat she wore as a fur-lined designer model from a Madison Avenue boutique. Reading *The New York Times* carefully from cover to cover and even the whole Sunday paper kept Laura Alice abreast not only of foreign and domestic affairs, but also of fashion trends and sources, nuances of the gay and straight community, the city's current political position on the homeless, what was hot on Broadway, and why one must buy a ticket to London to see a really happenin' show. She was in no way content to be a parochial Washington bureaucrat who read only the Washington *Post* and thought cogent life stopped at the Beltway.

They were about the same age. But it was one thing to be married, as Laura Alice was, to a professional man making $200,000 a year, with her salary bringing their combined income to almost $300,000. That made it possible to buy a nice house in Bethesda. But Reese probably didn't make that much more than Laura Alice, and an $80,000 or $90,000 federal salary didn't swing a big mortgage.

"So, exactly where is the place you're buying? I know Georgetown pretty well."

"Mmm," said Reese, "I don't like people to know that." She shot a quick glance at Laura Alice. "Sorry, but I'm a pretty private person."

"No problem," said Laura Alice. "I can see why you'd want to be careful." The constant terrorist scares had created ripples even down to administrative aides, she realized. As for Laura Alice, she lived on a street in the Battery Lane subdivision that fed into Wilson Lane, a sedate road controlled by a million speed signs that nevertheless was a state highway. Where she lived was open and known by one and all, and she didn't think twice about security. Maybe that was because she was pregnant, and she sensed there was still goodness in the world, and that she and her husband Jim and her baby were protected by it.

She smiled when she thought of Jim, with his bluff, Irish face and disheveled sandy hair. He was a stubbornly optimistic man: no personal or world troubles could shake his good spirits. It was why she'd married him in the first place, hoping to counterbalance her own acerbic outlook on life.

Reese Janning had finished talking about her condo purchase. Now she turned to Laura Alice and said, "But I mustn't just talk about myself. How are you? Of course, I envy you, you know. You're married. You're settled. You probably have children."

Laura Alice shook her head. "No, I don't have children. But I—"

"Well, you can always *have* a child," interrupted Reese. "Life is quite different for me." She turned another big smile on Laura Alice. "I live on the edge. The single woman in Washington."

"And a very successful one."

"Oh, yes," she agreed, and went on to talk about some of the business trips she'd been able to make with her boss, and the exciting things that were coming up in monetary policy. Laura Alice and Reese both worked in finance, so finding topics of conversation was no problem at all.

As they came into Bethesda by way of Little Falls Parkway, Laura Alice hadn't had a chance to talk about herself—about how well her husband was doing in his architectural work, about how they spent their evenings doodling out rough sketches for a "child" addition to their house, about how she was pregnant just past the stage where food smells in the morning made her sick to her stomach. . . .

No, she'd had no chance to reveal these things. Just as well. At the moment, anyway, Reese Janning was totally focused on herself. And then she found out why.

"Uh, this is very hush-hush," said Reese, "but I know you can keep your mouth shut. There have been some threats against Walter Freeman. Are you surprised?"

Walter Freeman was head of the President's Special Task Force on Monetary Reform, and with the economy so shaky, and corporate corruption dismaying investors, reform was the big deal in Washington: it was right up there at the top along with the fight against terrorism.

Laura Alice would guess that Freeman was about a "nine" in importance around Washington, on a scale from one to ten: just short of that elite group that was chauffeured in limos around town. "No, I guess I'm not surprised, not with the way things are these days."

Reese gave Laura Alice a long look. "I do work for him at home. Maybe somebody knows about that, maybe they don't. But that's one of the reasons I'm buying into a place with a doorman. With my family's help, of course. . . ."

Laura Alice mentally kicked herself: *Janning*. Probably Reese was of the millionaire Janning family. If she were, there would be no mystery as to why the gal had a fifty-thousand-dollar car and a Georgetown condo.

"So that's why I'm moving," Reese continued, "because it's not necessarily that safe for me in Bethesda. Unfortunately, Walter Freeman has deep roots there, with his house in Ledgebrook. It's different for him. He'll just have to depend on his neighborhood security guards."

4

Louise Eldridge pushed on the shovel with a heroic effort and gathered up a big scoopful of snow that was as thick as the sugary sludge in a snow cone. Whimsically, she reflected that trying to get rid of this mess from her driveway was going to kill her.

She dumped the shovelful on the edge of the driveway, then quickly straightened. Her little inner joke suddenly was no joke, for her chest had tightened as if someone had encased it in iron. It couldn't be, could it, that at forty-five she was having a heart attack?

She bent over like an old man, but the pain didn't subside. Her heart was beating at double its normal speed. She didn't need more clues as to when to stop this foolish pursuit. Why hadn't her husband, Bill, or her strong seventeen-year-old daughter, Janie, been around to help shovel on the snowiest evening of the year? She walked like a cripple up the path to her front door, and leaning the shovel against the side of the house, went inside. She kicked off her boots, threw her wet coat and gloves onto the flagstone front-hall floor, and stumbled in and collapsed onto the living room couch.

Feeling like a beached whale, she lay and tried to relax. After a few minutes of furious thumping, her heart quieted down and the pain disappeared. She slowly exhaled.

The old forty-five-year-old body was all right after all. Yet, she reflected, her heart might need checking. In the past few months, every time she had exerted herself—or scared herself to death in some fashion—she ended up with rapid heartbeats. Louise hadn't been to a doctor in two years: maybe it was time.

Her telephone rang. Fortunately, it was on the table next to the couch within easy reach. To her surprise, it was a friend in Bethesda, Emily Holley. She hadn't heard from Emily in months. Bethesda wasn't that far—thirty or so miles north, as traveled around the Beltway from Louise's house in Sylvan Valley, which was four miles south of Alexandria, Virginia. Bethesda was one of Washington's oldest, most prestigious suburbs, while Louise's was a Johnny-come-lately neighborhood, developed only a scant fifty years ago by a dreamy, liberal architect who had aggravated many staid people with his futuristic house designs. Louise's busy existence, balancing a career in public television with home and family life, made it difficult to stay in contact with her Bethesda friends. Emily and Louise had been classmates in graduate school at Georgetown University. It seemed like a century ago, and they'd lost the closeness of those special college days.

Emily had always been, and still was, the soul of politeness. "Louise, I hope I haven't intruded on your dinner hour."

Louise looked at her watch. Six-thirty, with her family gone, and not a sign of dinner in the house. "Don't worry, Emily. Tonight it's going to be a ham-and-cheese sandwich. Bill and Janie are both out for the evening."

She could tell from the tone of Emily's voice that this was not a dinner invitation: she was going to ask a favor of her. Emily began, "As you know, I'm a member of the Old Georgetown Garden Club . . ."

Louise, hostess of a PBS Saturday morning garden show, *Gardening with Nature,* jumped immediately to the correct conclusion: her friend wanted her to do a program on her garden club.

As Emily went on to describe the venerable old club and its cozy history, Louise's mind wandered to what her producer would say. Despite the good things Louise knew about garden clubs, she also knew about TV ratings. She could practically hear the acerbic Marty Corbin now, arguing that a garden-club feature shouldn't take up a precious slot on the schedule. "Be real, Lou," he'd say, "who wants to watch an entire hour on America's garden clubs?"

With all the hype that had crept into new TV gardening shows, even Louise wondered if people wouldn't think of those biddies in flowery hats Helen Hokinson used to draw for *The New Yorker.* She and Marty had been burned once before, losing ratings to another TV garden program with more pizzazz than hers. They always had to be concerned about avoiding topics that would have viewers flipping the channel. And now new "reality" garden shows were popping up with jazzy formats such as the one that involved instant makeovers of home gardens, performed in real time over two days and completed on the garden show in half an hour. Compared to that exciting format, a show on garden clubs sounded—*lifeless.*

"Umm, it's an interesting idea, Emily," she told her friend. "Let me pass it by my producer: he's the final arbiter. But I have to warn you . . ." She told her friend of the tremendous pressures of filling only twenty program slots in a season.

"Otherwise," she quickly added, "how are you? And how is Alex?"

Emily had always seemed to Louise a bit of a lonesome polecat, there in her splendid colonial house in Bethesda. Her husband, Alex, a patrician New Englander, so aloof that Louise had never felt close to him in the more than twenty years she'd known him, worked nights a lot as a high-level government official, doing something so secret she wondered if he didn't work, just as her husband did, undercover for the CIA. Bill used the State Department as *his* cover, and Alex, as Louise recalled, was in Commerce, but had moved to State. There were lots of differences between the two men. Bill was an amiable sort—a remarkably normal marriage partner, Louise thought, for a CIA undercover man. Alex was distant and difficult, into his own world, and away from home a lot. Emily seemed always to be pulled along by her spouse like the cart behind the horse. Her diminutive stature and genteel nature only accented this impression that she was more like an appendage than a player in the marriage.

"Oh, we're both just fine," said Emily, in that mannerly voice. "Uh, once in a while, I'm not so hot—you know, my condition. Sometimes I get depressed. But Alex says I'm doing pretty well, so it must be true."

Alex says—so it must be true? Louise wondered if her friend was slipping a bit into an invalid frame of mind, into being a person who was just too dependent on her husband-caregiver. Louise hadn't known rheumatoid arthritis was that debilitating.

"And you, Louise—how are you and the family?" A light little laugh. "Any crime fighting these days?"

"Not lately," said Louise, thinking that nonetheless it hadn't been too long ago that she'd been involved in a double-murder investigation. "The only thing new with me is total exhaustion, Emily. I just tried to shovel the driveway apron and it darned near killed me."

"Oh, my dear," said Emily, as if Louise were out of her mind, "that's a job best left for your husband or a service. But now, I'm excited that you'll take my idea up with your producer. Louise, people *need* to know more about garden clubs, and that they're not just a bunch of ditzy females in flowery hats."

Louise blushed at her end of the telephone. How could her friend have read her mind so accurately?

5

May

While Louise readied herself for the trip to Bethesda the next day, Bill and Janie packed for their week-long trip to East Coast colleges.

Feeling like a hall monitor in a college dorm, Louise traveled from her and Bill's bedroom to Janie's bedroom to check on the packing process. Gently ruffling through the clothes the girl had packed, Louise stood with one hand on a hip and said, "Don't forget to put in a little black dress. Remember where you're going: New Yorkers adore black."

"Ma," moaned her blond daughter, "don't you think I have any fashion sense at all?" Janie looked quite spectacular, tiny braids festooning her long hair, her simple jeans and shirt outfit transformed by her fresh beauty. Louise felt uncomfortable letting Janie out of the house. But at least she'd be with her father on this college-visitation tour.

Feeling she'd put her foot in it again, Louise raised her hands as if in surrender. "Sorry. I apologize. I know you know fashion. But you know you'll be invited to tea somewhere, the theater, upscale restaurants, all that—Okay, I'm going to see if your father is packing the right underwear."

"Very funny, Ma," shot Janie after her.

Bill's small suitcase was as neatly configured as a computer board. Louise went over and leaned against him. "Gone for a week—I'll really miss you two."

Her tall husband twisted around and gave her a hug, and she caressed his blond head. "Likewise, my dear. But do sit down." She sat on the bed next to him and he reached over and took her hands. "Something I want to tell you, before I forget, Louise. It's about Alex Holley. I want to warn you to try to get along with him, especially since you might decide to stay with the Holleys for a day or so."

"*Alex?*" she scoffed. That pristine—and rather snobby—scion of an important East Coast family, with his thin, aristocratic body and his high forehead? "Don't tell me you think he's dangerous. He's like a poster boy for an overbred, fast-dying-out Eastern establishment WASP."

Bill normally would have laughed at this effort of hers to be at once truthful and humorous. Instead, he stopped her with the seriousness of his look and the way he pressed her hands in his. "Not dangerous, Louise, in the traditional way. But I know him well, too well, almost—" He stopped, as if not wanting to reveal something crucial about the man.

Then she recalled the history of the Holleys and the Eldridges. Both were stationed in England at the same time, assigned to the American ambassador in different capacities. That was a period when CIA agents were being assassinated, as well as purported spies of foreign nationalities working for the United States. Alex, Louise was more certain than ever, was undercover CIA, just like Bill. "You worked with him when we were stationed in London. I see. You're not free to divulge why you think he has some unsavory elements to his character."

Her husband's gaze leveled on her. "That's it, Louise. Just take my word for it: don't get involved with Alex. There's something about him that I could never understand—and

I don't want you to be responsible for fathoming his hidden depths."

"Wow," she said. "Hidden depths. That will make my trip to Bethesda interesting."

He grinned at her. "Have a good time. You'll do your usual good job with the program on the plant sale. Just watch yourself at the Holleys. You and Emily are such good friends that you shouldn't have any trouble at all ignoring a mere husband."

6

Saturday

Walter Freeman looked up from his newspaper and peered at his wife over the top of his half-glasses. "It's getting on, dear. Are you almost ready? I'm afraid I'm due downtown at nine."

"Saturday-morning meetings seem such an unfair burden," said Catherine, in the smooth, slightly complaining voice that she'd commenced using lately, "especially for a man who serves his country so diligently and brilliantly five days a week."

"A very important little meeting of some of the governors," he replied, and glanced over at her curiously, trying to look objectively at this big woman that was his spouse. He thought of Catherine not as just a wife, but as a kind of institution. Like an institution, she needed a lot of funding—though much of it she provided through her own private fortune—careful management, and timely maintenance. She was doing the maintenance work right now, and he curbed the impatience a more ordinary man might have experienced.

Big, and also overweight, Catherine was as imposing as a monarch, reflected Walter, and as gracious as any queen. She dwarfed the brocade bench on which she reposed in front of her triple-mirrored French dressing table, her ever-increasing hips drooping over either side. He watched

impassively as she deftly applied the expensive creams and
dabs from jars of high-priced makeup—he'd found out
just how high-priced it was when he'd lifted a minuscule
little container with a translucent shell-like lid off the
glass-topped table and discovered a price tag of a hundred
dollars. To a boy brought up in relative poverty by immi-
grant parents, the extravagance produced a twinge of out-
rage. But the institution of Catherine Freeman knew what
it was doing when it spent half an hour and God knew *how*
much money in raw materials on her appearance: by the
time she was finished, his wife would have obliterated at
least ten years of wear from her pleasant baby face.

She took the same ultimate care of her business investments, thus always maximizing the sizable capital left to
her by her generous and successful father, Henry Fortnum. Even her azalea business made money—her rooted
plant starts raised in their backyard greenhouse commanding top prices from area wholesalers.

Yes, quite so, thought Walter, folding his paper neatly. He
fell easily into the thought patterns he employed at work,
so thus could summarize Catherine in a few words:
Catherine was a woman who parlayed her business and
personal strategies to optimize the results and create around
her ample self an effective halo of good health, success, and
beauty.

Measuring Catherine's pluses and minuses was something he had been doing more frequently of late.

And since he was thinking of halos, his gaze fastened
not so happily on his wife's hair. Catherine's hair, he noticed, had recently been treated at Emilio's, and *represented* a wavy halo around her head, as if she were a very
big, overweight angel come to earth. It was dyed what
Walter could only think of as the color of the manila en-
velopes delivered to him in profusion each day in his important office in the Federal Building.

Why women dyed their hair tan, he had no idea.

He narrowed his eyes slightly to see her better. She looked both amenable and a little vulnerable. Now might be the time to see if there was any negotiating room in her ideas about spending some time away from home . . .

"My dear, have you given any more thought to visiting your sister in Santa Barbara while the California weather is still reliable?"

"No, dear," replied Catherine. "In the first place, there's the azalea show in just two weeks. I *can't* miss that, or I won't win. And anyway, you know I don't want to leave you alone. Why, you'd probably develop ulcers. Martina would revert to Island food, and it would burn your poor stomach out again."

He didn't like to hear this. He loved the food their Jamaican housekeeper prepared for him when Catherine wasn't around—the spicy meat patties, the pepper pot soup, the ackee with salt cod, the Jerk chicken, the curried goat—always served up with Blue Mountain coffee grown on the island. It was probably true that it was not indicated for a man with incipient ulcers. "I could easily avoid her cooking, then. Bethesda must have two hundred restaurants with carryout. And a few people with more mundane cooks might invite me for dinner."

Her long-eyelashed gaze swept over him, and for a moment he felt that twinge of desire he'd felt ten years ago, when a not-so-expansive Catherine had gently lured him into marriage and a comfortable bed. Catherine's eyes had always been her most precious asset. At the moment, though, the eyes were rather cold, and did not match her mollifying words.

He decided on a different tack. "Now, another thing, Catherine. The economic summit is coming up in October in Geneva. I mean for you to accompany me, and I know you will be like Jackie was to Jack in Paris. But this means you must be careful to avoid more, uh, attacks. Is that agreeable? Your gardening activities—I hope you

don't overdo on them, with all these shows on the schedule. Is it not appropriate to think that you need a little
respite, a little time away to restore yourself?"

"Darling," she said, practically purring like a cat, "and
this is final. I'll not leave you alone and to your own de-
vices. Who *knows* what terrible crisis might occur that will
demand your expert help? You know when the president
beckons you in for meeting after meeting that it is hard on
your psyche." She widened her eyes. "Remember what
happened last time: you were rushed to the hospital. You
need me around to protect you. I should hate to think what
would happen if I left you alone. . . ."

Was the woman protesting too much? He answered her
in a docile tone. "You're right, darling."

Unfortunately for Catherine, Walter knew other women
more robust than she. Women not heavy with fat-laden
stomachs and giant hips, healthier women who weren't
rushed to the hospital with so-called digestive attacks that
were mostly due to not following the eating regimen of a
diabetic. Women more in tune with a lean, athletic man
who excelled at tennis and swam thirty laps a day at the
club pool and *liked* sex, and didn't treat it, as Catherine
did, as if it were a sinful pursuit of which her stern father
wouldn't approve.

Maybe it was because Catherine had been over fifty the
first time a man had penetrated her precious private parts.
Getting into those private parts these days was difficult.
Sometimes he suspected that Catherine knew *he* was entering foreign parts. When this thought crossed his mind,
it gave him an uncomfortable twinge, as if he were teeter-
ing on the edge of a building and about to fall off.

With his customary sense of discipline, he set these
thoughts aside along with his newspaper. His watch told
him that it was time to go, whether or not Catherine was
ready to go with him. His voice betrayed no sign that he
was impatient, and he wasn't really impatient: men of his

stature could not afford to register impatience over such paltry dilemmas as the failure of man and wife to be ready to exit the house at the same time—or failure of a husband to properly hint that *he* needed time alone, away from his mate.

Impatience. Only, perhaps, in a world economic crisis, which could come up any day now, might he permit himself to exhibit impatience toward some high-level fool who dared oppose his solutions to the world order. And it would be exhibited then only as part of a power play—*not* because he had lost his cool.

"Now, dear," Walter said, "let's stop talking about the future and consider the here and now. What will your decision be? Shall I be off alone now, in order to arrive downtown on time, or can you tear yourself away from your ablutions so that I can drop you off at the spring plant sale on the way?"

7

When Louise Eldridge drove from northern Virginia to Bethesda on Saturday morning, she noticed there was the usual surfeit of things in bloom, in spite of the drought. Dogwoods and shadbush. Carolina silverbell. Viburnum. Spirea. Late tulips and daffodils. Camellias and columbine. Japanese iris and trillium and meadow rue. They all bloomed their best, as if competing in some ultimate garden show. And the winners—no contest!— were the mountains of brilliant azalea bushes that slathered their bright colors over the suburban countryside. They managed to diminish all the other entries.

Perhaps because of the dry heat, everything seemed to have come into bloom at once. A fussy garden designer, thought Louise, might have torn out his hair and screamed, *Too much!* But she, like other Washingtonians, had grown used to the extravagant excess.

It was known as the month of May.

By the time she reached downtown Bethesda, with its Washington-style, limited-hangout skyscrapers, the exuberant floral displays were confined within planting boxes.

Now she stood in the yard of the Farm Women's Market, a cultural oasis amidst the office buildings. Her arms were akimbo, a frown on her face. She was here for the spring plant sale. It was the last place she'd expected trouble, at a spring plant sale, from women between the ages thirty and seventy whose main hobby was supposed to be digging in the dirt.

But trouble started as soon as her WTBA-TV crew pulled in with their big white truck full of equipment and started setting up in the small front yard of the old market.

Her producer, Marty Corbin, had warned Louise that this program idea of hers was flat. Louise had insisted on going ahead with it for two reasons. Partly, it was to please her soft-spoken friend, Emily, vice-president of the club. Partly, it was out of a certain hubris, a belief that through sheer personal charm she could make any garden topic come alive on her show—from worm culture to wisterias.

She'd argued Marty into it, and now she had to produce something good. Now, however, Marty was surrounded. He stood there, big, brash, and handsome, in white shirt with rolled-up sleeves, his curly dark hair ruffled in the breeze, his brown eyes twinkling with either mirth or malice, she couldn't tell which. On three sides of him, like an attacking army, stood a cluster of Old Georgetown Garden Club members demanding their fifteen minutes of fame. One was a tall, loud-voiced woman, her auburn-colored hair caught up in a bun. Another was a short, small-boned person with decorous gray curls and brown button eyes who spoke with a whiny voice. But it was the third woman who commanded the scene. High-cheeked and tall, with her blond hair done in a mass of waves and curls, she had a look in her almond-shaped blue eyes that alarmed Louise. It said, *I'll get my way, or else!*

Could people really care this much about appearing on a Saturday-morning TV gardening show? Louise had warned Emily to tell the club members beforehand: the shoot would feature club president Catherine Freeman and her famous azaleas, but these three had apparently chosen not to believe that.

Though Louise stood at her producer's elbow, the three ignored her and focused on Marty: they knew who was running this show.

"I've belonged to this garden club for ten years," claimed the redhead, who introduced herself as Meg Durrance, "and I have plants that are just as pretty or *prettier* than Catherine's. *See?*" She swept a manicured hand back toward a table filled with small shrubs with large yellow and green variegated leaves. "*Look* at those aucuba—do you see anything better looking at this sale? I raised them from slips and now they're *two feet high.*"

The woman with gray curls could hardly wait to say her piece. Louise suspected that she'd lived for sixty years without learning how to assert herself. Breaking in here must have taken a lot of courage on her part. Her forehead wrinkled plaintively as she said, "I don't want to seem uncharitable, Mr. Corbin, but I have a *real* gripe—"

"Your name, ma'am?" Marty asked.

"I'm Phyllis Ohlmacher. I run a small nursery north of town, and my whole *life* is dedicated to raising azaleas." She pointed down the row of tables. "You can see them right on the end there, and I hope I get time equal to Catherine's, who, after all, only does this for—" She turned to the blond woman. "You explain to him, Sophie. This is Sophie Chalois."

Sophie extended her hand to Marty and in a low voice said, "I'm so happy to meet you." Louise wondered why a woman her age was working at a plant sale in a dishy, magenta-colored, low-cut sports top, though she had to admit Sophie had a fine bust. The woman was happy to be spokesman for the group: "Phyllis is trying to explain that Catherine is not the only—I mean to say, she shouldn't *be* the only one featured in this show. Let me explain: Catherine raises azaleas as a hobby, in her state-of-the-art greenhouse in back of her home—while *Phyllis* does it as her profession; it is her *livelihood*—a humble livelihood, perhaps, but an honest one. If you want to get a real picture of the Old Georgetown Garden Club, you have to get more than Catherine's hybrids. I, for instance, have brought with me a wonderful display of ivies, representing several species. Some are very unusual."

Louise had a sudden mental picture of Sophie as a blond Medusa. The curls supported the picture, and she thought it appropriate that this woman raised plants that twined sinuously like serpents.

The woman bestowed a glowing smile on Marty. "I even have plants that are starts from one that came straight from George Washington's home."

Louise couldn't help laughing. "You mean you stole some ivy from Mount Vernon and now you grow it to sell here? That's enterprising."

Sophie sniffed. "Um, whoever you are, you're not only interrupting, you're *really* offending me."

With a big grin, Marty pulled Louise forward into the circle. "You'd better get introduced, because this is Louise Eldridge. Lou's the star of this gardening show—and she's the one who's gonna have to improvise if we decide to widen our scope and include you folks."

"Oh," said the blonde, and with great difficulty put away her pout and pulled out a smile. "I didn't mean to be rude, Louise, but *you*—"

"That's all right, Sophie," said Louise. "Some of my best friends have snitched ivy from Mount Vernon, even though I know it's frowned upon. I was tempted myself when I went on a tour there. But it takes a lot of nerve to propagate it and sell it at the Old Georgetown Garden Club plant sale."

Sophie Chalois's eyes darkened dangerously. Marty put up his hands, like a man who had just surrendered. "Okay, okay, ladies. So we've got Phyllis's azaleas and Sophie's ivy—"

The bold Meg grabbed his arm. "Don't forget my aucuba—"

He gave the redhead a big Irish grin. "Naw, I won't forget your aucuba, Meg. I know just what you ladies want.
With Louise's cooperation, it's gonna be no problem." He
looked expectantly at Louise.

She nodded. "No trouble at all, if you cooperate." She
glanced over Phyllis and Meg and fastened on Sophie. "As
we're taping, just follow my lead and answer questions—
briefly." She coughed. "I don't think we should mention
that some of the ivy came from Mount Vernon. Not a good
thing. The rest should be easy."

As the women returned to their plant tables, Louise
and Marty exchanged a glance. There was a devilish look
in her producer's eye. "Lou, I'm thinkin' something. I'm
thinkin' we can use this visceral moment of savage competition to our advantage."

"I could tell you were thinking that."

"At least it will give this shoot a little pizzazz."

"We've been strong-armed by a clutch of garden dollies."

"You'll manage it," he assured her. "You always do." He
grabbed her arm and squeezed it. "I'm beginnin' to get
into this garden club stuff: we may just end up with something great! We can tell the promotion department to tag
it 'Cutthroat Gardeners Contend for Customers at the
Spring Plant Sale.' "

She laughed. "Okay, then let's include everyone. Maybe
if you do a slow pan of each aisle, we just—"

"Yeah," agreed Marty without hearing the rest, "stop for
a while at each stand—or whatever you call it where these
ladies peddle their plants—"

"Station, I guess."

"All right," said Marty, rubbing his hands together. "We're
on the same page. This is gonna be a dynamite show."

Emily, as manager of the sale, was a small, busy figure

helping people unload plants. She'd noticed the complaining women but couldn't break away. Now she rushed over to Louise and cast a nervous glance at Marty, who was already back to work directing the cameraman on lighting details. She looked up at Louise and said, "Do forgive me. I'm so *mortified*. What did Meg and Phyllis and Sophie *want* of your producer? Here I persuaded you to do this program, and now to have them bothering you."

"It's all right, Emily, don't worry. Marty talked them right through it. He knows just how to handle things."

Emily shoved back a wisp of light brown hair that fluttered like a stray butterfly in the breeze and sighed. Her pale eyebrows over her large gray eyes descended in remorse. "I am *so* sorry. I know you people are superb professionals, and do things the professional way—that you have a script and a plan. I hope this doesn't spoil things for you and Marty."

"Don't apologize, Emily. Everything's going to be fine."

But Emily couldn't stop apologizing. She looked around, to be sure no arrivals had slipped into the parking lot, and said, "Catherine's late, and I'm sorry about that, but I know she'll be here soon." With a final remorseful glance and squeeze of Louise's hand, she hurried off, like the harried Rabbit in *Alice in Wonderland*.

But nothing could spoil things for Louise, for it was a great day for a shoot. Spring had brought perfect weather to the Washington, D.C., area. A stranger in town might have been fooled into thinking this was normal weather when, in fact, steamy, unlivable humid days were just around the corner. But for now, spring, with its deceptive livability, was here. The front yard of the Farm Women's Market was filled with warm, dappled sunlight that came through the leaves of the tall sycamore trees. These ancient trees, with their mottled and peeling bark, reminded Louise of soldiers in combat dress.

Beyond the yard with the plant sale stood the old market itself, a modest, white, one-story building. People flowed out from it, arms laden with packages containing fresh produce, free-range chickens, Maryland farm cheeses, and big bouquets of cut flowers. One man had an antique side chair tucked under his arm. This market was a vestige of Bethesda's rural past, which otherwise was obliterated by the skyscrapers that loomed on either side of the market and throughout the downtown.

Louise reflected that some might think the venerable Old Georgetown Garden Club was another vestige of the past. But her petite friend Emily had sold her on the fact that it was up to date and "on the cutting edge of gardening issues, just as a garden club *should* be."

As they videotaped, Louise and the camera crew would have to proceed carefully, for the small compound was jammed with tables containing the women's wares: pots and flats of flowers, shrubs, and trees brought there for the annual plant sale. Savvy customers already crowded into the small space, knowing the early bird got the worm. Stylishly dressed yuppies in Saturday sports togs, a silver-haired man in a suit who looked as if he'd stopped on the way to an important appointment in downtown Washington, plant-loving people in frumpy clothes. They'd all come because they knew they'd find things here that they'd never be able to buy in a nursery—slips of precious plant species dug out of the yards of the garden club members.

Louise wandered over to the refreshment table in the corner of the yard near the parking lot. She passed up the pot of water for making tea, and went to the fifty-cup coffee urn and poured herself a big cup. Carefully, she positioned herself in back of the big urn where no one could see her. After that scene with the fretful women, she needed a moment to recoup. Who'd have thought a plant sale would bring out the beast in people?

She allowed her eyes to settle into a soft focus, and the

bustling yard became like something an impressionist artist would paint—a scene of amiable human activity conducted under tall trees and a brilliant but cloud-cluttered sky.

A gray Jaguar pulled up in the nearby parking area not six feet from Louise. Her eyes went into sharp focus again. From the driver's seat stepped a tall, slim man in a business suit. Though his face was plain and lined, his alert, intelligent eyes behind his horn-rimmed glasses gave him a distinctly attractive aura. Even the old-fashioned horn-rimmed glasses, on him, looked chic. Because she'd seen him so frequently on TV, Louise recognized him immediately: Walter Freeman, the man who told the country what it should do to keep on a firm economic course. His position as head of the president's task force on monetary reform made him one of the most powerful men in Washington during these economically jittery times. He constantly upstaged the Fed Reserve chairman, and the buzz in town was that he soon would take over that job, thus making an honest man of himself by retiring from the job of the snapping dog at the chairman's heels.

Emily had mentioned to Louise that their club president was married to the important Mr. Freeman, but she hadn't given it much thought. Now, to see him dropping his wife off today gave her a good feeling. It made her realize he didn't spend every moment worrying about the finances of the country. Important men and women also had private lives, lives that included chauffeuring their family members to mundane events like garden club plant sales. This probably served them well in bringing them down to earth, and within the scale of ordinary human beings.

But was Walter Freeman ordinary at all? Louise watched his every movement. As he walked around the car and approached the passenger-side door, he impatiently muttered something to himself. They were words that only

Louise heard, though she could not distinguish them. Someone in the car wouldn't hear them because the passenger-side window was closed. He opened the door. A heavyset woman with an elegantly coiffed head of beige hair laboriously pulled herself up out of the seat. This was Catherine Freeman.

An interesting-looking pair, thought Louise. Her friend Emily had given her the inside scoop: Catherine had a sharp business mind, and had parlayed her inheritance into a real estate fortune by buying Bethesda commercial property decades ago and watching it grow exponentially in value. Her husband of ten years, son of immigrants, succeeded on his brainpower, leaving the private sector to become a public servant decades ago.

As the regal Catherine stepped from the car, the man stood in back of her. On his face was a dismissive look that only Louise was close enough to see. Startled, she felt as if she'd intruded on an intimate moment. She should have turned away, but she didn't. The big woman turned affectionately toward her husband, her pudgy hands out as if expecting an embrace. Instead, he stepped back a tiny step, bent, and gave her a peck on the cheek.

Emily scurried over to greet the woman. But her keen eye recognized Louise skulking behind the coffee pot, and she called out, "Louise, come out from there and meet Catherine"—she looked patiently up at Walter Freeman—"and her famous husband, too."

With a start, Freeman looked over at Louise. "Oh," he said, "I didn't notice you."

Catherine Freeman extended her hand to Louise. "What a pleasure," she said. "Emily has told me all about you." Louise felt as if she'd just been presented to the queen. The woman clutched at her husband's suit jacket. "And do you know Walter?"

Freeman's face had become an impassive mask. "Nice to meet you."

I'll bet, thought Louise. She'd caught the man in an un-guarded moment, and he couldn't have liked that much.

As if he needed coaching, Catherine said, "Louise, you know, is the star of the TV gardening show that we're film-ing today."

"Really? I'm afraid I'm not familiar with that show."

Louise said, "I'd be surprised if you were."

Although not overtly, Freeman was giving her the once-over: her checkered cotton blouse, her flared denim skirt, the breezy kerchief at her throat. "Uh, tell me about the show, Louise. I hear Catherine's flowers are to be fea-tured."

"Yes, they are. The show appears weekly. The Washing-ton PBS station, WTBA, is the sponsor, and it's syndicated, so it appears in about two hundred markets . . ."

She was annoyed to see that Freeman wasn't listening. He didn't even notice that she hadn't completed her sen-tence. She felt like stepping on his fancy tasseled loafer and telling him to pay attention. Instead, she stole a glance at Emily, and realized her friend was similarly be-mused by this self-important man.

Freeman slid up his coat sleeve and studied his watch, which he clearly thought of as his escape from this female gardening klatch. "Well, ladies," he said, "I see the time is fleeting, and I'm due downtown. Catherine, you have a ride home, I'm sure."

"Oh, yes, darling." This time, probably because of the spectators, he leaned over and gave his wife a warm kiss full on the lips. A wide wave at the plant-sale crowd in the background, and he was off in his Jaguar. The nation's economic hero.

8

While Louise was meeting the Freemans, the disruptive trio of Meg, Phyllis, and Sophie had assumed their stations and were busy selling plants, maybe to bolster their argument that they should be part of the TV shoot. At least all was quiet on the Western front. Then Marty gave her a heads-up: he was ready to let the video-cam roll.

The clever Marty took plenty of time taping the entire scene. The camera stopped at each table, so that Louise could describe its plant wares. Winging it, Louise injected a little of the spirit of competition into her dialog—"An air of healthy rivalry exists as club members strive to produce the most beautiful plants and shrubs for sale to the public. They'll compete again, in events such as the Garden Club of America's annual flower arranging contest, and other plant-of-the-year events."

There would be plenty of tape so that the station could send consolation videos to those who ended on the cutting room floor, though the only ones who probably cared were the three who'd not minded breaking all those middle-class inhibitions people usually had, and had contended like schoolgirls for their moment in the sun.

Since she was improvising dialog, Louise was fortunate that she had an old-time club member, Dorothy Cranshaw, standing by to help her. The woman was in her sixties and had no pretensions: her wavy, gray-streaked brown hair was in a simple bun, and over her sweatshirt and jeans she wore an old denim gardening apron that looked like her grandmother had used it before her. Like an adviser to a king, Dorothy literally whispered into Louise's ear things about people and plants. She knew everything and shared the information humbly. "At the next table you have Laura Alice Shea, one of our younger members. She's brought lots of wonderful epimedium starts from her garden. . . ." or, "Coming up on the right are some very generous-sized pots of blooming Virginia bluebells . . ."

Laura Alice Shea was quite a contrast to the plain Dorothy. She was small and muscular, and very pregnant, with stylish brown hair cut in a bob close to her head. Her running clothes looked as if they came from Chicsport, the ultimate source of sports togs—though Louise wondered if Chicsport catered to pregnant women, and decided they must have been purchased in a maternity shop. Although probably about to have a baby any minute, Laura Alice seemed the type who still would take a run around her neighborhood after she got through working at the plant sale. Most likely in her mid-thirties, she was one of the younger members of the club that Emily had told Louise about, who had careers but still managed to come to garden club meetings. They were somewhat outnumbered by the graying heads in the group, the women who stayed home.

The interview with Catherine Freeman was easy. It was apparent that the woman was accustomed to being in the public spotlight. As the videocam rolled tape, she stood before her table of gardening goodies and held up a pot of elegant, blooming azaleas. Her hands were as graceful as the rest of her, with curled pinkie fingers. She explained, "These plants are from years of hybridizing. It took me that long to get the perfect petal shape, the per-

fect flame of color in the throat of the flower, and the perfect size."

The woman was captivating, her large size no drawback
to her beauty, since her face was so handsome and kind,
and her movements so refined, in spite of a shortness of
breath that sent her into occasional paroxysms of cough-
ing. This woman was classy, thought Louise, despite what
that husband of hers might think of her.

In one of the final shots, the cameraman caught a club
member arriving with a car full of annuals that would re-
plenish what already had been sold. Louise noticed they
were America's favorite annuals: marigolds, impatiens,
and petunias. Immediately, a half dozen club members
went to help the newcomer carry the heavy flats and put
them on tables. Louise used that as her close.

"And so it goes, this spring plant sale, one of the most
popular community events in the Washington, D.C., area.
Club members bustle in all day with plants dug up from
their own gardens or purchased from local nurseries.
Customers pour in from all over the metropolitan area to
buy them. From this sale, the garden club will net between
five and ten thousand dollars. The Old Georgetown club
has spent a great deal of its proceeds on a garden for crippled children at the Davis Special Needs Library in Bethesda. Complete with delightful bronze animal statues,
this garden was specially designed by the Old Georgetown
Garden club for the delight of the children. So when you
think of garden clubs, forget the image of a woman in a
fancy hat drinking tea with a crooked little finger: garden
club members are not like that. They plant trees and gardens. They protest and make speeches, and even sue
counties and cities, when they have to, to protect the environment and America's countryside. The prestigious
Garden Club of America, of which this club is a part, pro-
motes and financially supports plant research and ecolog-
ical restoration. Garden club women are in the forefront

of the greening and forestation of America. They help to make trees and flowers a vital part of people's lives."

Marty called out "That's a wrap, folks. Nice work, everybody; nice work, Mrs. Eldridge." He put a big arm around her shoulder. "You did good, Lou. After all my misgivings, I've gotta say that was a great program. I particularly liked that big redhead's take on the flower-arranging contest: a good-humored loser, who still thinks she might win one of these days."

"For the camera, she was good-humored," said Louise. "I wonder what she really feels about always losing. Nobody likes to lose constantly."

They walked along together, Louise making the interior passage from being on camera to being just an ordinary human being. Thus, she was unprepared and shocked when the tall Sophie Chalois cut right in front of her path and fell into step with Marty. In a low voice, Sophie said, "You are so *creative*, Marty. What magic you have wrought here!"

He stopped and laughed and made a little space for Louise. "*Ha*, you have it all wrong. You have our star to thank for the magic, Sophie. Louise is the one who invented stuff out of whole cloth."

Sophie deigned to look at Louise. "Of course, Louise, you, too—" Her gaze went back to Marty, and those blue eyes, when they softened, Louise knew, were capable of melting men's hearts. "But truly, Marty, she'd be nothing without a producer like you." She extended a thin, beautiful hand and said, "I shall remember you always."

Even her producer's hard-boiled New Jersey upbringing and years in the television industry hadn't prepared him for this onslaught. He blushed and stammered, his brown-eyed gaze casting around for something safe to look at besides Sophie's decolletage. "Oh, gosh—aw, thanks, Sophie. I don't think I'll forget you, either, mighty soon."

In disbelief, Louise turned away to say good-bye to

other members of the crew; they would return to the studio in Fairfax, Virginia, forty minutes around the Beltway. She herself was staying in Bethesda. Since Bill was away on the college scouting trip with Janie, Louise had accepted Emily's invitation to stay—maybe even two nights—instead of returning to her empty house in Sylvan Valley. After all, she had no work on the docket for the coming week.

Marty quickly caught up with her. "Can you believe her?" he muttered to Louise in a low voice. "I haven't had anyone come on to me that strong for at least ten years—"

"Lucky you," she said. "And lucky me: I get to spend the rest of the afternoon with her."

He squeezed her arm. "You can handle her, Lou. I'm going home before she hits me up for a rendezvous in the back of the truck."

Louise went into the quaint Farm Women's Market to use the restroom, then browsed for a while in the big, pleasant, enclosed market. Delightful odors barraged her from all sides—the smells of herbs, flowers, and freshly baked cakes and cookies that she wished she could sample. Instead, she went outside to rejoin the women at the plant sale.

Glancing around at the women's faces, she could see that now that the TV cameras were gone the glamor had also gone out of the annual plant sale. What was left was hard work. Louise became a plant peddler, and she even fraternized a bit with Meg Durrance and Phyllis Ohlmacher.

Sophie Chalois stood her ground at her table full of ivy, and didn't come anywhere near where Louise was selling flats of annuals. If Louise thought the woman would be grateful for anything, she was wrong.

Catherine Freeman won Louise's heart by coming over at one point and telling her, "You're a jewel, Louise, to work so hard all day. It's a shame that you don't live nearby so that you could become part of our club. You'd be a splendid member, the kind who brings *spirit* and fun to gardening."

Hours later, her feet and back were tired from standing. Louise had only stopped briefly when someone brought in hot dogs for lunch. Though Louise wasn't fond of hot dogs and thought their ambiguous ingredients appalling from a health standpoint, today they tasted like manna must have tasted to the ancient Israelites starving in the desert.

Just like the New York Stock Exchange, the event closed promptly at three. Louise did a double take when Catherine solemnly removed a small bell from a box that also held a record of sales and proceeds and insistently rang it, nodding her head to further confirm the message that time was up. She, Emily, Catherine, Phyllis, and the helpful Dorothy were the only ones who had stayed for the entire sale, the others taking two- or three-hour shifts. A number of members, however, reappeared at the end of the sale to help clean up. They were accompanied by their amiable husbands. The only sour face was on Phyllis Ohlmacher's bald-headed spouse, whose name was Al. The Ohlmachers had plenty of leftover azaleas on their table to cart back home, and the seemingly shy Phyllis was not shy about giving orders to Al on how to do the job.

Another male helper was Dorothy Cranshaw's tall, jeans-clad son, Jack, a plain-looking man with a stolid expression on his face. Louise saw that despite his disinterested look, he was very efficient. He arrived in a big pickup and pitched quickly in to get the job done, as if he'd done it many times before.

There were lots of plant leftovers, despite the club members' best attempts to gauge their needs. While they took samples of these plants home to use in their own gardens, the bulk of them went to Dorothy Cranshaw, who intended to plant them in the garden on the grounds of the Davis Library.

Louise had begun to feel an integral part of the team by the time she helped load plants in cars. Emily bustled about like a stevedore, hoisting flats as if she'd done it all her life. Catherine Freeman limited herself to small loads, and Louise realized she was not in the greatest health. Catherine was moving other people's plants, for her beautiful azaleas had sold out hours earlier. She told Louise that she called her plants her "pets." For some childless women, dogs and cats were substitutes, thought Louise. For Catherine Freeman, apparently, plants filled the void.

At the last minute, Meg Durrance and Sophie Chalois drove up and claimed some plants to take to their own gardens. Then they got into a prolonged and amiable conversation with Catherine.

The work was nearly done, with just a few big pots remaining. Louise, feeling strong now, decided to move two three-gallon plants at a time. Suddenly it felt as if her back ligaments had separated from the bone. "Oh my God," she muttered, as the pain shot up her back. She pulled in a painful breath as she struggled to reach the car.

Emily hurried over. "Careful, Louise! What are you doing? Silly girl—each one of those pots weighs twenty-five pounds. Let me take one of them." And she adeptly moved one to her own arms and set it in the back of Jack's truck.

Louise tried to smile through the pain. "This is my trial by fire. Do you think I've passed the test for becoming a garden club member?"

Emily laughed. "I do—and I think it's high time you joined a club down there in the Alexandria area. Now, soon we'll go to my house, Louise, and then we can shower and relax. But I have to warn you: it will be a quiet week-end. The biggest excitement we'll find in Bethesda on a Sunday afternoon is an author-signing at the bookstore."

Louise was having a hard time picturing Bethesda as quiet. After all, didn't Walter Freeman, Sophie Chalois, Meg Durrance, Phyllis Ohlmacher—all those non-quiet people—live here?

9

Louise had forgotten how perfect Emily's house was. Its deep, many-paned windows were framed in dignified crewel draperies, its rooms outfitted with priceless dark-wooded Early American furniture that came to them via Alex's New England ancestors.

She took her SportSac off her tired shoulder and was about to rest it on a half-moon mahogany side table. Then she gave the table a second look. It had a shell motif that announced its special nature and a patina a half-inch thick that practically shouted, *Don't dare scratch me!* Louise put the bag back on her shoulder, looking around for some other place to set it. "Umm," she said to Emily, "maybe I should I put my things upstairs?"

"Why don't you?" agreed her hostess. "The first bedroom on the left is yours, with the bath next door. While you freshen up, I'll fix tea."

Louise went upstairs to the bedroom, which was a colonial bower in white embroidered linen, complete with a canopy-covered bed and another one of those antique tables alongside it on which she wouldn't dare to place a thing. She felt like flopping down on the bed and taking a quick nap, but she was too dirty, and anyway, tea was being prepared. Though Emily had talked about hot baths, she didn't think her hostess was really serious, hunger being a bigger consideration.

She freshened up and returned downstairs to join her hostess. Emily had prepared a repast of tea and tiny, delicious-looking pastries. She had also freed the family's large yellow Labrador retriever from his crate in a back hall; he apparently spent his time there when they were away. Now, two-year-old Lancelot happily cavorted over the pristine wood floors and Oriental rugs, and followed them out onto the brick patio to enjoy snacks, which included a few dog biscuits for him.

Unlike the patio at Louise's northern Virginia home, which was closed in with huge sweet gum trees and pines from an uncut forest, Emily's was right out of a home-gardening magazine. A few majestic shade trees looming above to modulate the sun's rays. A few charming, smaller garden trees. An irregular flower bed surrounding it, with plants that looked good even close up, including spectacular, candy-pink wild orchids that Louise would give her eyeteeth to have growing in her own garden. Nothing seemed to have suffered from the drought that the Washington, D.C., area was suffering—not yet. Maybe by August the Holleys' bluegrass lawn might lose its emerald luster.

Louise gratefully sank into one of the comfortable, handsome chairs to relieve the back pains she'd acquired at the plant sale.

"No," Emily told Lancelot, who had gobbled his treats and then begun to beg. The dog magically obeyed, turning its attention to sniffing the flowers, then trailing down several wooden steps into the backyard.

When a woman next door came out on her raised porch to shake out a rug, Louise could see her above Emily's stockade fence. "That's Laura Alice Shea, isn't it?" asked Louise.

"Yes. A very nice woman. Except sometimes we wish they didn't have that raised porch, because the noise of social activities up there carries to our yard. Alex hates the sound of neighbors."

"Do they have noisy parties or something?"

"Laura Alice herself is a very quiet person. But when they have family parties, there's quite a bit of racket. They love to play games, and you hear these peals of laughter from their yard." She smiled reminiscently. "Jim Shea is so charming, and his laugh is so infectious that I always wish I were over there with them. I envy what goes on there."

Laura Alice's gaze flicked over at Emily and Louise, and she gave them a wave before she went back in her house. Louise realized that soon, very soon, in fact, a bumptious baby also would be making noise on that porch. She wondered how Alex, who liked the sound of silence, would handle *that*.

They had barely taken a biteful of pastry when they heard a door slam and a man call, "Emily. Where are you?"

Emily checked her watch with a faint frown on her face. "Four-thirty. Alex is home a little earlier than I expected." And then her husband walked out onto the patio, tall and thin, with reddish hair, his long face wearing a look of restrained disapproval. Louise suddenly understood: it was one thing for Louise to visit with Bill at the Holleys' elegant dinners for eight, but quite another to hang around with Emily by herself. After all, maybe she'd influence Emily to stand up on her own two feet.

He greeted the two of them with kisses on the cheek. Equal kisses, as though they both were distant friends.

"Louise, so good to see you again."

She gave him a big smile, determined to make this encounter with her good friend's husband go better than previous attempts.

The dog reported enthusiastically to his master's side, and was rewarded with a few rough caresses that left the animal wanting more. Then Alex noticed the tea things.

"Tea, so late? I suppose this means dinner's going to be

late." There was a little smile on his face, as if to take the sting from his words.

Emily explained to Louise, "Alex is the type who needs to eat five times a day—and have his three squares right on schedule."

Archly, he replied, "I didn't know I was a *type* at all, just a reasonable person who needs reasonable nourishment."

Unruffled, Emily offered him the plate of miniature sweets. "I didn't mean to offend you, darling. Come and have an éclair."

"I'll join you for just a minute, but I don't intend to spoil my dinner by eating éclairs." His wide-eyed gaze turned on his wife. "Now, Emily, I hope you were careful today not to overdo."

"I was," she said, in her good-natured voice. "Louise will confirm it: I let others do the heavy lifting, and I simply bossed people about." Since this wasn't exactly true, Louise looked out on the yard, and watched the dog chase a squirrel.

As there was an hour until dinner, Louise had a chance to lie down for a few minutes. Emily had declared she needed no help preparing dinner. She had bought ready-to-eat foods for the meal, easy to warm in the oven and microwave and serve promptly at six-thirty. This regular schedule, apparently, was what her husband was used to.

As soon as Alex began eating, his mood improved, and he even told a couple of jokes. Louise marveled to herself that it was almost as if he were a new man—but maybe she shouldn't judge so quickly.

They soon got onto the topic of Bethesda, and how their neighborhood contrasted sharply with Sylvan Valley. Louise hoped that her neighborhood was not going to suffer by the comparison.

Alex said, "Since the subway arrived, the neighborhoods of Battery Lane and Ledgebrook have become the handiest and most desirable places to live in all of Washington,

D.C. And our Bethesda Downtown is not only a business and convention center, but it has two hundred restaurants—can you believe it?" He was like a small boy reveling in having more marbles in his bag.

He laughed. "In contrast, I believe your neighborhood south of Alexandria has changed very little over the years. Stayed static, as it were."

"Not exactly," said Louise, her guard going up as if she were a knight protecting the Holy Grail. Damnit, but she had to defend her territory. "There's *lots* more business on Route One since you've been down that way—and multiple housing, that sort of thing." She didn't mention that places like Romantic Village, a tacky pink motel on Route One only two miles from the Eldridge house, still operated, offering people a place to have quick sex. "But you're right," she conceded, "I guess there's no comparison."

Emily said, "The number of house renovations around here is phenomenal, but not all of them successful. Some people don't know what to do with millions of dollars in their pocket when they put it into a home, and some nice colonials have been totally ruined."

"You exaggerate, my dear, as usual," reproved Alex. "As a person who holds architecture as his avocation, I can tell you most do-overs are vast improvements over the pedestrian colonials that were there . . ."

Louise had had her fill of house talk; she wondered if this was the thing the two of them usually discussed on a Saturday evening. They turned to the subject of who lived in Bethesda, and she had to admit she was impressed: Alex ran through the roster of ambassadors, congressmen, and political writers of note who made their home here, of course mentioning Walter Freeman.

Why did Alex Holley bring out the worst in her? For now Louise felt obliged to throw in a competitive word about Sylvan Valley. "We don't have the roster of prestigious people that Bethesda does, but there are some well-

known people living there. Newspaper editors, that sort."
She laughed. "Most of them are the free-thinking variety,
Democrats and liberals, because conservatives aren't at-
tracted to Sylvan Valley."

Alex waved one of his thin hands. The other was busy
caressing the dog. "It's the architecture," he drawled,
"those modular, glass-walled homes, surrounded by uncut
woods. Too uncontrolled for us conservatives, Louise. Of
course, it was conceived by Sven Gorensen, a very innova-
tive—you might say, *radical*—architect, as a paean to new
ideas and has attracted liberals ever since."

"I agree that's true," said Louise.

He sniffed. "Sylvan Valley's known best for its wife-
swapping movement in the sixties."

"That was far from a *movement*, Alex," she said, and
could feel her face flushing. "Wife-swapping went on
other places besides Sylvan Valley during the touchy-feely
sixties. The way I heard it, it was only four couples."

"Louise, I'm sure that's true," agreed Emily, giving her
husband a rebuking glance. "Furthermore, you have a
charming neighborhood. And as for the prestigious people
in Bethesda, some of them around here are not all that
nice. And I'm sorry to say that this includes Walter
Freeman."

"What a way to talk about him," scolded Alex. "I know
you've gained a rather poor impression of him, my dear,
but it isn't the proper thing to do to share it with Louise.
Walter is a wonderful man—you just don't know him. I
don't see him much around here, but I do see and talk to
him downtown at the club. He is a man of exceptional
qualities, and I for one don't want to see his name be-
smirched."

Emily's head was bowed. "I'm sorry to offend you, Alex,
but I happen to know he's a bit uncaring."

"*Really,* Emily."

She turned her plaintive eyes to her spouse. "He doesn't

keep appointments with his wife, then doesn't call and worries her to death. Isn't that a bit uncaring? *You'd* never act like that, Alex, you know it: you're too much the gentleman."

Alex was temporarily stopped by his wife's compliment. Then his forehead knit up in a frown. "Just because you happen to be privy to Walter's failures in communications with his wife because you're over there for trifling garden club business doesn't mean you should be carrying *tales.*" His pale-skinned face had turned red with anger.

Trifling? If Alex were her husband, Louise would have thrown a rock at him.

But Emily was not like Louise. She looked at her spouse remorsefully, as if she regretted her words. "Sorry, darling. I didn't mean to offend you by gossiping about your friend. Let's go on to something else." She turned to Louise. "What do you say we watch the special on public television, and then take a nice walk in the neighborhood? Actually, we can take you by Catherine Freeman's house, and maybe a couple of other houses of people you met today."

A shimmer of fatigue ran through Louise's body. She would just as soon have had dinner and gone to bed with a book. But no such thing would do, for it turned out Alex, and the dog, *needed* walking.

"It's their nightly routine," explained Emily, with a smile.

Louise felt fondly toward her friend Emily. But the perfect, uptight house, and its territorial, less-than-friendly host threw a damper on her visit. It made Louise determined to head for home first thing in the morning.

10

It was after eleven when the three of them, with Lancelot in tow, started their walk. Louise hoped Alex wasn't the sort who did three or four miles at night.

With the enthusiastic dog pulling at his leash, they took off down the street and crossed Wilson Lane. Louise had been amused over the years to see how Maryland Highway 188 could be tamed by the efforts of high-powered neighbors on either side into a quiet road. Once they crossed the two asphalt lanes, they were in Ledgebrook.

"Even though Emily is loath to leave Battery Lane," said Alex, "this is where I hope we can move one day soon. The houses tend to be larger, but even more important, the yards are more private, and as you could see, we have absolutely no privacy, especially since the neighbors built that porch." He sniffed derisively.

If Alex was this starchy about things, Louise decided Laura Alice Shea might be happy if the Holleys did move into Ledgebrook.

They walked down a curved lane, and Louise noted how deadly silent it was. She checked her watch: eleven-fifteen. It was moist and cool and energizing, a lush spring night in Washington. The colors of the day were drained away, and everything appeared in shades of dark and light. Crabapple trees glowed white in the moonlight, though Louise knew the blossoms actually were pale pink. Manicured lawns were smooth planes of black, while the houses were large lumps of gray in the background.

In this forgiving night light, the houses seemed unblemished, no matter how much dry rot, peeling paint, or mildewed walls they might actually suffer: all imperfections were blotted out. She guessed that Ledgebrook homes were better maintained than average but was sure some of them suffered from lack of attention, which would be remedied only when a new owner took over and poured thousands of dollars into repairs. The same thing happened in her more modest neighborhood time after time. The truth was that Washington-area homeowners, like those in other damp parts of the country, had to be like sentinels to keep their houses from falling into the clutches of destructive flora and fauna: mold, dry rot, carpenter ants, termites. The only advantage of the Washington, D.C., area's long spell of drought was that it was slowing down the rate at which houses were rotting away.

The night universe captivated the three of them, and caused them to fall into silence. Only the jingle of the dog's metal choker interrupted the stillness. As they moved down the street, Louise noted the glitter of the back bumper of an SUV wagon. It was shoved crookedly into a small, vine-covered alleyway, and she speculated that a teenaged child of one of the privileged families around here had driven in drunk and given up at the alley.

They were a few paces beyond the alley when they heard two muffled pops. The sounds were so out of character with the peaceful evening that it took a moment to register. Alex and Emily kept on walking, but Louise, on hearing them, stopped in her tracks.

The couple turned back to look at her. "Louise, what on earth—" began Emily. "It couldn't be—"

"Someone's shooting," said Louise. "Let's *go.*" They

hurried down the street, first walking, then breaking into a run, as the downward grade increased. Lancelot, trotting with them, emitted throaty growls.

As they approached a cross street, Alex slowed his stride and said, "Hold up a minute. Those sounds are from directly ahead—"

"That's the Freeman house," cried Emily.

"Yes," said Alex, "and there's no way that I'm going to let you go closer."

Louise looked at him. "We have to. Someone may need our help. In fact, call nine-one-one right now on your cell."

"A better idea than just bumbling on," he said. He slipped his phone from his belt and dialed the emergency number, his voice steady as he relayed the location to the operator.

Then they heard the frantic call. "Help—help . . ."

Louise said, "Let's get *going.*" With the dog straining in the lead, she and Emily sprinted across Glenbrook Road, Alex in the rear.

"There's the Freemans' car in the driveway," said Emily. It stood under the glare of outside lights that lit the scene like a stage set. In the distance, Louise could hear another car start up. Other than that there was silence. She ran across the street toward the house. It sat on a small rise and seemed to loom up in the air, four stories of white brick elegance. The driveway was on the lowest level. Walter Freeman's gray Jaguar stood beneath a portico, its nose about fifteen feet in front of the open garage door.

She could hear Alex's footsteps behind her. He caught up with her and grabbed her arm so hard that she winced. "Damnit, I mean what I say. You and Emily hold back for a minute. I'll go ahead. It's hard to say what I'll find."

Louise was not used to being told to hold back, but Alex's grip held her fast. "Okay," she said, more out of regard for Emily, whose face under the streetlight had become a mask of fright. Maybe her friend was as sick as her husband intimated. She pulled herself loose from Alex and put a hand around Emily's shoulder. "It will be all right."

Alex approached the car. "My *God,* what's happened here, Walter?"

"Alex—help!" cried Freeman in a weak voice.

Louise could not contain herself. She ran up to the car, well-illuminated with powerful outdoor lights. She pulled in a breath and put a hand to her mouth. Walter Freeman, in black tie, sat in the driver's seat, looking stunned. Next to him was his wife, Catherine. She wore a long, beaded dress, her head tilted awkwardly so that Louise could see she'd lost a good part of the back of her skull. The bullets had gone in neatly, making two holes in her forehead. Around the holes was a stippling of black specks, like pepper. Blood, brains, and pieces of cranium bone had blown out of the back of the head onto Walter Freeman and the interior of the car.

Louise stood there, trembling, trying not to scream. It was hard to believe that this atrocity—this *cadaver*—she saw before her was the gracious and friendly Catherine she'd met today under the sycamores at the spring plant sale. She knew Emily was right in back of her, sobbing, and trying to restrain the agitated dog.

Then something moved in the car, and Louise jumped. Walter, who'd been sitting silent as a stone, was swiveling his blood-spattered head toward Louise. Their eyes met, his begging for her compassion. "I—I drove in—a gunman wearing a hood—"

"Yes—" started Louise.

"Never mind talking, old chap," said Alex, from beside her. "I've called the police. They'll be here in minutes."

Louise continued to stand there, wanting to help, wanting to reach out and give the man a friendly touch. Freeman appeared to be in such a state of shock that she was doubtful he'd be able to leave the car, even if he wanted to. The best thing she could do was to be a witness to his grief. Her gaze traveled over the scene in the car. The driver's-side window was all the way down. The air conditioner emitted a low hum. A well-dressed man and his well-dressed dead wife. A ghastly but genuine tableaux in that no one was moving: Catherine Freeman was bent forward, Walter Freeman was sitting as if plastered to the back of his seat. *So would I be,* she thought, *if someone began shooting in a car window at me.*

Alex Holley turned to Louise and, as if noticing her for the first time, firmly shoved her back from the car. This caused Emily to lose her balance and lurch back, and the dog to bark in confusion. "Best for us to stay away," he said. "Give the man air, even though I don't think I can get him out of that car. What a *barbaric* thing this is!"

Having shooed them away, he went back and started to rest a hand on the windowsill. Louise called to him, "Best not to touch the car, Alex." He shot her a dirty look, withdrew the hand, and bent down and talked soothingly to Freeman.

In less than a minute a patrol car cruised into the driveway, lights flashing, and Louise realized what superb police protection this upscale neighborhood enjoyed. Within moments more police came, sirens crying into the night.

They rushed over to the Freemans' car. One patrolman ordered the three of them to step back, then said to Louise, "Do you have any idea of what happened here?"

"Not really," she said. "We were a couple of blocks away when we heard two muffled gunshots. Later, there was the sound of a car starting up."

Alex stepped up to the officer. "Some drive-by thug came along and accosted them as they were returning from a Washington social function."

The patrolman looked at him oddly. "You don't say. So that's what you think?"

Alex stood a little straighter. "It's *obvious,* Officer."

"Fine. Detectives Kovach and Girard from the county's Major Crime Division will soon be here. They'll want to question you, sir. But right now I want you people to step out of our way, please. This is a crime scene and we can't allow you to contaminate it."

Alex dutifully joined Emily and Louise at the edge of the driveway. Louise cast another look at the Freemans' house: French manor style, she noted, with that flaked-off painted white brick so fashionable in the Washington area.

"How cruel," she said to Emily, "to come home to a beautiful house like this, and then get murdered in your own driveway."

11

Sunday

Louise spread orange marmalade on a piece of toast and popped it into her mouth, the sensory delight of it flowing through her whole body. Delicious: the height of breakfast luxury.

"Nothing as good as runny marmy," she said, as she carefully licked her fingers. Only then did she notice Alex Holley's disapproving look, and she reddened with mortification. It was vulgar to revel in the pleasures of good jam on morning toast when a friend of her host's family had had her brains blown out a little less than twelve hours before.

Better, perhaps, to discuss the murder straight out, and show how much she cared. She wiped her mouth and said, "You know, Alex, Catherine's murder was horrible. And the more I think of it, the more it seems that the shooter could have been aiming at Walter Freeman. Look at that controversial speech he just made on the economy."

It was eleven o'clock. The two of them were having an uncomfortable late Sunday-morning repast together. Emily was still in bed, because, according to her husband, she was "a sleepless wreck." The dog was somnolent in his crate in the back hall. Louise sat at Alex's right at the breakfast table, which was laden with fruit, breads, and quiche prepared the day before by her hostess. With his guidance, she'd pulled the food out of the refrigerator and heated up the quiche while he made coffee. Thank God they agreed on a couple of things: coffee should be caffeinated, and strong.

Alex didn't reply to her comment on who might have been the murderer's intended victim, so she continued. "After all, that speech of his last week dropped like a thunderbolt. Recommending a complete revamping of the way the markets operate is an idea that galls lots of people in the big financial institutions."

He slid another glance at Louise, and then, what she now began to think of as The Frown overcame his face. Just a little frown this time, but enough for her to know she'd stepped on his toes again. As far as this overachieving polymath was concerned, Louise was seldom if ever in the right—just like his wife.

He picked off a crumb that had had the impudence to land on the sleeve of his maroon dressing gown and set it on his plate. She could see he was working up to a smart comeback. "Louise, how would you possibly know what was in the killer's mind? I don't think it's our prerogative to speculate about Catherine's murder, and whether or not the person was after Walter."

Her jaw dropped, and then she burst out laughing and slapped a hand against her denim skirt–covered thigh.

Her chuckles continued until her host asked her, "And what's so funny about what I said?"

"Oh, asking people not to speculate. You might as well ask them not to breathe, Alex."

He rolled his eyes. "In your case, I'm sure that's true. I might expect a person with your reputation would have all sorts of theories worked out as to why this tragedy happened." He leaned forward with a sincere look on his face. "Why can't you just accept that it happened, and not question why?" He took a look at his watch. "Why isn't Emily up yet?"

The Frown again. Where *was* Emily? And more to the point, how could Emily stand to live with this difficult man? For sure, Louise had better pack her bag and go home before Alex threw her out.

As if on cue, they heard Emily's shuffling step on the stairs. She soon appeared in the breakfast room, rubbing her eyes, looking childlike in her fuzzy robe and sheepskin bunny slippers. "Good morning—or is it noon yet? Sorry to be so late, Louise. I just couldn't get to sleep after that horrible scene last night—"

Louise got up and gave her friend a hug. "It's not surprising. I had a tough time myself, letting go of the images in my head. Let me get you some coffee and heat up a slice of quiche." Louise turned to the counter to fill a cup for her friend.

Emily gently touched her husband's neck as she passed him. "Darling," she said in a dutiful tone. Then she tucked herself in her chair, while Louise brought her coffee and quiche.

Alex set his napkin aside, a disapproving look on his face. "Emily, I'd thought you'd dress before coming down. It really is best that *one* of us is dressed, in case someone should drop by with all this excitement in the neighborhood. I'll go upstairs and put some clothes on."

"You do that, dear."

Louise enjoyed another cup of coffee and a companionable silence with her friend. She could tell that Emily had taken a sleeping pill last night, for she had that devil-may-care look about her that she'd had when she got numbly drunk at student parties more than two decades ago. Emily Holley hadn't always been the wispy, dependent woman that Louise now saw before her. She had been a derring-do graduate student who ranked at the top of her classes but who also liked nothing better than going out on the town and raising a little hell.

"Life is so sick, Louise," said Emily, in a monotonous tone. "Who could have done that to Catherine?"

Louise could see her friend needed a diversion. "I don't know, and right now I'd rather not try to figure it out. You know what I was thinking about this morning? Our days at Georgetown. Remember those great parties we went to? And remember that neat Professor Hazelton?"

Emily slowly smiled, and for the first time seemed to come awake. The gates of remembrance were opened, and she looked like a new woman as she recalled their happy days in grad school. "Do I remember *Hazelton?* It's like asking me if I remember Franklin Roosevelt. I always thought it amazing that someone so sexy could actually teach us so much about political science."

Those days at Georgetown had lasted for two semesters, and then Bill had come down from Harvard, met and wooed Louise, and taken her off to Europe as he started his career in the Foreign Service. Alex had just been awarded a Princeton graduate degree. Unlike Bill, who seldom bragged, Alex always found a way to mention that the degree was "summa cum laude"—lightly, as if ridiculing his brilliance, but actually turning the spotlight on it.

He'd persuaded Emily to drop her master's studies when she became his wife, apparently on the premise that one super-bright scholar in the family was enough to go around.

"I have to admit, Louise," said Emily, "that my life hasn't been as exciting since then. Not like yours, raising two girls, living abroad, and then becoming a TV star."

Louise laughed. "I don't know about *that.* Hosting a Saturday-morning PBS show with a limited audience doesn't exactly qualify you as a star."

"It's better than keeping a neat house in which there are no children," said Emily.

For a moment, Louise had no words for her friend. This was the bitter, unvarnished truth from Emily.

Finally, Louise said, a roguish tone in her voice, "Helping the police out in Fairfax County has been by far the most exciting thing I've done." She laughed. "Maybe you and I could check out Catherine's murder."

Emily raised her eyes heavenward. "I could no more do that than fly. Alex would absolutely flip out."

"I guess he would at that," agreed Louise. The questions of Detective Tom Kovach and his partner Peter Girard last night at the murder scene were perfunctory. Kovach, big and dark-haired, and Girard, a red-haired, freckle-faced man, worked smoothly as a team. They had taken Louise, Emily, and Alex each separately into their unmarked car for an off-the-cuff interview, Kovach acting as more of a heavy, while Girard's easy Irish charm smoothed his partner's rough edges.

The only thing Louise had to contribute was the mention of the SUV parked crooked in the alley, and the fact that it hadn't been there when they walked back home. When she couldn't provide identification beyond the fact that the back bumper looked sleek and expensive, the detectives appeared to lose interest.

Later, she'd told Alex what she'd told the police, and he'd given her a reproving look. It bothered her that he would be offended by this. Could he possibly have known who owned that car, or was his nose out of joint because he hadn't had any similar tidbits to offer to the investigators?

Although she'd prodded Detective Kovach with questions, he was understandably mum about what he thought of the murder. Yet she couldn't help bursting out then with her opinion, and she repeated it now to her timid friend.

"I'd like to know why Catherine Freeman was shot when her husband, not sitting two feet away, was the logical target."

Emily flinched. "Oh, *Louise,* you're so much tougher than I am. I only wish I could forget the way Catherine looked." Then she seemed to sink in her chair, raising her coffee cup to her lips as if it were some kind of protection from probing questions about murder.

Louise suddenly realized she could learn more about this crime by phoning New York. Her husband was there, almost through with squiring daughter Janie around to see colleges. Bill, through his job, always seemed to have the pulse of people like Walter Freeman.

"Um, Emily, I think I'll dash upstairs. I want to phone Bill before I leave for home—tell him what's happened."

"Of course. But Louise, please don't go home just yet."

"I really should."

Emily looked warily around, as if what she was going to say might be traitorous. Alex was not in sight, having gone upstairs. "This murder's got me awfully nervous—I mean, this happened in *our* neighborhood. Of course, Alex is expecting me to keep a stiff upper lip. Couldn't you please stay through the day?"

Louise wondered if Alex's distaste for her could grow any stronger and decided it couldn't possibly do so. "If you put it that way, of course I'll stay."

She went upstairs to the guest bedroom, where she'd already neatly made the bed. She plopped down onto its whiteness, feeling like a proper colonial woman, although she doubted colonial women sprawled on beds. Fortunately, she caught Bill at their friends' apartment where he and Janie were staying. The Hunters themselves were on a trip, so Bill and Janie had a Manhattan pad to themselves.

"This place is unreal, Louise," said Bill. George and Kay Hunter had money, and were into art collecting. "You wouldn't believe the throwaway sketches from famous artists on the walls. On the other hand, you'd hate the windowsills: they're thick with grime."

"New York, New York. How does Janie like the city?"

"She loves it. I don't think there's any other choice for her than somewhere near Manhattan."

"Can I talk to her?" Louise felt a little left out, as if the college decision were being made without any input from her.

"She can't get on the phone for a hello, I'm afraid, because she's out prowling the streets. She loves the Big Apple, Louise, and is seriously infatuated with NYU."

So far, their daughter had proclaimed each school her favorite immediately after visiting it; maybe that was why Bill had suggested leaving Princeton until last—because he had a feeling that the girl would choose it in the end.

Once he'd completed this update, Louise told him about Catherine Freeman's murder. "Bill, it was tragic—the most horrible sight I've ever seen."

He was very sober. "I'm very sorry to hear about this."

She told him about the gore at the scene of Catherine Freeman's death, with her brains scattered all over her designer dress and her husband's elegant tuxedo.

Suddenly, her stomach pitched, and she thought she was going to be sick. "Just a minute," she told Bill. "I need water." She reached over to the bedside table, where Emily had carefully placed a small tray with carafe, and took a drink. "I don't even want to think about it, but I can't stop thinking about it."

"Louise—" Her husband's concern carried over the phone line. "Do you want me to come home?"

"No, no. Please, stay with Janie and finish the college tour. I'm trying to block the bloody picture from my mind; so is Emily. But I *can't* block out my concerns about what happened. It looks so fishy."

Bill groaned on the other end of the phone line. "Oh, no, Louise. You can't get involved in this thing." He laughed. "Anyway, you're out of your jurisdiction."

"I know that, don't worry. Just the same, to satisfy my curiosity, tell me something about Walter Freeman. I told Alex that it didn't make sense to kill Catherine Freeman. From what I've found out, she was quite a businesswoman, active in charities, and a good wife and hostess. She also raised azalea plants and was president of a garden club. Who'd want to murder her?"

"That's the first thing police should ask," agreed Bill. "Walter's the logical target of a gunman, just having made what some people call a very inflammatory speech. Freeman's new proposals were opposed by the big players in the nation's leading financial institutions. One of them easily could have hired a hit man to kill him."

"That's what I intimated to Alex. But he told me in no uncertain terms that I shouldn't speculate."

Bill said, "I'm not surprised to hear that you two are getting along poorly."

"I miss you, Bill. Now I realize that you neutralize Alex when the four of us get together—help him mellow out or something." She lowered her voice, suddenly fearing that Alex was outside the door eavesdropping. "He's *so* difficult, Bill. Sort of mysterious, just as you warned me. I can tell he thinks I'm a wild woman who doesn't follow the Holley Covenant, the one where the woman walks three paces behind."

"Just remember, tread carefully."

"I will. But go ahead now and tell me what you know about Freeman. Do you know him at all?"

"Never met him. I'm not going to be much help to you, Louise. But wait: I did listen in at a congressional hearing last year when Walter was being questioned by the Senate Finance Committee regarding fiscal policy. I was impressed with how witty the man was. I'd heard about his wit but had never seen it in play. No wonder he's so influential—his charm is unbounded."

Charm. That was what these Washington figures seemed to have in abundance. Louise remembered the aura of sex and power she had noted in every visit she'd ever made to the Hill—watching Congressmen and women walking or riding their private little train, with handsome and beautiful aides at their elbow, serving their every wish. Sitting, as it were, at the right hand of God.

It suddenly came to her, an old adage from Louise's professor father: *Where you stand depends on where you sit.* It meant that he or she who sat in an important seat of power was influenced in his or her thinking by this position. During her youth, her father had dished axioms out regularly. Occam's Razor. Murphy's Law. Old Irish adages that had come down through his family. "Bill," she said, grasping at straws, "who was sitting near Freeman at the hearing? That is, who's his chief aide, a man or a woman?"

"A woman. But a very severe, no-nonsense-looking woman, who looked like she'd haul off and hit someone who hit on her. I didn't get any vibrations off the two of them, if that's what you mean. The man is very powerful, as you know, the type you expect to be above reproach. But funny that you should ask. I have seen the two of them together in a Washington restaurant, too. Yet it's not unusual for a man like Walter to include his top aide among his lunch companions. And now, I have a word for you, my dear . . ."

She knew what was coming. Bill hated for her to get involved in police matters when he was in town, and hated it worse when he was out of town. "Stay out of this, will you, please?"

"Honey, I'll try. I'm going home later today, so you don't have to worry about it."

She hung up the phone. Everything told her that she should go home, from Alex's attitude to the fact that she had a pile of reading to do as background for her future TV shows.

Then she sat up in bed. She had to call her producer— though Marty already realized they had to junk all the work they'd done Saturday. They'd taped a Gardening with Nature show with a now-murdered woman as its main focus. Even though they had shot enough material to slice out the parts with Catherine Freeman and still have a half-hour program, it would be just too macabre to even visit the subject of Old Georgetown Garden Club's spring plant sale.

Louise sat on the edge of the bed and thought things over. Maybe she'd better stay over another night in Bethesda for her friend Emily's sake. While she was here, who knew what she might learn about this murder?

12

Dick Rugaber needn't have worried about rousing Charlie Hurd. The Washington *Post* city editor found the thin young reporter hovering near his office when he struggled in at eleven o'clock this Sunday morning.

"Charlie. Just the man I've been thinking about."

"I thought you'd need me, Dick. That's why I zoomed in as soon as I heard the news."

"Yep. I want you over there, helping them out in the north suburban news bureau. Northern Virginia will have to get along without you for a few days, till we get a bead on this Walter Freeman assassination attempt."

"So that's what it was, huh?" said Charlie, his sharp, long nose practically quivering with excitement. Charlie, assigned to the northern Virginia suburbs normally, would do fine to help interview Bethesda neighbors of Walter and Catherine Freeman.

Rugaber stood before his office door and looked down on the shorter Hurd. "Well, Charlie," he said, in a smooth, sarcastic voice, "on the one hand, we have the overweight sixty-year-old wife, Catherine. A sharp businesswoman with heavy investments, especially in Bethesda, and with a little specialized nursery business of her own to boot. But a nice lady, we hear, president of her garden club, Cultural Women's League member—all that. On the *other* hand, we have Walter Freeman, fifty-eight, head of the president's task force on monetary reform. A man who says, 'Kiss my ass,' and everyone kisses his ass, so to speak. Who says, 'The economy's improving, you dumb shits,' and the economy improves"—Dick snapped his fingers—"just like that. Who has foreign princes and diplomats cooling their heels in his outer office, while he tinkers with interest-rate decisions that affect the whole global economy." He could hardly keep from sneering at this reporter who'd crept onto the news staff through sheer influence with the publisher—but admittedly did good stories on occasion because, granted, he had balls.

Dick performed the coup de grace: "Now who do you think the shooter intended to kill? That nice garden club lady, or that important man who makes the world economy sway to his snake-charmin' ways?"

Charlie Hurd stood there, rocking back and forth from heel to toe. His pale face remained without expression, his pale blue eyes merely blinking occasionally, like a lizard's. "Well, I dunno, Walter. The guy who makes the whole world economy behave didn't get *his* head blown off. The nice garden club lady did. All I can say is, if this was a hit, the people who hired the gunman sure didn't get their money's worth."

Rugaber was exasperated, at the insolence, and from the paucity of caffeine in his system. "Think what you want—I don't care. Just get up there and help interview the neighbors. And if you do good work, Charlie, you'll share a byline on the sidebar."

The editor turned away, but he knew Charlie would insist on the last word.

"Good," said the young reporter. "Then maybe I'll have a little extra time to figure out what really happened. When I do, I'll phone it in to Rewrite."

13

Alex Holley waited until after he'd eaten his lunch to make his announcement to his wife and her guest. He had to go to his office to pick up some papers and would be home promptly. Giving Louise a pointed look, he said, "But if you leave while I'm gone, do have a safe trip back to Alexandria."

Foggy Bottom on Sunday? Since Bill worked in the State Department Building, too, Louise knew that week-end drop-ins by employees meant going through lots of security. Bill himself never bothered to go back to the office: he simply brought the papers home in the first place. Interesting, thought Louise, that Alex seemed to do everything the hard way.

After her husband went out, Emily's face relaxed. "I have an idea. How would you like to pay a condolence call on Walter Freeman? You could even put on your detective cap, if you want to, as long as you don't—"

"As long as I don't embarrass you by asking probing questions?" Louise said with a smile. "No, I won't do that. But I doubt that Mr. Freeman will even be home. The house is a crime scene. And do you know the man well enough to just drop in on him?"

"I certainly know him well enough. We garden club

members were in and out of his home all the time. I'd planned on doing it; I *have* to tell him how badly I feel about Catherine, though I know it's mostly for me. I want to visit the inside of the house again, to see the little things that made it distinctly hers. Who knows if I'll ever see those things again? The quilt she'd pull over her legs sometimes, the bouquets she always put around on her end tables. Why, the bouquets probably will still be there—" Her lip quivered, but she went on resolutely. "But it's not only for me; maybe I'll be helping Walter, too." She gave Louise an intent look. "Despite what I said about him not being my favorite person, that doesn't mean I don't like him. I like him, and I certainly respect him. I'd be doing this for Catherine. We won't stay but a minute, and I know he'll appreciate people dropping by. I would, wouldn't you?"

Louise couldn't even imagine being in Walter Freeman's shoes, having his spouse massacred in front of his eyes. "I guess I would."

It was about two o'clock when they set off on foot with the dog. By the time they'd crossed Wilson Lane and headed down Glenbrook Road, they could see the yellow police tape that swathed both the corner Freeman property and the portion of the streets that fronted it on two sides. Evidence technicians bent to their work in the driveway. Several television trucks were parked down the street from the house, as if the murder drama were still going on, and for them it was, until the case was solved.

A group of reporters and cameramen approached Emily and Louise as they walked on the sidewalk opposite the Freeman home. In a low voice, Louise told Emily, "Look, I'll get rid of them. I've done this before." Then her eyes widened as she saw the familiar face in the crowd. The omnipresent Charlie Hurd from the *Post* was standing at the back of the clutch of press people, a wide smile on his face.

"Hey, Louise," Charlie Hurd called out, "what are you doing at the site of another murder?"

Louise pulled in a breath. "We're . . . friends of the family. We're paying our condolences to Mr. Freeman."

The other news people stared at her, then quickly lobbed questions at Charlie, trying to get a handle on who she was. She looked dubiously at the yellow police tape, then saw that a big police officer had noticed them and was slowly approaching.

Charlie shook his head. "No way are you getting in there, Louise, friend or not. If you two are looking for Freeman, he's camping out at the neighbors' while the cops check his house."

Emily turned to Louise and said quietly. "You know this reporter?"

"Yes," murmured Louise. "I have quite a history with him, and it's not all been good." Then she called out, "Which neighbor, Charlie?"

He pointed to a dark house next door, constructed of somber wine-colored brick. It was dwarfed by the size of the Freemans' place. "He's in there, and he isn't talking to us, unfortunately."

"Thanks," she said. They went to the door of the house, and as if he'd seen them coming, the front door opened, and Walter Freeman, in business suit, stood there.

The widower's greeting to Emily was distracted but friendly. "I'm staying here for a couple of days while the police do their work," he explained. "My neighbors have gone to their second house in Deale and kindly turned this place over to me for my use. Martina and I probably will be permitted to go home on Tuesday."

"You surely remember my friend, Louise."

He put out a gracious hand to Louise, and then, remembering the events of the previous night, took both of her hands in his and bent toward her. "Louise, my dear," he said, and fixed her with an expression so sad that she could have burst into tears.

"I'm so sorry for what happened, Mr. Freeman," she said. "Your wife was a wonderful woman."

He started to usher them in, when he noticed that Emily was holding the young dog. He said, "I'm afraid you'll have to leave the dog outside, Emily, do you mind?" Lancelot was cinched to an antique device for scraping mud from shoes and given a firm warning by Emily not to bark. Then they entered.

When they reached the living room, two men in suits rose from a couch, and Louise wondered if calling on this fresh widower was a good idea. Not only did he have to deal with the horrible fact that his wife was just murdered, but also with the many details that accompanied a death in the family. Without introducing them, Walter went over and guided the men out a doorway and said, "You can work in the study across the hall. I'll be with you in a bit."

Then he came back and joined Emily and Louise, waving them to be seated. Louise noted two small bouquets in crystal vases situated on a big coffee table. Emily leaned over to look at them and cried out, "Those are *Catherine's* bouquets!"

"Yes," said Freeman, and bowed his head. "The police permitted me to bring them here with me. Otherwise, they'd just die there in our house. Forgive me if I seem befuddled, my dears. A thousand things to be done, you can believe that, can't you? Soon my assistant, Reese Janning, will be here to help me with the phone calls and so forth. And yet, Emily, I'm glad you came. I'm sensitive to how close you'd become to Catherine, and how keenly you shared things that were close to her heart."

"The reason I came, Walter, is that I wanted to know if there was *anything* I could do for you." Tears welled up in

Emily's gray eyes and overflowed down her cheeks. "I'm shattered. I couldn't sleep, seeing what happened to Catherine. Never in my life have I seen anything so terrible . . ."

Freeman reached over and clasped her hand, whereupon Emily began sobbing. He said, "You're a genuine friend, Emily. I'm so sorry that you had to see it. I've had a bad night, too. The reality of her death hasn't even sunk in yet." Then, as if just remembering there was a third person present, he turned and gave Louise a strange, haunted look. "I keep thinking it should have been me. Why wasn't it me?"

Louise opened her mouth and nearly opined on that, then closed it again. Neither the time nor the place. But she agreed with him: why not *him*?

Emily said, "I didn't mention, Walter, that Louise has been responsible for solving several crimes that happened in Fairfax County, where she lives. In fact, she's quite well-known for being a crime-solver."

He looked at Louise more closely through his horn-rimmed glasses. He said, "Would that you could solve this one. Unfortunately, the police are wondering if it wasn't a hit man, who in fact intended to murder me, and made a dreadful miss. And if that is so, it might be very hard to find the culprit."

"I was wondering that, too," said Louise, and with great difficulty resisted pursuing the subject further. She was finding it easy to sympathize with Walter Freeman; he seemed vulnerable—genuinely wounded by the terrible events of last night. "I only met your wife at the plant sale yesterday, but I could tell from talking to her that she was a woman of great character. You must be simply devastated."

"Thank you, Louise."

There, they'd both said their piece, more than once. She rearranged her purse on her shoulder, hoping Emily would take the hint, but she didn't. In fact, Emily had a need to talk—and talk. "I want you to know that Alex, too, sends his deep condolences," she said. "The only thing that interfered with his coming today was some emergency work to do downtown. But we're right here, Walter, within three blocks of you. You *must* call us if you need anything—or even if you should just want to stroll over—remember when you and Catherine once did that? You might want to get away for a moment, or perhaps dinner—"

The doorbell interrupted her litany. When Walter hurried out to answer it amidst sporadic barks from an impatient Lancelot, Louise whispered, "Don't you think we should leave? The dog's restless, and the guests are beginning to pile up."

In the hall there was a period of silence and muffled sobs as he silently greeted someone. Walter ushered in his next guest. It was Sophie Chalois, her blond hair straggly and her blue eyes with dark circles under them. Obviously, she'd gotten the word last night some time of the murder in the neighborhood, and the news must have interrupted her sleep, too. Their host said, "You know each other—or do you? Louise, have you met Sophie Chalois?"

Sophie stepped over to where Emily sat and gave her a peck on the cheek. Louise got a little smile, which was more than she expected; grief must have softened the Chalois woman's heart. "Isn't it just awful about Catherine?" she said. "I heard the terrible news, and I have to confess, Meg and I came over and stood by in the crowd for God knows how long." She cast anguished eyes at the new widower. "I knew poor Walter would need company, and I guess you did, too, Emily."

"We were just thinking of leaving," said Louise. "The dog, you know . . ."

"No, no, you mustn't leave yet," said Walter, gracefully heading for the kitchen area. Over his shoulder he said, "Martina is managing this borrowed house rather well. She has tea things ready—I'll alert her. You must have a cup of tea before you go. I insist."

14

Sophie insisted on pouring when the tea tray arrived. It had taken her a while to discover just where Walter had gotten to while the police blocked off and searched his house, but finally the news media people told her. The minute she heard Martina was there, too, she'd known the housekeeper would prepare tea—Walter loved tea—and she'd planned to angle herself into the position of pouring. She'd worn just the thing for the occasion, a long mauve gauze dress with sandals. The mauve, she was sure, reflected a proper mood of mourning. The full skirt moved gracefully along her thin body as she bent and moved. Today, she was Walter's hostess, and she intended to continue that role.

It was not a surprise to see women already hovering around Walter; she was just surprised at who they were—the harmless Emily and her rather obnoxious television hostess friend. There could have been one of the females who had designs on Walter. They were bound to show up by and by. But this time, by God, he was hers. She'd earned him, done things for him that she'd done for no other man. Now was the time for him to equalize things. He had treated her shabbily ten years ago, when he'd loved her and left her, choosing to marry Catherine.

Sophie had never been a graceful loser, and she knew

from the minute that marriage took place that someday she'd see it end and would assume Catherine's place.

As for other women, including that young harridan of an aide of his who must fancy him—Reese, or whatever her name was—they just weren't going to win, to take over Sophie's charming and brilliant Walter. Charming and brilliant, as far as the whole world was concerned, and the best lover she'd ever had: a lover who seemed to study how to please a woman as closely as he studied the economic industrial charts. But his clandestine late-night visits were becoming less frequent, so it had been imperative to act, and act boldly.

No other woman would claim Walter this time. She wasn't going to let it happen again. Not over her dead body.

15

Fortunately, the reporters had vanished by the time Louise and Emily completed their condolence call. The newshounds apparently had found a more interesting line of research. And Lancelot was ecstatic to be released from his entrapment on the front porch, and knew just where home was.

They strolled by the Freeman property, where police activity hadn't seemed to have let up, and then back across Wilson Lane.

"Walter Freeman is a very warm person," said Louise.

"I thought you'd like him," said Emily.

"Why do I sense that he and his wife were not happily married?"

"You sense that because it was probably true. Walter is just too busy, and maybe too self-important to be a perfect husband. He's too caught up in his job. But you can't blame that on him, poor man." Louise wondered if that was how Emily justified her own husband's behavior.

Her friend was carrying one of the little cut-glass vases of flowers, a small basket containing miniature tulips and sprigs of baby's breath. Walter had pressed it on her as they left. It weighed less than a pound, but its emotional weight was enormous. Louise noticed her friend's attitude toward Walter—somewhat judgmental last night before the murder of his wife had taken place—had softened in those few minutes since he gave her Catherine's favorite vase as a token of their friendship. According to Walter, his wife had arranged these flowers Saturday evening, just before they went off to Kalorama Road for dinner with the French Ambassador. Louise suspected Emily would dry them and keep them in perpetuity.

"Marriage is difficult," continued Emily, as if obliged to carry on the defense of Walter Freeman. "Half of all married people are probably unhappy, anyway—certainly not you and Bill, of course, but lots of others. So the Freemans were just one more less-than-happy couple."

Louise found it depressing to hear about the high number of less-than-happy marriages, just as it distressed her to hear divorce statistics. She and Bill got along so well that they couldn't even imagine what it would be like to be at each other's throats, and then spiral downward into divorce. . . .

"Louise?"

"Oh, sorry. I was so busy thinking about marriage stats that I didn't hear you. What were you saying?"

"I said even if they weren't *supremely* happy, I get the sense that Walter feels very guilty that the assassin missed him—"

"—and took out his innocent wife, instead," finished Louise. "I do, too. The man was filled with remorse."

Emily looked slyly up at Louise, far, far up. Louise realized what an odd pair they were, Louise being a head taller than her friend. "How about that Sophie?" said Emily. "What did you think of her showing up so soon after Catherine's death? Of course, I suppose she felt the same as I did. . . ."

Louise smiled. "I don't think Walter Freeman is ever going to be lonely."

Emily looked dreamily into the distance. "Who knows? Maybe he and Sophie will renew their romance. They were quite close, I hear, before he met Catherine and married her instead."

That was an interesting wrinkle, thought Louise. She couldn't quite picture the chubby Catherine beating out a romantic opponent as beautiful as Sophie.

Emily chuckled. "I know what you're thinking. Back in the early nineties, Catherine looked much different. She was a very stunning woman, really—*curvy*. That's when I first met her. Gracious, beautiful, and bossy, that was Catherine. She gained tons of weight over the years—well, maybe not tons, but fifty or sixty pounds. She had a lot of health issues, so not all of it's her fault—or rather, *was* her fault."

Louise took a quick glance at her friend. Emily's eyes had filled with tears again. She wiped them away with a handkerchief that was already soggy. "Well, what I tried to say before I began blubbering is that Catherine was fighting diabetes, and not very successfully. She couldn't seem to stay on a diet."

They were approaching Emily's house and saw a Cadillac stopping in front. "I think we have company. That's Meg Durrance."

Meg hopped out of her car and approached them. "My God, Emily," she called, in a loud, dramatic voice, "isn't it terrible about Catherine?" With that she enveloped Emily in a huge embrace, and kept her there while tears flowed from her big brown eyes.

Emily pulled away, carefully protecting the bouquet and the vase, and said, "I know how upset you must be, Meg."

"*Me* upset? How about *you*? Sophie and I went over there last night once we heard the news—but I hear *you* were around when she was shot!"

"Not exactly," said Emily. "Come inside and we'll talk."

They went in by the front door and found that Alex had returned home from his quick trip to the office. He was puttering around the kitchen, but anxious to give the job over to his wife. Brusquely, he said, "Here, take over, Emily. You have two guests already out on the patio. I was making them iced tea and dragging out the leftover pastries. And I also need a private word with you."

"How nice of you, darling," his wife said smoothly. "You're an exemplary host." She gave him a warm peck on the cheek, and suggested the women precede her to the patio.

Phyllis Ohlmacher and Dorothy Cranshaw called out greetings. Lancelot went over to sniff Meg in a private spot, and she rudely pushed him away. "Damned dogs," she muttered.

Soon, the five women were drinking tea and eating sweets and trying to ignore the begging dog. Finally, Emily commanded him to "lie," and all his puppy training and previous admonitions clicked into place, like a computer sorting data. He found a place at the edge of the patio near the columbine and slumped into submission, his body still, only his big brown eyes continuing to beg.

Emily talked about the weather; after all, weather was a safe topic. "It's the kind of perfect spring day that makes people want to roam, or else sit around and do nothing but look at the crab-apple blossoms." Her face darkened. "But I suppose you weren't just roaming. You came over because of what happened last night. I'm not sure I want to talk about it. What happened last night is like a bad dream that I'd like to forget."

Meg sat, long legs crossed, looking indignant, ignoring Emily's desire to forget the matter. "As a resident of Ledgebrook just like Catherine, I'm *appalled* that our private security people couldn't have prevented this tragedy. Imagine, having your head shot off in your own driveway!" She turned cautiously to Emily. "It must have been awful. We heard from someone who arrived earlier that her brains were all over the car—"

Emily raised her delicate hands to cover her face. "Oh, please don't, Meg."

"Oh, sorry."

She lowered her hands to reveal teary eyes. "It's just that I can't stop seeing her there in the car. I couldn't sleep all night thinking about it, and I don't want to dredge it up now."

Louise realized Meg wouldn't let it alone until she had someone's first-hand account. She turned to Emily, as if seeking her permission. Emily, still on the verge of tears, nodded.

"Let me tell you briefly what Walter Freeman just told us. He and Catherine attended a dinner at the residence of the French ambassador—I believe you already knew they intended to do that, since Catherine mentioned it at the plant sale. A little after eleven o'clock, they drove home. When they pulled into their driveway, a gunman wearing a balaclava jumped out of the bushes, came right up to the car, and shot through the window at Catherine. Her head was terribly injured. Emily and Alex and I were on a walk and quite near their house. That's why we all saw her. It's like a bad dream, and that's why we try to get our mind off it as best we can."

Meg nodded. "Oh, I understand, I understand. How terrible. But we must think about Catherine as she was— one of the foremost women in the community; a woman whose modernization ideas were going to make our wonderful club even better."

Phyllis Ohlmacher looked at Meg strangely. "Let's go back to that security system: I bet you pay a lot for that, don't you?"

Meg nodded grimly. "You bet," she said briskly. "And, as I said, I just wonder where those people were when Catherine needed them."

Dorothy Cranshaw was matter-of-fact, and in Louise's

opinion, classy in her comments. "What's done is done. Why don't we let the Ledgebrook Community Association take care of asking where the security folks were? What we garden club members need to think about is how to honor Catherine; she was our leader for more than twenty-five years, so she deserves a memorial. We'll need to talk about that, maybe at a special board meeting."

Phyllis nodded her gray curls. "She worked hard for the club, that's for sure, the way she helped raise money to modernize the building."

Meg sat back jauntily. "Well, Emily's our new president. How about it, Emily? What do you think?" She looked over the fence. Laura Alice Shea had come out on her high porch. "There's Laura Alice: she's young and sprightly—she'll have some ideas." Her loud voice grew louder as she called out, "Hi, Laura Alice. Do you want to come over and join us?"

Laura Alice called back over the thirty feet that separated them. "Sorry. Can't make it just now. But I know what you're talking about—I'm terribly sorry about Catherine." Then she ducked back in her house.

Louise couldn't blame Laura Alice; Louise wasn't enjoying this little postmortem much herself.

16

Phyllis stacked the dessert dishes neatly on Emily's immaculate counter. Phyllis was the kind of woman who would never leave another's house without helping clean up—just as, at the spring plant sale, she stayed to the very end cleaning up. Maybe this was because as a plantsman, she was used to the never-ending work of stacking shelves, moving and pruning and pricing plants, to say nothing of the other less physical but mentally arduous tasks of keeping books and ordering and cataloging that were involved in running a small retail business.

Just now Phyllis would have liked Meg and Dorothy to come right out and tell this Louise Eldridge woman that their dead president was no saint. But no one would ever do that, so Louise would never know the real story. She would never understand that Catherine Freeman *deserved* being killed. Nervously adjusting two stacked cups before they fell and broke, Phyllis had a jolt of remorse: she supposed God didn't think *anyone* deserved to have one's brains shot out.

But the truth was that one couldn't even talk about Catherine in anything but glowing terms. She sniffed, and rinsed the dish of some messy person who'd left crust fragments and eclair filling smeared across the plate surface, as if looking for a treasure within the pastry that they'd never found.

The truth was that Catherine Freeman had been a spoiled woman her whole life. She went about in a cold-hearted fashion, paying absolutely no attention to how many people she injured, including Phyllis. She had *deeply* injured Phyllis, year after year! Whereas Phyllis was the daughter of an honest farmer, and her father had shown her how to work, how to be fair with people, and how to swallow disappointments until it seemed the bitterness just gathered within her like a cancer.

Phyllis had come by a bit of business success, such as it was, honestly, by the sweat of her brow and the work of her strong hands. And yet Ohlmacher azaleas took second place to Catherine Freeman azaleas year after year after year in plant shows. It only showed the vicious favoritism Catherine enjoyed because of her station in life. Even if she had been a smart woman, Catherine hadn't achieved that station in life all by herself: she'd done it by being the daughter of a rich man, and marrying a prominent husband. And now she was gone—

Phyllis suddenly felt dizzy, aware that she was somehow responsible for Catherine's death. She had wished it, willed it, *dreamed* it—resented Catherine practically every living day for the past twenty-five years. But did anyone really deserve to die that way? She gripped the inside of the porcelain sink hard and shook her curly head, as if to shake the guilt away, to absolve herself of sin.

She would *not* feel guilty. Catherine Freeman was dead, and it was good riddance.

17

Meg slipped into the restroom off the kitchen. With slightly trembling hands, she swooped her deep red hair into a fresh, new, opulent bun, pulling out tendrils to fall down on either cheek, and several in back to curl over her pale green linen dress. Narrowing her eyes, she looked in the mirror, and liked what she saw. And yet the next moment her face fell, and she thought she might scream from the tension. The last thing she'd needed was a big, stupid puppy smelling her crotch, but fortunately Emily's dog had soon settled down and left her alone.

Totally fatigued after playing the voyeur at the scene of the crime last night, she needed to go home and take a nap. This false face took enormous amounts of psychic energy. Within, she exulted over Catherine's demise, but she had to try to conjure up a sorrowing, sentimental countenance for the world to see.

It would get better day by day, but on this day after the Mighty One's fall, it was hard for her to sit around and talk about Catherine and how wonderful she was and act like she meant it. Not when she had thought so many nasty thoughts about her, planned so many plans against her. . . .

But soon the woman would be forgotten, though her shadow would remain. At least with Catherine gone, it left some breathing room in this world. As a smoker, Meg of all persons knew she needed breathing room.

She dabbed a little rouge on either cheek and noted that she looked much more together than she felt. That made her feel good about herself. Her imagination began to soar. She could visualize the fantastic arrangement she'd submit in the September flower show: a dream arrangement of white orchids, small pink roses, a hydrangea or two, a twirling twine of philodendron, all arranged against a spectacular piece of driftwood she'd found on the South Carolina shore, and set in a rough, free-form bowl she'd had especially made.

She'd steal Catherine's best design ideas and incorporate them with her own far-out, ingenious ones, and she bet that now it would be her turn to win "best of show."

18

Alone on the patio after the women had gone, Emily looked Louise dead in the eye. "You don't have to pretend with me: you don't like those women, do you?"

"Oh, of course I-I—" Louise stammered, then fell silent. "No, not much, I guess. I like Dorothy the best. As for the others—"

Emily, sitting in a patio chair, then seemed ready to relax. She crossed her legs so that her skirt rode up on her thighs, and she grinned, as if daring to be devilish. "Neither do I, not this bunch. There're lots nicer people in the Old Georgetown Garden Club, women who are really *together*, who're intelligent and very nice, who lead quiet lives with their spouses and children. One of them is our neighbor, Laura Alice—though in fact she works so much that I've never gotten to know her well. Too bad *she* didn't wander over today."

Louise was enjoying the last dregs of her tea. "I've been thinking about what happened last night, Emily. What bothers me is why such an important man as Walter Freeman would drive around Washington at night with his car window rolled down, exposing himself to the world."

"I see what you mean. Had the window been up, his wife might still be alive." Emily put a hand on her mouth and looked in horror at Louise, as if she'd just profaned

God. "I didn't mean to say that. *You're* not implying that, are you, Louise? I couldn't think that Walter had anything to do with this."

"I'm not saying that. On the other hand, until the police know who did it, anyone could be a suspect."

Emily's eyebrows curved downward as an anguished expression overtook her face. "Oh, Louise, Alex warned me just now in the kitchen that you might do this. . . ."

"Do what?"

"Get involved in Catherine's murder."

Louise smiled. "You make it sound as if I'm about to commit a crime myself."

Emily shook her head. "It's just that Alex is loath for me even to *talk* to him about what happened, much less get involved along with you, or even watch you get involved."

Louise kept her voice mild and neutral. "Talking about it, Emily, isn't the same thing as getting involved."

"But you don't understand, Louise. I have certain physical liabilities caused by my rheumatoid arthritis. I can't overdo or I might bring on a painful attack and then"— she shook her head—"I'm practically bedridden. When that happens, it really gets me down. I need special hot-wax treatments on my arms and legs, and I can hardly do a thing around the house. You see, I haven't talked about my condition much over the years. But now I'm getting to the age where it might flare up again."

"What age is that?" asked Louise.

"Fifty is what they say."

Louise smiled. "You still have five years to go, Emily. Why not enjoy yourself first?"

Emily looked at her strangely, as if Louise were a little mad. "At any rate, Alex doesn't want me to pry into this, and what Alex doesn't like, I generally don't do."

Louise looked at her trim, attractive friend. Her skirt was now pulled down again, her legs crossed at the ankle as demurely as a debutante. She even had her big, bouncy puppy under control. Everything about her, including the expression on her face, was proper, polite, a little re-mote—safe in this proper little world where her husband was boss and her main mission in life was to avoid hot-wax treatments. Since Louise arrived, Emily had shown an occasional flash of the spirit she'd exhibited as a grad stu-dent. But the Emily who now sat before her was a throw-back to a generation ago, when women hadn't heard the term women's liberation.

Emily leaned forward and looked earnestly into Louise's eyes. "Seriously, you mustn't criticize or have suspicions of Walter. I wish you'd forget what I said about him not checking in with Catherine—that was nothing serious. You have to understand the man: he's perfectly nice—he's a *neighbor.*" A little nervous laugh. "Next, I suppose you'll suspect a garden club member of having something to do with Catherine's murder. That's even funnier."

Louise's hostess might think that was laughable, but it was just what Louise was thinking. That was why she gave in to Emily's pleading and agreed to spend another night in Bethesda.

19

Monday

When Louise woke up on Monday morning at eight, Alex had gone to work, and Emily was still asleep. Lancelot was making whimpering noises in his crate, but Louise didn't think she should interfere with the pup's routine.

She had thought a great deal about the murder before falling asleep last night and knew she wouldn't be satisfied until she talked again to those homicide detectives. Pulling out of her pocket the card one of them had given her Saturday night, she phoned and learned that Detective Kovach, at least, would be in his office.

The Major Crimes Division of the Montgomery County Police, which was handling Catherine's murder, was in Rockville, ten miles north of Bethesda. After leaving a brief note for Emily, and grabbing a cup of coffee left in the pot made by Alex, she took off, traveling north through the rush-hour Washington traffic. Why, she wondered, were so many people rushing *away* from Washington, when all the action was supposed to be *in* the capital?

After walking through a warren of office cubicles that reminded her of a mouse maze, she sat across from Detective Kovach in a conference room. She noticed the furnishings in this interview room were luxurious compared with those in the Mount Vernon substation on Route One near her northern Virginia home. That was where her old friend, Detective Mike Geraghty, operated. The man across the table did not seem particularly friendly on this Monday morning: probably annoyed because this nosy woman wanted to talk about a murder case. He was a remarkably large man, probably six feet six, and carried enough weight to qualify him for major league football.

"I thought of something else after Saturday night, and I really wanted to, um, talk to you about it." She nearly said "share it with you," but Kovach didn't look amenable to sharing anything with anyone this morning, with his puffy eyes and generally sleepy demeanor. He seemed like a man who was sleep-deprived and hadn't had his morning coffee. His short, straight black hair was in need of a comb, though his white shirt and solid blue tie were impeccable.

As if to confirm her thoughts, he gave her a smile and said, "Late night last night, and I just rolled out of bed. They've run out of coffee in the lunchroom, but the coffee's on its way. Want a quick cup? I've gotta make this quick, I'm afraid, because I have a load of work to do."

"No coffee, thanks." She'd tasted police coffee before.

He leaned back in his chair and tried to relax. "Well, Mrs. Eldridge, something must be pretty important to bring you out first thing on a Monday morning."

"I was curious about one little detail about the shooting Saturday night."

"What detail is that, Mrs. Eldridge?"

"The matter of the driver's-side window on Mr. Freeman's car, and why the window was open. The murderer shot Mrs. Freeman through the open window."

Kovach's large face froze in a frown. "Is that all you came here for? The lowered window is all part of our record. What are you really here for, Mrs. Eldridge? Your friend, Mrs. Holley, took great pains Saturday night to tell

Peter Girard and me that you're some kind of amateur sleuth. Is that what you're her for? You wanna get in on the case?"

Louise shook her head. "Not at all. I only came on the matter of the window, even though I know it sounds trivial. Another related question: if he had the window down on the trip home, then the air-conditioning should have been turned off. But when I recall standing by the car that night, the motor was still running and the air-conditioning was still on."

Kovach loudly cleared his throat. His impatience now seemed to be running over, and his hand went up like a traffic cop's. "Just one minute, Mrs. Eldridge. You said your friend at the Mount Vernon substation was Michael Geraghty?"

"Yes."

"Hold on." And then, while she reddened with embarrassment, he got the number from her—she almost knew it by heart—and by luck found Mike Geraghty at his desk.

"So, Detective Geraghty, we have this friend of yours here. She seems real interested in helping us with a case . . ."

Face still flaming, Louise looked out the window into what was another perfect day in the outer environs of Washington, D.C. She wondered why she hadn't just spent the morning with her friend and then breezed home and forgot the grisly murder in Ledgebrook.

But Louise couldn't forget. The fact was that Catherine Freeman had touched something in her. She had been a beautiful woman with a great zest for gardening, an intense pride in the azaleas she'd created, and a loving concern for her gardener friends. Not that Louise disliked Walter Freeman—quite the reverse, in fact. She'd liked him and found him a sympathetic figure when she talked to him yesterday. It was just that there were these *questions.* . . .

Now Detective Kovach was chuckling into the phone, behind his big hamlike hand. "Uh, maybe a *little* off-base," he murmured into the phone.

Louise sat up straighter and gave him a neutral look that she hoped masked her revulsion. Was Tom Kovach one of those people who made women hate men? Luckily for Louise, she'd felt the imprint of wonderful men like her father and her husband to balance her judgment for those occasions when she met a man like this policeman.

"Thanks, Mike," Kovach said. "I understand more now." He hung up the phone and leaned both forearms on the conference table. "O-*kay*, Mrs. Eldridge. Mike Geraghty really likes you, and apparently you've been a real big help to them down there in Fairfax. But just one thing you have to understand: we don't need your help with this murder—we're coming along just fine. Though we do appreciate your pointing out the matter of the air conditioner. I'm sure there is a simple explanation." No promise to relay that information to her when he got it. He rose from his chair, and she realized she was being dismissed.

She said, "He wasn't accustomed to driving with his window down."

"Now how would you know that?"

"I saw him Saturday morning, and his window was up and the air conditioner was on, although it was a day when one could have gotten along without air-conditioning."

Kovach leaned over the table, staring down at her, and she had a sudden fantasy of him leaping over it and throttling her. As one of his tools, Detective Kovach obviously used the intimidation created by his enormous size. An officer came in with Kovach's coffee and set it in front of him, and the detective's face softened with gratitude. "Thanks—I really needed this," he told his associate.

Louise had already risen from her chair. She said, "Well, I'll leave now, Detective Kovach, and let you get to work.

Maybe none of this is important. I just keep thinking of how funny it is—"

"Yeah, what's so funny?" said Kovach, standing and practically gulping down this first cup of coffee.

"If he'd had his window open during the drive through Washington, D.C., he could have been mugged before Catherine Freeman ever had a chance to be murdered."

The detective looked at her distractedly, as if there were lots of thoughts running through his head.

"Anyway, I wish you luck in solving the case, Detective Kovach."

"Oh no, ma'am," he said, "it won't be luck that'll do it. It will be hard work. The best outcome would be to find the murder weapon—a Glock Nineteen nine-millimeter semiautomatic. It's a fairly popular smaller-model gun— costs about four hundred fifty dollars these days. We'll, of course, check recent sales on that model."

"Oh. Well, thanks for sharing that with me."

She was almost to the door when he said, "And one piece of advice."

She turned. "And what's that?"

"You shouldn't interfere with the police as they do their investigating. We know how to do our work, and need to be left free to do it. We know, for instance, that spouses have to be seriously considered in murder cases like this, and it is standard that we request lie detector tests from them. You might be interested that Mr. Freeman agreed to cooperate fully in that regard."

"Oh?" said Louise, her face reddening. Was she playing the complete fool? All her questions to the detective reflected suspicion on Walter Freeman. Yet here Freeman was, eagerly agreeing to take the police's lie detector test. Guilty people didn't do that.

The detective ploughed on: "We also will be talking to Mrs. Freeman's friends and business associates, *and* Mr.

Freeman's. That's what we *do*, Mrs. Eldridge, good, solid police work. And we could get very suspicious of someone who showed too great an interest in one of our local crimes. As to that, you people did show up conveniently soon after the shooting of Mrs. Freeman."

She stared at him, hardly believing her ears. Then she turned and went out the door.

20

Louise reached Emily's house with every intention of packing her bag and leaving for home. She found her hostess sitting on the sofa in the living room reading the newspaper. It was ten-thirty, but Emily was still wearing a blue satin robe and nightie. Lancelot was roaming the house and bounded to greet Louise as if she'd now become an elite member of his circle of friends.

Refreshed by a good night's sleep, perhaps, Emily had a slightly different look about her today. When Louise told her of her plans for departure, Emily laid the paper aside and said, "Please don't decide just yet. First tell me about it: you went to the *police* station way up Rockville Pike? What a gutsy lady you are."

From a description of the Major Crimes Division offices to a summary of her conversation with Kovach, Louise told her the highlights. An open window meant Walter Freeman was suspect. Yet Emily didn't want to connect the dots. She didn't want to hear anything that hinted that Walter Freeman was involved in the crime.

What galvanized her friend was Louise's description of the detective's phone conversation with Mike Geraghty. She cried, "How *obnoxious!* What a male chauvinist! Here you are, a citizen trying to help. How dare he treat you like that? I bet he wouldn't have treated a man that way. But tell me more. What did he say after that?"

As she gave Emily more details, Louise saw her friend's mouth tighten, and the expression in her eyes harden. This was a woman who once was a serious student, one who was going to study international law. "He warned you not to interfere with the police? I might be naive, but I thought people had a right to speak up when a crime has been committed. You can bet people all over Bethesda are talking about this."

"I bet they are, too—but just not bugging the police about the details." Louise started to get up from her chair. "Well, that's the story, and now I really have to go home."

"Hold on for a minute," said Emily, sitting forward and looking earnest, her robe falling in silky folds around her like a princess. "Louise, this murder not only frightens me, it makes me really *mad*. It happened right here in my neighborhood. How dare someone come into our neighborhood and just *slaughter* someone?" She whacked her hand down on the newspaper. "I just read the *Post* story, and it's filled with all this speculation about how some bigwigs tried to assassinate Walter. How about mentioning my friend *Catherine* a little more? She's the one who got killed."

"Drive-by shootings are hard to solve," said Louise. "And that's what they call this murder."

Her companion's eyes narrowed thoughtfully. "What if you didn't go home right now? What if you and I went over to Walter's and just looked around?"

"But you said that Alex—"

"I thought it over during the night—couldn't get to sleep for hours. I stayed awake and fantasized that you and I were detecting together—saving the neighborhood, catching the bad guys."

Louise took in the unlikely picture of her petite friend sitting there in delicate nightclothes, suggesting that they do some hard-bitten detecting. Emily was changing in front of her very eyes. "I'm warning you that it isn't as easy as just marching over to Ledgebrook and thinking we can find clues. The clues probably are somewhere else. Anyway, your husband would hate me if I got you involved in this."

"We won't tell him. We won't *have* to tell him, because we'll be very discreet. How about it?"

Louise thought of Kovach's warning. Then she looked at Emily's determined face and had a suspicion that she might go off on her own even if Louise didn't come with her. It wouldn't hurt to hoof around the neighborhood with her friend and chat with a few people. And it would be therapeutic for Emily, who at least had caught on to the fact that action was better than sitting around and mourning.

"All right, I'll stay until tomorrow."

Emily came over and gave Louise a hug. "Now I need to get on some *detecting* clothes."

"Uh, it doesn't matter what you wear—" she called after her. But Emily was out of earshot. The dog, sensing the humans in the house were ready to do something interesting, followed his mistress upstairs to see if he was going to be part of it. She dashed back downstairs holding the downhearted animal by his collar, and he knew he was headed for his crate again. Then she rushed back upstairs and reappeared in five minutes wearing dark navy jeans, a short-sleeved navy T-shirt, and a navy bandanna holding back her hair. On her feet were heavy-soled walking shoes. Louise smiled but did not laugh; she sensed it would come off as ridicule.

"And what's more," Emily said, handing Louise a small black device, "I even dug out of my drawer this *equipment* we can use. It's a voice-operated tape recorder Alex gave me." She grimaced. "He hopes I'll get on the Internet and do some research and write a family history, but I just don't want to; it's too *sedentary.* Almost everything I do is sedentary. It's much more fun to go investigate!"

Louise could hardly believe the change in her friend. Right now Emily reminded her of the bright, lively student she'd known years ago. But would it last? Since part of the reason for Emily's depression seemed to be her lack of purposeful things to do, any activity seemed better than none. The garden club appeared to be the extent of what Emily did outside of keeping house, cooking, and playing the occasional hostess. From Louise's observations, her friend suffered from the fact that Alex insisted on treating her like an invalid.

As the two women walked over to Ledgebrook, Louise told Emily how they would operate. "First, we have to keep a lookout for Charlie Hurd. He's the kind of person who will dog our footsteps if he thinks we're trying to find something out about the murder."

"Really? He sounds like a creep."

Louise slanted a look at her friend. "Just remember, you can't trust him. He will do almost anything for a story. Now, as for us, we're going to try and learn something by talking to Catherine's neighbors."

"It'll be cinchy," said Emily. "I know some of them."

They made a wide berth around the Freeman house in order to avoid newspeople. Then they cut across the street and aimed for a house two doors away, where an elderly man was hoeing a flower bed.

"I think I know him," said Emily. She called out, "Mr. Dietz—isn't it?"

The man took off his straw hat and scratched his bald head and gave her a good looking over. "Actually, it's Rietz, Howard Rietz."

"Oh, sorry. Mr. Rietz, I'm Emily Holley—I live just over Wilson Lane in Battery Lane. And this is my friend, Louise Eldridge . . ."

Expertly, Emily led the conversation to the topic of Catherine's murder. "We wonder what you make of it all."

Mr. Rietz shook his head. "Well, I didn't want to tell those TV and news reporters anything, but I'll tell you two what I think. He's a fast mover, that Walter Freeman. Mixing with the powerful, going all the time to Washington parties and meetings, traveling overseas, enjoying the fact that people hang on his every word. Sure he's right about everything." He peered down at Emily. "My view is they were after Walter. He wasn't a very nice man, anyway. Never said hello to me on those few occasions when he could have done so, even when he was pacing the neighborhood in the evening."

He paused to replace his hat on his head. "Now, as one who has his savings tucked safely away in bonds and cash, I don't have to worry. But with his wild ideas I don't trust him to call the shots on the economy. No, I can see that a certain number of people would want him dead and not ascending to become Federal Reserve chairman. Not Mrs. Freeman, though; everybody liked her. She was a princess of a lady. Walked down the street here as friendly as you'd please. Once she brought over a cake when my wife was sick. In my humble opinion, the murderer was a bad shot: missed Walter and took away a woman who sure didn't deserve it."

After they talked a while longer, Emily broke away so gracefully that she left Mr. Rietz with a big smile on his long face. Louise said, "Good work, Emily. You're a natural."

Her friend beamed. "Thanks. So, did you get all that on the recorder?"

"Oh, sorry. I forgot to turn it on. I can pretty much remember what Mr. Rietz said without a tape."

Emily gave her a doubtful look. "Louise, how can a person like you avoid modern technology? Why, you don't even bother to carry a cell phone. Even I have a cell phone, and a computer, and a fax . . ."

"I know. Back in the Neanderthal age, aren't I? I was thinking of stepping up to the plate on this phone business. There have been a couple of times when I could have used a cell phone."

Next, they threaded their way through one side of the block and back on the other, discreetly peering into every backyard but failing to turn up other neighbors working outside. Louise had to dissuade Emily from knocking on people's doors, for after the unpleasant encounter with Detective Kovach, she was reluctant to be too aggressive.

Emily had no such qualms. She cocked her head up at Louise, a challenging look in her eyes. "I think that detective has intimidated you. Do you normally hold back this way when you're investigating crimes?"

Louise laughed. "Not normally, but you'd be intimidated, too, Emily, if you'd had Kovach threatening to wring your neck. Just remember, I'm a stranger in a strange land. One of these people will call the police if we start questioning them in their houses, and then we'll be in trouble."

Her friend clutched her arm. "We still have plenty of garden club members to talk to. And tomorrow we can talk to Walter's housekeeper, because she and Walter will be allowed back in his house. But I *know* you think there are possibilities among the club members, or at least I do." She chuckled. "Among our members are a few, what you might call, 'witches.'"

They'd just crossed Wilson Lane again when Louise realized how to crack this case. She said, "We'll get nowhere with our investigation until we get some help. What we need is someone who has the inside scoop on the club members. The one that's been around the longest, and one whom we can trust. Someone like Dorothy Cranshaw."

They stopped and looked at each other and smiled,

then gave each other a high five. "Dorothy!" cried Emily. "Of *course.*" Then she hurried on, beckoning Louise to catch up. "Dorothy lives at the clubhouse: she's the caretaker there. Maybe she's home right now. And she knows more than anybody about the Freemans, as well as the garden club members—as well as everyone *else* living in this area. All we have to do is ask her and she'll tell us. I'll call her from home."

"She lives in the clubhouse?"

"In the basement—or rather the lower level. That's where there are stacks of club records for decades past. Oh, the apartment's not what it sounds: it's very elegant, even luxurious, I hear. It even has a walled garden. Dorothy gets it rent-free; otherwise, it would go for two thousand a month in this pricey part of the world. Poor thing lost her husband years ago, and she's been on her own ever since."

"Why this largesse on the part of the club?"

Now they were in sight of Emily's house, and she speeded up, like a horse getting near to the barn. "For one thing, she's worked like a soldier for the club. She used to live in Ledgebrook, just like lots of garden club members, but she sold her house after her husband's death, I guess. And then about ten or fifteen years ago, her son Jack wanted to go into business for himself—"

"I met Jack at the plant sale."

"Yes, he shows up once a year, to help her ferry plants to the library garden. Dorothy gave him most of her capital to open a restaurant near DuPont Circle—you know, the diplomatic neighborhood. I heard even Catherine Freeman lent him money to help him get started, because he needed a huge amount of startup funds. He did all right for a few years, but proved to be a poor businessman, and maybe not the chef he was touted to be. He eventually went bankrupt and the restaurant closed. Since then, Dorothy's been painfully short of money. Catherine took Dor-

othy over as her favorite project, and for a while she even
worked for Catherine as housekeeper. After Walter came
on the scene, it seemed better to have another housekeeper, I guess. Who knows? Walter probably didn't like a
social contemporary of Catherine waiting on their table.
But Catherine gave all the perks she could manage to
Dorothy—free rent, free garden club membership"—
Emily laughed—"though that only comes to thirty-five dollars a year. Leftover food from club luncheons."

She looked up at Louise. "That doesn't sound very nice,
does it? It's as if Dorothy's begging crumbs from the table.
But food from the club luncheons is always very good, and
there's lots of leftovers. Now her caretaker job is being
phased out since Catherine engineered some big changes.
The clubhouse is being renovated, and we're getting security entrance cards."

"No more free housing for Dorothy?" said Louise.

"She doesn't mind. In fact, she seems relieved to be
moving out—and ending this gracious charity that Catherine had extended. She's launching some whole new career, about which she is very excited."

"What career is that?"

They went to the back door and Emily unlocked both
locks. "I don't really know. She's keeping it under wraps;
Dorothy is pretty close-mouthed, but she's also very clever.
She says it will earn her good money. Anyway, let's go in
and give her a call."

Under Emily's direction, Louise rummaged out frozen
lasagna for lunch and put it in the microwave.

Emily phoned Dorothy.

"She'll come over right away," reported Emily.

Louise gave Emily a droll look. "Surely you didn't tell
her we wanted to snoop into the lives of garden club members on the supposition that one of them is the murderer."

"I surely didn't. I said you were here for an extra day
and wanted to visit Phyllis's greenhouse, and maybe look

around the neighborhood a bit. She needed to talk to me anyway. She's down in the dumps over poor Catherine." Emily shot her a guilty glance. "I have to admit, Louise, I've forgotten completely about being sad about Catherine's murder, because we've been so busy investigating it."

"It's good for focusing your mind."

"But first, I'll have to satisfy Dorothy that, as the new club president, I've done the right thing about the flowers we send to the funeral home. Visitation apparently starts tomorrow."

"A funeral bouquet," said Louise. "That's pretty standard. It shouldn't be too hard."

Emily shook her head. "Oh, no, Louise, you have it all wrong. *This* is the trifling, seemingly insignificant thing you have to do right if you're the head of our garden club. Catherine warned me about this aspect of garden club etiquette: always respect plants, as well as the living and the dead. This bouquet—or wreath, if we decide a wreath is better—has to stand out with pride. It has to say, 'We loved and respected Catherine, our great leader, and to show it, here is this lovely floral offering.' So I've phoned the best florist in Washington."

Louise smiled, a flood of remembrance overcoming her. "And who's that supposed to be, Richard Ralston?"

Emily's eyebrows ascended. "How did you know—oh, I suppose you do know such things. I usually only deal with Bethesda Florist and let it go at that."

"I happen to have met Richard."

"Oh, have you? This bouquet has to be the very best bouquet at the wake. And Richard—who's very charming, don't you think?—said he'd whip up something 'terribly poignant.' His exact words: weren't they nice?"

"Richard will do well by you."

They sat on Emily's pleasant patio and silently ate their lasagna and salad, both lost in their own thoughts. Louise found herself longing for home but had the feeling she wouldn't be able to extricate herself from this place for a while. Bethesda was a different world from her woodsy neighborhood. Or was she kidding herself? This place might suffer from conspicuous consumption and a certain smugness on the part of residents who thought it was the new center of the Washington universe. But her neighborhood, the deceptively bucolic Sylvan Valley, had its own intrigues, pretensions, and hang-ups, helped along by a plethora of media executives, Democratic pols, and State Department types.

Maybe it wasn't Bethesda that made her uncomfortable, but rather Emily's house, or rather, the man of the house. Louise had a serious spiritual dislocation with Alex Holley. She considered him the very agent of the devil, with his devilish sandy brows that came down in such scorn and disapproval, as regularly as a clock ticking the minutes.

But Alex was at work, and not due back until six. All Louise had to do was sit back, relax, and enjoy her next investigative foray with Emily and a new member of the detective team, Dorothy Cranshaw.

She'd liked what she'd seen so far of Dorothy: smart, plain, down-to-earth. Maybe Dorothy could help them shed light on Catherine Freeman's demise. She and Emily this morning certainly hadn't done so.

Then Dorothy drove up in her car.

21

Dorothy Cranshaw got out of the car, took her bandanna handkerchief from the pocket of her blue denim shirt, and carefully blotted the perspiration from her forehead. The day was growing hot, and she was growing nervous, for she didn't like uncertainty.

Catherine was dead, and who knew what would happen now? Would they find Catherine's killer? And what was to happen now to her beloved garden club? Would the changes in the club still take place without Catherine there to guide them through? Emily Holley was taking over, but she was a hothouse flower, with a husband who wouldn't let her carry a gallon pot of flowers when she was in his sight.

And this Louise—why was she still here? Dorothy thought she knew. It would have made her feel better if Louise had just gone home, for she appeared to be sticking her nose into the neighborhood business. Of all the people who respected neighborhoods and their sacrosanct quality, it was Dorothy.

What was most important was keeping up standards. That meant that at Catherine's funeral, protocol and tradition had to be preserved. Club members and others had to turn out to honor her, and that included Dorothy's son, Jack. After all, Catherine had helped him when he needed help; so he owed Catherine that much. The woman had not even put pressure on him to repay the loan she made him after his business went belly-up.

The garden club's funeral bouquet, of course, had to be the grandest arrangement available in Washington, D.C. Old Georgetown Garden Club must show that it had class.

And difficult as it would be, she must talk with Emily and Louise about the people in the garden club. When Emily phoned, she said she merely wanted to show Louise around town, but Dorothy knew better. They were fishing for murder suspects, and not a bad call, since Dorothy knew several club members with good motives to murder Catherine. The Eldridge woman apparently was some kind of police informant, she'd heard. But such matters were better left to the police, not women, in Dorothy's opinion. People who snooped could get in trouble. Indeed, leave it to the police; if they couldn't solve the crime, then so be it.

To tell a stranger like Louise Eldridge what she knew about her fellow garden club members would be hard for Dorothy, seeing as she knew the information could be used against people. She respected garden club members as much as the elders in her church.

As she walked into Emily's house, Dorothy gave Lancelot some affectionate pats, then rubbed that place on the chest that dogs liked rubbed. She loved dogs and they loved her. Then she looked up at Louise Eldridge and, taking her time, spoke in a deliberately methodical voice. She found that this tone slowed other people down and made them more thoughtful. She sensed that this Louise person needed slowing down, for she appeared to be a bit manic: she talked a little too fast and moved a little too fast. Maybe that was what ailed television personalities like her—they wanted action all the time.

"So you're curious to know more about Bethesda,

Louise? Then why don't we take a little tour? I can drive, if you don't mind a car that's not very new."

With this agreed upon, Emily crated her dog and they set out. Dorothy knew just the route she'd take, first, past Meg Durrance's house in Ledgebrook, then a swing through "Old Bethesda," so Louise could see what was left of the triangle of shops that constituted its early business center. Next, they'd go up to Phyllis's nursery, where they'd stop and visit for a few minutes and inspect Phyllis's plant stock. A quick trip east of Wisconsin Avenue by the homes of a few club members, and finally, they would return by way of exclusive Ledgebrook, passing the house of the person who would make the most likely suspect in any murder, Sophie Chalois.

Actually, the more Dorothy thought about helping solve Catherine's murder, the more excited she became, but she wouldn't admit to these two that she was on to their game.

She smiled at her passengers. "Is it cool enough in here for you? I could turn on the air, but it doesn't work too well."

"I like it with the windows down, don't you, Louise?" asked Emily.

"Yes, I do."

Dorothy slowed down as they passed a large white colonial. "This is where Meg lives."

"A magnificent old house," commented Louise.

"It was one of the original homes around here. She's restored it beautifully."

"Quite a formal yard, isn't it?"

"I think she tried to replicate the Mount Vernon garden, to some extent," said Emily. "She's espaliered pears on her split-rail fence, and they're wonderful."

Dorothy wasn't into garden talk. She got down to the more convoluted parts of Meg's background. "Meg came here about ten years ago, maybe eleven, after a difficult divorce from a very rich husband. She's worked real hard since then to do things in flower arranging, and she's very good at it. She hasn't achieved what she thought she'd achieve, I'm afraid."

"Oh, what's that?" asked Louise.

Dorothy cocked her head at Emily, sitting in the passenger seat beside her. "Emily knows all this. Tell her, Emily."

"Oh, you mean because she's never won the top prize in flower arranging?"

"That's what I mean," said Dorothy.

"I didn't think it was such a big thing with Meg," said Emily. "Do you think it is?

"Oh, *yes,*" said Dorothy. "Very big. Apparently she won the blue ribbon every year in Winnetka, where she came from. It just . . . bugged her that she never got to the top in her chosen hobby after she moved here."

"I'll bite," said Louise. "Who tends to win the blue ribbon?"

"Oh," cried Emily, "that was always Catherine. She was a great flower arranger."

"A talented woman, wasn't she," commented Louise.

Dorothy interrupted to activate her role as tour guide. "Now we're coming to old downtown Bethesda, the triangle . . ."

Once they'd done their little town tour, Dorothy headed north. "Phyllis specializes in azaleas," she explained. "You'll see that when we get to her nursery." She shook her head, as she expertly took the turn from Montgomery Avenue onto Wisconsin Avenue. "Phyllis Ohlmacher, always the bridesmaid, never the bride."

"Um, what does that mean?" said Louise.

These women were looking for suspects. Dorothy had sketched in a motive for Meg Durrance. Now she'd give them one for Phyllis. "Well, she's sort of like Meg: always second or third in the local azalea show."

"Yes," chimed in Emily, "those gorgeous, dark-throated, fluffy-petaled plants of Catherine's always do better than Phyllis's hybrids—I mean, *did* better."

"How disappointing for her," said Louise.

Dorothy said, "The azalea show comes up in about a week, and obviously Catherine's plants won't be there."

"Sad," said Emily.

Dorothy had expected more of a rise out of their visitor from northern Virginia. Louise had hardly reacted to anything said about the club members. Dorothy couldn't tell whether these two women were snooping about or just innocently spending an hour on a pleasant sight-seeing trip, but it didn't really matter to her. She looked at the car clock. Two. In any case, she would have to get a move on or they'd get caught in the vicious late-afternoon traffic, and her car might overheat.

Just to put things in perspective, Dorothy threw in a word about herself. "You know, I'm going into business soon, just like Phyllis Ohlmacher. I have some pretty extensive plans—I'm moving from the clubhouse, too, of course, at the same time. I think it will be quite a profitable enterprise."

"*Oh?*" said Emily, her tone showing that she would welcome more information from her. Dorothy kept her peace, knowing that it was not good sense to give out details of an upcoming business venture. Someone, anyone, might want to copy her idea.

When they got out at Phyllis's modest greenhouse, Dorothy realized she could have elaborated a bit on the extent of the woman's disappointment at losing each year in the Washington Azalea Show, but it wasn't her style to gossip. Maybe later. But right now she wouldn't tell about those furious private words from the small, strong-as-a-horse Phyllis about Catherine—those tears and suppressed screams of rage in the ladies' restroom after the judges' decisions. Dorothy was always there to support the smaller woman, since Phyllis's indifferent husband didn't want to hear about it.

The reason she didn't want to bad-mouth Phyllis was that Phyllis was an old friend, too, just like Catherine. Besides, who'd believe a woman would kill over losing an azalea competition? Would Louise Eldridge believe that?

Because Phyllis was skimping on water, her plant stock didn't look quite as sprightly as it might. And then it turned out she'd just received a half-truckful of annuals— multicolored zinnias, yellow marigolds, blue lobelia, and impatiens in all the red shades. Unfortunately, thought Dorothy, this nursery only carried the most popular and pedestrian plants. As a result of the delivery, Phyllis had little time to talk to them before she put away her stock.

Probably to show they were good sports, Louise and Emily offered to help. But Phyllis shoved back her gray curls with a gloved hand and proudly declined. "Thanks, girls, but I have plenty of help," she said, nodding to two swarthy men who'd come around the building. "And my husband Al should be somewhere around here, too, to lift a hand."

22

Louise drifted away from the conversational group and walked around the nursery building. A tall, balding man with thin shoulders and a paunch was leaning against a locust tree, smoking a cigarette and sipping on a canned drink. She smiled at him but didn't approach. It took a minute for her to realize he hadn't noticed her, so caught up was he in his own thoughts. It was Al Ohlmacher, whom she'd met briefly at the plant sale on Saturday. Al looked bored with life, and in no hurry to join the work going on in the backyard of the nursery.

Then she heard the angry, hissed words: *"There* you are, you lazy s.o.b!" It was Phyllis, who'd rushed around the building, her face brick red with anger, her gray curls tousled and wet with sweat.

Louise crouched behind a mature ligustrum bush.

Phyllis obviously scolded her husband a lot, and had learned to do it in a low-key, menacing tone. "Listen, you, it's not enough I'm working my tail off, and having to get ready for the azalea show as well. But now we have company—some gals from the garden club. And they're going to wonder why I'm out back with Ramon and Feliz busting my back hauling flats while you stand around sipping beer and smoking. *You get out there now,* dammit, and help me!"

As she turned to go, Al brought her to a halt by saying,

"Clear up a mystery first, will ya, Phyllis. Why're those wholesalers calling us inquiring about your azaleas? Did you think there was gonna be a big hole in their supply? Is that what Catherine's death means to you?"

She approached her husband, and he shrank back just enough so that if she lashed out a fist, he was too far away for it to connect with his jaw. "You foolish man. Of course it will shrink the supply. And *our* stock—of which you know there's a hell of an oversupply—is going to zoom right up."

She moved closer and was standing now under her husband's nose. "Quit speculating, Al. It doesn't become you."

He stood there, arms out, a smoke in one, a beer in the other, looking helpless and yet full of guile. "What's done is done. Do *I* care who killed Catherine Freeman? Okay, okay, I'll come and help." He gave her a boyish grin that might have worked sometime in the past but wasn't working now. "Just let me swig down the last of this beer."

Louise thought Phyllis was going to hit her husband, for she stood in front of him with hands on either hip. Not a good harbinger: Louise had personal experience with people who got angry and put their hands on their hips; the next logical thing was for them to sock someone.

But Phyllis apparently thought the better of it. Her voice even softened a little. "Al, dear, I'll forgive you everything if you come heave some flats and meet the ladies. And under the circumstances, it wouldn't hurt you to turn on a little charm, either. Don't forget: you're in this with me."

Then she reached up and gave him a quick peck on his cheek before turning to go. When she turned away, he swiped at the spot with the back of his hand.

A marriage made in heaven, thought Louise. During the conversation, neither of the Ohlmachers had noticed Louise. She continued to watch as Al stamped out his cigarette, set his unfinished beer into a crotch of the locust, and strolled around to where the truck was parked and others labored.

Lots of tension in that marriage, thought Louise. She would have despised living in such a relationship.

And all this talk of wholesalers—that was directly related to the fact that Catherine Freeman was no longer going to be competition for the Ohlmacher Nursery. *How convenient for them,* she thought.

When they'd arrived, Phyllis had painstakingly shown them her row upon row of hybridized azaleas, and though adequate, they didn't compare with Catherine's stock. In fact, Phyllis said something to that effect: "Of course they aren't quite as fancy as Catherine's, but they sell steadily, and there's a lot more of them available than Catherine ever had, because I work day and night to keep up the supply!" In her brown button eyes was real anger. Was it sufficient to murder?

23

On their way back to Emily's house, Dorothy decided to show Louise the good works of the Old Georgetown Garden Club. She stopped at the Davis Library garden that was maintained by the club and that she had so recently beautified.

As the three women got out to look at the garden, Dorothy couldn't help smiling, for it was such a pretty place. Dominated, of course, by those bronze statues of deer, bear, squirrels, and chipmunks, though her gaze went to the garden itself, which was gorgeous, thanks to Dorothy.

"Many of the annuals," she informed Louise, "are left-overs from the Saturday plant sale. I put them in myself Saturday after the sale; didn't finish until six."

"Did anyone help you?" asked Louise.

"No," said Dorothy matter-of-factly. "Everybody else had somewhere to go that evening."

"How cleverly you've placed them," said the visitor.

Subduing her pride in the fact, Dorothy informed Louise that garden club members had a combined experience of more than seven hundred years. "Of course, I'm still counting Catherine into that figure, since she—"

"I understand," said Louise.

Dorothy tucked back a strand of gray-streaked hair that had escaped from her bun. "I personally have gardened for more than forty years. Maybe our long experience is the reason that we club members can take a bunch of left-over plants and make them into something beautiful."

"You should be proud," said Louise.

"You really should," agreed Emily.

Flushed from the praise, Dorothy added, "Well, it wasn't easy this year, with the water restrictions put on because of the drought. I added polymers to the soil to help retain water. And, of course, soaker hoses help a lot."

"And mulch," added Louise.

"That goes without saying," said Dorothy, just a trifle annoyed that Louise had to have the last word.

They loaded back into the car, Louise sharing the front seat this time, and Dorothy headed for the next destination. It was the most interesting one on the trip. She'd saved the best until the last. Dorothy could feel her palms sweating, for the afternoon was growing more exciting. She looked over at the tall, brown-haired Louise and saw her looking back with those big hazel eyes. She sensed this woman was shrewd enough to figure out that Sophie Chalois had the strongest motive to get rid of Catherine Freeman. And she'd probably already recognized Sophie was a woman with hidden purposes.

She dodged back into Ledgebrook, surprising her passengers by not turning down Exeter Road, the route to Emily's house. Dorothy knew every house in Ledgebrook, and why not? She and her husband had lived there long ago.

"Didn't you take a wrong turn?" asked Emily. "I thought—oh, I see. You're going by Sophie's."

"I thought Louise would like to see the house." She shot her a glance. "It's one of a kind." It was coming up now on the right, and Louise made the proper "ooh" and "ahh" sounds. Caught among the lovely colonials and the re-done colonials, the house was modern, with a hidden entrance, a fancy stonework facade for which she must have paid dearly, and a modern sculpture set out in a small forecourt.

"Now, Sophie's an interesting person," said Dorothy, as if throwing live bait to sharks. But these women weren't very sharklike. What kind of detective was Louise, anyway? There was no earthly reason for her and Emily to angle for this tour of Bethesda if Louise weren't investigating.

No one took her bait, so she continued. "She dated Walter Freeman before Catherine stepped in and snatched him away. I don't mean to talk idly about poor, dead Catherine, but that's the fact of the matter."

"I had heard that," said Emily. "Walter must have been a very desirable bachelor."

"Oh, he was, indeed. I, for one, thought he and Sophie were definitely headed for the altar, but Catherine had many desirable things about her. Beauty. Money. Though, mind you, I'm not saying those were the crucial factors. Catherine had a heart of gold, and a fine character."

Louise said, "From the look of her house, Sophie herself is a woman of means."

"Oh, but nothing like the money Catherine inherited from her father." Dorothy shook her head. "A very large fortune. Which, by the way, she took and invested very smartly indeed."

Then Sophie herself swung around the side of her house, from behind a screen of hemlock. Probably she came to inspect her grand bed of New Design tulips. Dorothy had always thought the variegated leaves, combined with the pale-pink-with-white striped flowers were a bit over the top, but she had to admit they looked beautiful in Sophie's front yard.

But Dorothy was almost embarrassed at Sophie's attire: a colorful bra, short shorts exposing her long legs, her feet in tennis shoes. It was a warm day, but not *that* warm.

Dorothy herself was dressed in a long-sleeved old sweat-shirt and pants, prepared for any cold snap that might come along.

Dorothy slowed the car to five miles an hour and went by, hoping Sophie would invite them for a yard tour. Sophie waved and smiled, but then her eyes met Louise's and she seemed to lose her friendly enthusiasm. After hesitating and giving them a long, pointed look, she slipped around a hedge.

"There she is—or was," said Dorothy, feeling a little as if she were pointing out a local tourist sight, or a rare and skittish bird that had taken flight. She turned the corner and stopped at the curb so that Louise could catch a glimpse of Sophie's backyard. "Oh well, guess she doesn't want to talk to us today. That's Sophie, through and through. Hot one minute, cold the next. Anyway, take a look at that yard."

Louise had her hand thoughtfully supporting her chin. "Beautiful," she said, "what I can see of it."

Then, just as Dorothy was about to start the car moving, the half-naked Sophie appeared again. She flitted out to the street, put her hand up in a commanding gesture, and ordered, "Stop."

With a slight squeak of brakes, Dorothy did so. Sophie came over to the driver's-side window and slouched there with her arms on the windowsill. *"Ladies,"* she said, "did you come by to see me?"

"Yes," said Dorothy, a bit off-put by the woman's antics.

"You have an intriguing yard," said Louise.

"Want to see it? Pull over, Dorothy, and I'll give Louise a tour."

It was a spectacular display, Dorothy had to admit. Out of ivy-carpeted beds—Dorothy knew the ivies were care-fully propagated from the sprig Sophie bragged that she'd stolen years ago from the Mount Vernon estate—sprang small trees and evergreen and deciduous bushes. Drifts of flowers were set here and there. The yard was one surprise after another, divided by hedges and groups of trees. Finally they came to what looked like an oasis in the center of the backyard: an amoeba-shaped pool surrounded with brunnera and bamboo plants, and other water plants that Dorothy had never seen before, because she wasn't into water plants.

"How truly delightful," exclaimed Louise.

Sophie gave her a hard look and coolly replied, "I'm so glad you appreciate it. That's one advantage of your having been around: you can appreciate quality when you see it. Not everyone around here can."

Dorothy was taken aback at this remark. Sophie'd managed to insult fellow club members and at the same time compliment this Louise Eldridge, when a moment ago she appeared to dislike Louise. Oh well, Sophie was one of those temperamental females that Dorothy simply could not identify with but just had to accept.

The three women thanked Sophie for the tour, got back in the car, and drove off. They soon reached Emily's house, and neither Louise nor Emily had said one thing that would indicate they were trying to solve the neighborhood murder—though Catherine's death loomed in their consciousnesses like an eight-hundred-pound gorilla.

Dorothy was puzzled, feeling a mixture of relief and disappointment. Relief because it was best not to step into things that weren't one's business. Disappointment, because she was curious to know herself just what these two were going to do next.

24

Sophie slipped the secateurs from the tight back pocket of her shorts, careful not to scratch her butt on the pointed blades. She crouched down and resumed snipping off the dead heads on the orange osteospermum. Although her movements were calm, her heart was pounding. She could have used a pill, but she'd been avoiding the use of pills since the events of Saturday. Calmness and complete rationality were called for in these difficult days.

That damned Louise Eldridge. Why hadn't she gone straight home after that WTBA-TV program of hers? Instead, Sophie had already heard from Meg how Emily and Louise had been hanging around the neighborhood, talking to people. They were about as transparent as a plate-glass window, the Eldridge woman an incurable snoop, pathetic Emily Holley carried along in the excitement.

She'd heard about Louise and her little claims to fame as a detective and found herself disliking the woman the minute she'd met her. Especially after she'd ridiculed Sophie for swiping ivy from Mount Vernon and then propagating it for sale. The dumb woman didn't realize that *everyone* who could manage it snitched pieces of ivy from George's old house. The only good thing about Louise

Eldridge was that she appreciated a fine garden when she saw one.

That producer of Louise's, though, was another matter. Marty Corbin was smooth as velvet, the kind of man one could imagine in bed. Great eyes, and eyebrows, a darling face, really. And he exuded sex. Sophie could have spent more time working on *him,* but he'd dodged off and hadn't even seemed interested in a follow-up. Maybe he was happily married, but she knew that in time, he could be had. She could always tell this about a man.

As for Louise, she had that cocky, know-it-all way about her that Sophie despised. Maybe she could tell that Sophie had designs on Walter. Maybe she suspected things about Sophie.

What Sophie didn't want dredged up was what had happened two decades ago in Princeton, New Jersey. If, by chance, she came to the attention of the Bethesda police, they might look into it, and tie her to Catherine's death, and to that other incident ten years ago in Washington.

She was getting tired of selectively deadheading. She made a vicious grab for a cluster of osteospermum in one gloved hand, and with the other snipped off their heads with one quick movement of the shears, removing the living blossoms with the dead.

That afternoon twenty years ago, her car had broken down as she left for an all-day trip to New York City. She'd returned home to her Federal-style house unexpectedly and come upon her adulterous professor husband making noisy love to his assistant in the canopied master bed. Running downstairs to the kitchen, Sophie'd picked up a chopping knife—and damned well with the intent to do bodily harm—but unfortunately, he'd heard her and headed down the back servants' stairs. Screaming profanities at him, she'd pursued him out the back door and into the street, until the neighbors halted the travesty by calling the police.

Days later, when they'd sat in a lawyer's office while her husband agreed to drop the charges, she'd asked him why. "How could you do it with that little frump?"

He'd replied, "Because unlike you, Sophie, she cares about me. She's kind to me, whereas you treat me like a piece of clothing you're about to give away to Goodwill."

She'd told him, "I wouldn't treat you that way if you acted as if you cared—as if you were interested in building this marriage into something vital."

He'd said, "What about all the trips I've taken you on? The attempts I made to get you interested in my activities?"

"I'm interested in neither golf nor geology," she'd answered, "nor in your incessant prattlings about the French deconstructionists."

Then he'd struck at her heart: "Unfortunately, you're not interested in anything, Sophie, outside of the image of yourself in the mirror. The ladies' lunches, the workouts at your club: you only do things to satisfy your own self."

What a mismatch it had been, the golden-haired debutante and the nerdy English professor. That humiliating scene in the bedroom and its unfortunate outcome had led to a divorce from which she'd never recovered. After that, men seemed to treat her like a dangerous commodity—someone who wasn't worth getting involved with, someone treacherous and unsteady, who would take a man's affections and trash them, and then blame *him*, not herself. Who might even come after him with a knife or a gun.

At least, that was what they'd thought in Princeton. Eventually, she'd moved away and carefully reestablished herself in the Washington, D.C., area. Kept a low profile. Just barely avoided having her name dragged in the mud after that incident in Cleveland Park. Joined the right clubs and organizations, including the very hoity-toity Cultural Women's League. Had her romantic skirmishes, then wooed, and lost, Walter.

Now she was in jeopardy again, she realized, as she gathered up the flower heads. But she was determined that this time she wouldn't lose Walter. Even that aide of his, Reese, was not going to win, not this time. Walter must know in his bones that Reese Janning—why, she couldn't be any older than about thirty-three to his fifty-eight—was out for herself, and not going to be dedicated to an old guy who'd be seventy-five and doddering when Reese reached fifty and was still in her prime.

Sophie walked proudly to the garage to dispose of her tools and garden debris, knowing that she cut a youthful figure despite her age. At fifty-five, she knew she was the perfect mate for Walter: a sexual dynamo when she wanted to be, demure at other times. A perfect hostess, known throughout Washington for her occasional but always delightful dinner parties. She'd planned her life carefully over the past ten years, and made the right connections. The way was now paved for Sophie's ascendancy to the role of Mrs. Walter Freeman. And the nosy TV hostess of a gardening show was not going to stand in her way. Nor would Reese Janning. She'd seen the woman once and noted how ugly she was. A prototypical Ivy League overachieving female graduate—Sophie should know. She'd seen whole campuses full of this type of woman and knew what they were all about. They were out for themselves, out to *succeed*. Men and husbands were simply appendages to help them reach their goals.

No, neither Reese Janning nor Louise Eldridge would stand in the way of Sophie's plan.

25

Louise was in charge of the risotto, while Emily flew around the kitchen preparing pan-fried, Cajun-style tilapia, homemade biscuits, broiled tomatoes stuffed with thyme-flavored goat cheese, and asparagus. Louise's mouth watered with hunger as she slowly stirred the pot. One good reason for hanging around Emily's house was her superb cooking. Another was having a nice dog to pet. Louise and Bill now owned a cat, Hargrave, courtesy of an old friend, and she loved that cat. But Hargrave wasn't good for walks in the neighborhood, nor did he exhibit the rank enthusiasm and lack of critical judgment that she found so charming in young Lancelot.

The dog sat now in the corner of the kitchen, giving Louise a friendly eye, fantasizing, perhaps that she'd toss a dog biscuit across to him—which she would have done if one were handy. Yet the slow stirring of the risotto was like a metaphor for her present existence, which was going much too slowly for her tastes, but possibly getting somewhere, just like the risotto.

Since no one had asked Louise and Emily to poke around in this murder investigation, she felt a sense of discomfort. Things had taken a negative turn this afternoon, somehow, and it was as if she'd fallen into a maelstrom of gossip.

Was her pursuit of unsolved crimes usually this seedy? Or was it that she was dealing mainly with female suspects today—seemingly innocent women, the kind who liked to beautify the world and their own community, planting thousands of trees and bulbs and native plants. Weren't these her sisters in gardening? Somehow she was ashamed to think that one of them could be a killer. That was why she'd asked no leading questions about specific garden club members—though Meg, Phyllis, and especially Sophie were the kind of people the police might want to interrogate further. Dorothy'd shown her that with the tidbits she'd thrown out.

Louise had thought she would like Dorothy Cranshaw, but there was something about the way Dorothy gossiped about people that turned her off. Then she realized what it was: Dorothy knew what Louise and Emily were up to, even though the two of them hadn't been honest enough to come right out and say, "We're investigating." Dorothy had tendered the stories of all those personal tiffs and romantic disappointments strictly for the two of them. No, Dorothy wasn't maliciously gossiping; she just saw right through them.

Even though Meg, Phyllis, and Sophie might have had serious gripes with Catherine Freeman, the garden club members, to this point, anyway, were off the police's radar screen. If one of them had done it, she was safe from scrutiny for now. Maybe, when their other theories were exhausted—a random drive-by shooter or drive-by gang, or perhaps a hit man who'd aimed at Walter and hit Catherine—then the police might delve into Catherine's garden buddies.

Then the phone call came. Emily answered it and handed the instrument to Louise. "It's Dorothy, and she wants to talk to you."

Dorothy got right to the point. "I know what you and Emily are doing. And I want you to know that I don't have any qualms about it. I mean, we'd all like to see this murder solved, because until it is—well, the murderer could strike again, right?"

"Uh, right," agreed Louise.

"In fact, Louise, it's kind of interesting checking out people. You're looking into club members, thinking one of them might have something to do with Catherine's murder. Well, just to help you, let me tell you this: Sophie Chalois is having an affair with Walter—I mean, up to last week, though I don't know about *this* week. I doubt they'd get together at a time like this. I'm not an expert like you, but I'd say that that gave her a good motive."

"How do you know this, Dorothy?"

"Friends. I ran into a woman I know after I left you and Emily. She's a live-in nanny for a Ledgebrook family across the street and down one from Sophie. We got to talking about the murder, and she was only too happy to tell me about how she saw Walter coming and going into Sophie's house, real late at night. He was very secretive, she said. He apparently snuck out of his own back door and walked to Sophie's—it's only half a mile. She noticed him more than one night. He'd only stay an hour, and then hurry back home. I bet that was for cover. He could always say he'd gone out for a constitutional."

"Well, Dorothy, you're quite helpful. I don't know what to say, or where any of this information will take us."

"Just remember this: if you and Emily need any more help, call me. I know how to keep my mouth shut, and I know my way around every street, alley, and cranny for a radius of three miles."

After thanking her caller again, Louise turned to her busy friend, who'd taken over the serious task of the risotto. "Dorothy's an eager sidekick: reminds me of Nero Wolfe's Archie Goodwin." She told Emily about Sophie's affair.

Emily busily stirred while she stared into space and figured it out. "A heavy affair? If they love each other, that means either Walter or Sophie or both could be involved in the murder."

Louise looked at her approvingly. "I think you're right." As an amateur sleuth, Emily was doing just fine.

Later, when dinner was finished, Bill phoned Louise. She went upstairs to take the call so that Alex wouldn't hear, for he had come home armed with dark suspicions of Louise and Emily.

Her husband said, "Just thought you might want to know a few facts about Freeman's aide. Her name is Reese Janning. I'd forgotten this, but it's an interesting story, and was quite public a few years ago. Janning writes financial books, the first one at age twenty-six: she was quite the prodigy. But about three years ago, plagiarism charges arose when she published another book. You've read of how ambiguous and difficult those suits can be. Walter Freeman, of all people, stepped up and took the woman's side and got her nicely off the hook."

"How'd you find that out?"

"I had to call the office, and I mentioned Reese Janning to one of my compatriots. He said she was a brilliant grad student who'd gone on to attach herself to famous men and campaigns. When she followed her sources too closely in that book of hers—"

"You mean, plagiarized—"

"Yeah. Walter Freeman apparently very much admired the young woman's intellect and bold new ideas, and went out on a limb for her, making some fancy case for her, since she'd actually given credit through footnotes."

"I thought quotes helped," said Louise sarcastically. "Quotes, or outright attribution."

"Me too," said her husband. "Reese Janning must be eternally grateful to Freeman for essentially cleansing her of wrongdoing. After that, she joined his staff. That represented another big step up the ladder for her."

"And she now perches there—at the top of the ladder

with the country's economic oracle. *Thank* you for this, Bill—you're a honey. Now, let me tell you about my day— you wouldn't believe it. I've been tramping around with Emily and another garden club member, hearing gossip about still *other* garden club members. It almost makes me feel unclean. But finally, tonight, things are beginning to make sense. What seemed to be mere gossip could be quite serious."

"Now look, honey," he replied, "the only reason I told you this about Reese Janning is because you could find it out anyway with a simple computer search. But you be careful how you use this, hear me?"

"Of course, darling. Don't worry. I am so discreet you wouldn't believe it. The cops here don't seem to like me."

"Oh. How did you piss them off this time?"

"They questioned me, of course, the night of the murder. Today, I went to see Detective Kovach. He was annoyed with me from the minute I walked in the door and pointed out a few things to him." She told Bill about the open window on Walter Freeman's car. "So I agree with what he said, that that may be unimportant. But *now,* don't you see? Now there are two aggressive women in Walter Freeman's life. It brings up two questions. Wonder if one of *them* killed Catherine? Or wonder if he wanted out of that marriage and hired a hit man? The only thing I'm sure of is that he didn't take that gun and shoot his wife himself."

"Louise, *stop.*" Her husband's tone brooked no opposition. She could almost picture his troubled face. "I know that the spouse is always suspect in murder cases, but I'd advise you to go easy on Walter Freeman. Look for someone else as the perp. Look at those two women in his life, if you want to. Freeman has much too much to lose if it were discovered he murdered his wife."

She groaned. "I know you're right. But even so, maybe I'll hang around another day and see what turns up.

Anyway, detecting's good for Emily. She's come alive, and, believe me, it's great to see it."

Across the phone lines, Bill's voice was philosophical. "I'm glad to hear that. But whatever you do, it may be useless. My guess is that the police will find it was a botched attempt to kill Freeman. Now let me tell you about Janie . . ." After a report on their visit to Princeton, and more admonitions to be careful, Bill said good-bye.

Louise called home to pick up messages, and among them found an anguished plea from Charlie Hurd. *"Louise, ya got me over a barrel again. Have pity and call me. I'm guessing you have some inside stuff on Catherine Freeman's murder, because you have friends there in that neighborhood. Look, in a sense, we're an investigative team, aren't we? Forget the bad times, and try to remember the good times we've had, the times I helped you out . . ."*

She shook her head and couldn't help admiring Charlie's perserverance. He probably was being stone-walled by the Montgomery County Police on details of their investigation. He apparently had no idea Louise was still in Bethesda, and she had no desire to tell him.

When she returned downstairs to the Holley living room, Alex's suspicions had deepened. "Do I sense some-thing going on here?" he asked. "What are you women up to? And, Louise, is Bill feeding you information?"

So like an undercover agent, thought Louise, to suspect things like that. Louise was now convinced that Alex was CIA, or maybe NSA, snuggled away there in the otherwise unexciting State Department job. Anyway, Bill's warnings before she started out on this Bethesda journey had al-ready hinted at Alex's covert life.

"Of course not, Alex," she said smoothly. "He's just giv-ing me a report on Janie. Now she's in love with Prince-ton."

A graduate of that university himself, Alex lost his com-bativeness for a moment and smiled. "Well, you don't say.

And does she have the grades to get in?" His hawklike nose pointing in the air annoyed Louise no end.

"She's at the top of her class at Groveton. I suppose that will help."

He sniffed. "Groveton isn't the same caliber as a fine prep school. Are you sure you're being realistic?"

She shrugged. "How about SATs in the seven hundreds, then?" Why was she rising to this man's bait? She was becoming as small and petty as he was. Taking on the face of the enemy, she guessed that was called.

"Fourteen hundred in SATS?" he said. "Not bad, not bad." Yet he was not about to be put off his original track. He turned to his wife and said, "I'm concerned about what you two are doing, Emily, and don't forget it. Just remember that I sometimes work with Walter Freeman. I hope you're not snooping into that murder."

Emily insisted that she was merely showing Louise the sights and visiting friends' gardens. When Alex turned back to his newspaper, Emily turned to Louise and gave her a big wink.

26

Tuesday

Tuesday morning Emily stood at the tall living room window and watched Alex pull out of the driveway in his car. When the car had disappeared down the street, she turned to Louise, a sparkle in her eye. "All right, Louise, what comes first today?" Her formerly pliant friend had become like a bossy assistant, prodding her superior to get busy.

"Walter Freeman and his housekeeper probably have been allowed back in the house. I'd guess Walter's gone downtown to get back to work. Why not go talk to Martina?"

"Great," enthused Emily. "Martina Reye is a wonderful woman. What's more important, she knows me, and she'll trust me."

With the dog in tow again, they made the quick walk to the Freeman house. The police tape had been removed from around the property, but some of the press people lingered in the neighborhood. "How can we avoid them?" Louise asked.

"Let's come in from the next street and get in through the alley," said Emily. When they finally reached the kitchen door, she plucked Louise's arm. "Now remember to turn on the recorder this time. This woman was devastated by Catherine's death. She adored her. She might really *tell* us something."

Louise looked back at the large, forested backyard, and could just make out the top of a glass greenhouse at the far end of it. This was the repository of Catherine Freeman's famous azaleas.

The kitchen door opened noiselessly, and there stood Martina, probably wondering how the two of them found their way through the privacy hedges and other little fence barriers that kept strangers out.

"Martina, we came to see you," said Emily. "It must be good to be back in the house. Do you remember Louise from our visit on Sunday?"

"Of course I remember," said Martina in a musical voice. She bent and gave the dog a pat. "I'm so sorry, but dogs are not welcome here." With Lancelot tied to the porch rail, they were ushered into the spotless, modern kitchen, whose recent update left no traces from an older kitchen. This was Martina's headquarters, and she stood proudly in its center, near a stunning cooking island topped with a solid piece of deep green granite.

If Jamaica had princesses, Martina would have been one. With a graceful, long-fingered hand, she welcomed them to sit with her at a table in the carpeted breakfast nook.

Having said no to tea or coffee, Louise and Emily accepted glasses of water instead. Emily explained that Louise had sometimes helped the police with crimes. "But we didn't come particularly for that, just to visit." She made the perfunctory speech of regret over Catherine's death.

In a slow voice, Martina said, "I feel her here still. Her spirit will remain until they find those who slayed her."

Louise shivered as she looked in Martina's smoldering brown eyes. They stared straight at her, as if daring her to disagree.

Gently, Louise asked her, "Do you think they'll find the person?"

Martina was looking into the middle distance. Then she transferred her gaze to Louise again. "I do believe they will find them. You see, Mrs. Freeman was a *giant* woman."

"A giant woman?" Why would the housekeeper refer to Catherine's physical size?

"Yes." She pointed a long finger at her head. "She cut a big path in the world. Very smart. Very smart at business. Very smart at gardening. A caring woman, but not very strong." She shook her head. "Sometimes a caring woman doesn't see things clearly."

"Um, you said you believe the police will find *them*," said Louise. "Do you think there was more than one killer?"

Martina closed her eyes, as if bone weary, and shook her head, to make it all go away, including Louise and Emily. Louise sat very still, waiting. Finally, the woman said, "I see them after her."

Momentarily speechless, Louise and Emily exchanged looks. Best to get along with this interview, since Martina appeared to be fading. Emily began a little tale of remembrance—of the first time she'd been in the house ten years ago. "Can you remember ten years ago, Martina? Catherine's friend, Dorothy Cranshaw, was the temporary housekeeper here. But you arrived soon after that. Do you remember?"

Martina nodded. "Of course I remember." The woman's handsome brown face did not break in sorrow, even as Emily brought up her employer's little garden club parties, the fun-filled garden club work sessions—"we made the most whimsical things, Santa Clauses out of clothespins, little figures out of home-made dough, as favors for the old folks' home"—and the neighborhood parties that drew in thirty or forty from Ledgebrook and a few from Battery Lane.

"And you were always there, Martina, Catherine's unconditional support, to make each occasion wonderful."

Try as they might, they didn't elicit a word that could be construed as criticism of Walter Freeman. If Martina had had any gripes, Louise suspected that he'd suppressed them a long time ago in the same way he'd suppressed criticism from Emily—with gifts or, who knows, perhaps money.

On the contrary, she praised her employer. "He's a big man," said Martina, as the subject came up naturally, "a big brain, a big heart. He doesn't know yet how much he will miss her. Even his work and his business associates won't fill his life as she filled his life."

After a while, Louise made silent eye contact again with Emily. These premonitions of Martina Reye were scary and interesting, but what they really needed was something more factual that would point to a killer.

"Um, Emily, you talked about the way you did crafts in the recreation room," said Louise. "I'd love to see it."

Martina looked at her as if she were reading her mind. "Would you like a tour of the house?"

"The entire house?" said Louise. "That would be nice." She gave Emily a quick look.

"Even I haven't seen the whole house," bubbled Emily, "nor the greenhouse out back."

Martina gave Emily a somber look. "Mr. Freeman says the greenhouse must be seen by no one."

"Oh, of course," said Emily. "Whatever Walter wants." They started with the basement level, descending carpeted stairs to a walnut-paneled recreation room. Louise was impressed with the smell—or lack of smell. Washington, D.C., basements could smell as foul as two-day-old fish.

Comfortable chintz-covered couches lined the walls, all aimed at a large entertainment center, of which a gigantic television was the focal point. A long table stood at one end of the room, and Louise could just imagine garden club members hovering around it, doing worthy community projects such as making bouquets for the elderly or home-bound.

When the women went back upstairs, they passed slowly through the elegant, two-story living room, which was hung with fine paintings by nineteenth-century American artists. Next they came to a large dining room with a long mahogany table where Louise was sure some important people must have wined and dined and basked in Walter's intellectual glow and Catherine's gracious hospitality. A winding staircase took them upstairs. The master bedroom, largest of five, was bedecked in colonial style with crewel draperies similar to the ones in Emily's house.

Living in a modern house herself, Louise enjoyed looking at the fussiness and formality of this style—though she wouldn't want to live with it.

Martina opened the large suite for their inspection. Antique furniture added an elegant touch. Next to this room was one with modern furniture, decorated in navy and maroon. Louise wondered if it was the nightly retreat of Walter Freeman. As Martina showed Emily some feature of the view out of the bowed window, Louise covertly opened the closet door and spied an array of Walter's business suits. She quickly shut it again, but not before the sharp-eyed Martina saw her.

"Mr. Freeman stores his clothes here," she explained with a smile, "because Mrs. Freeman has—I mean, *had*— many gowns. They fill the closets next door."

"Of course," said Louise. "I only wish we had more space in our house so that Bill could do that."

Louise had seen nothing in the house that was irregular or sinister. It was time to go, and Emily made another tactful exit, giving Martina a warm hug and promising to come back and visit her again.

The housekeeper shook Louise's hand and fixed her with another smoldering look. "The detective must look for the answers," she said.

"Answers," said Louise. "Yes. I'll do my best." It was all she could think of to say. Since Louise was cynical about people with sixth senses, this interview turned her off. It made her wish she could head back to northern Virginia right now.

But instead, back at Emily's house, there was still the matter of Reese Janning to explore. Louise had filled her friend in on the information Bill gave her. They did a quick computer search, pulling up a review of the woman's latest book from the *New York Times* Web page and a recent biography. From the way Reese had progressed from being a brilliant grad student through financial management jobs into posts as economic adviser to high-profile political candidates, it was obvious that Reese knew the road to the top. The article mentioned the plagiarism charges and how instrumental Walter Freeman had been in minimizing them.

They printed out the stories. Their eyes had been glued to the screen for a half-hour, but now they looked at each other. "A woman bound to succeed, don't you think?"

Emily looked pensive. "I could use a little bit of her gumption. But this article makes me want to know more about her and Walter. Yet we can't jump to conclusions, just because he glossed over her stealing someone else's scholarly work."

"There's also the matter of Sophie and Walter Freeman."

"That could just be rumor," said Emily, giving Louise a firm stare.

"You're right. There are other people, too, that we can't forget. There's Phyllis, who seems so oppressed by that nursery business of hers. It's as if she has to carry it alone even though her husband is there in body. She must have felt terrible when Catherine swept all the azalea awards each year."

"Especially since it means she sold her plants at a fraction of the price that Catherine commanded. And let's not forget Meg. I've always had the uncomfortable sense that Meg can be very mean."

Louise sat back in her chair and a faint smile crossed her face. "Mean enough to kill because Catherine arranged flowers better than she did? It sounds almost ridiculous."

"Meg has very little in her life—no husband, kids, no job. She holds as a point of pride the fact that she won all those best-of-show ribbons in Illinois. Then she comes here and is beaten out all the time."

Louise sighed, feeling as if she were falling back into that vortex of female gossip. "What do you say we call Detective Kovach and put it in his hands? We may have discovered some detail he doesn't know yet."

Emily turned big gray eyes at her. "Do you dare, after what happened yesterday?"

Louise gathered herself out of the chair and said, "Sure. I've developed a very thick skin where police are concerned." She kept to herself the humiliation and discomfort she'd felt during her encounter with the detective the previous day.

She found Kovach's card and dialed his number at the Major Crimes Division. Surprisingly, he answered; Louise had expected him to be out somewhere detecting. "Detective Kovach, I, uh, I've learned some new information that you might want to know."

"Oh, you have, have you? Just what have you learned?"

With great circumspection, she disclosed the fact that Sophie Chalois had late-night meetings with Freeman. After hearing his skeptical voice fill the phone, she skipped lightly over her ephemeral theories about Phyllis Ohlmacher and Meg Durrance, then heard an explosive sound at the other end of the line. As she feared, the big detective was laughing at her, or else choking to death because he was suppressing laughter. And it *was* laughable to think either Phyllis or Meg could commit a capital crime.

The noises subsided, and then there was silence for a while on the other end of the line. Then he drawled, "Mrs. Eldridge, I dunno what to say to you. I thought I'd made things clear to you yesterday. You're out of order. As it happens, we have on our list of people to interview some of these garden club people you're mentioning, and even including your friend, Emily Holley. We also will be in touch with Catherine Freeman's associates on the Crippled Children's League, her friends at the Foxcroft Club, her Bethesda business partners, certainly, and even her fellow elders at the Bethesda First Presbyterian Church. Mrs. Freeman's activities were very widespread. Now, will you let us do this work? Just because you play amateur detective down there in Fairfax County is no sign you can do it up here in Montgomery County." He paused for a breath, and possibly to regain a modicum of politeness. "I don't mean to insult you or anything, but we don't need your help on this one."

Emily, who had been listening in on the kitchen phone, looked angry. Louise said good-bye to Kovach and said little to her friend after this new rebuff. But she could tell that Emily felt as she did—more determined than ever to solve Catherine's murder.

Suddenly the humor of it overcame Louise, and she chuckled. "The trouble with Detective Kovach is that he can't get his mind around it."

"Mind around what?" asked Emily.

"He just can't believe that a garden club member could have anything to do with a drive-by shooting. I can't say as I blame him: I have a hard time getting my mind around it, too. However, the police will be questioning club members eventually—after they get through with Catherine's business cohorts, the Crippled Children's League, the church board, and all that."

It was lunch time, and Emily headed for the kitchen, while Louise's mouth watered in anticipation of another tasty meal.

As she stood watching Emily rip apart spinach into a salad bowl, Louise said, "I'm surprised Kovach is so unwilling to listen. He's not at all like Mike Geraghty, or even George Morton, Geraghty's partner. I think the spotlight has to be turned equally on everyone, not just a few favorite suspects. Otherwise the truth may never be found. That means we look at everyone in the garden club—especially the high-profile members like Sophie, Meg, and Phyllis. Even Dorothy, and your neighbor, Laura Alice, have to be considered."

Emily giggled. "Laura Alice is preggers—why, she looks about ten months. Do you really think a pregnant woman would kill?"

"Just want to play fair with people, pregnant or not."

"So that means we also can't rule out Walter, no matter what Bill says," added Emily, as she added plump shrimps and finely chopped onion and celery to the spinach. Louise had related her conversation with Bill, and his view that Freeman was too smart to risk everything by murdering his wife.

Even if Walter paid a hit man for the murder, Louise knew she was in no position to prove it. The Bethesda police were holding their cards very close to their vest, and probably treading very circumspectly with the man.

The back doorbell rang, and Louise went to answer it, finding Laura Alice Shea standing outside the screen door. She was off work for a couple of days. When chatting at the gate in the fence earlier this morning with Emily, she'd been asked for lunch.

Laura Alice was the picture of good health, her short

brown hair gleaming, her body clad in pink plaid shorts and big pink shirt, so that one hardly noticed she was within weeks of giving birth.

The visitor's eyes twinkled as she gave Louise a grin. "I've come over to eat—and boy, can I eat these days—and to give you two Sherlock Holmes characters a little bit of help."

27

Laura Alice Shea had spent yesterday and today working at home, and had noticed the two women next door—coming and going, walking the dog, their heads together with Dorothy Cranshaw out on the patio. She quickly figured out what they were doing: they were snooping into old Catherine's murder—or at least talking it into the ground.

Laura Alice had to admit that she found it hard to like her neighbor. She had had as little to do as possible with Emily Holley in the three years since she and her husband had moved in next door. Just from idle observations, she'd concluded that Emily was a dysfunctional, middle-aged woman with a prick for a husband and no children to give her joy or distraction. When Laura Alice saw her, Emily was either frantically gardening, or else slumped in a patio chair reading big books—probably Victorian romances—and resembling nothing so much as a small, dying swan. She only came to life when gardening or when scurrying around to obey her husband's loudly stated commands.

And so it cheered her to see that this visitor, Louise Eldridge, had at least stirred her out of her torpor. The two of them had been running in and out of the house almost constantly over the past three days, looking a little silly, it was true, but at least doing something. Better than doing *nothing*, which Laura Alice had noticed was Emily's normal routine.

The three of them settled down on Emily's patio, and Laura Alice found herself ploughing through the excellent lunch with the abandon of a truckdriver, and guzzling glass after glass of herbal iced tea. As she did, though, she kept a wary eye on her companions. Just the two of them today, but there were three yesterday, when level-headed Dorothy Cranshaw had joined them. Laura Alice was amused, but wary. Women in groups tended to gossip, and she'd been burned too many times when growing up as the youngest of four strong-willed girls.

She didn't like "girl talk," nor girl groups. As for the Old Georgetown Garden Club, she kept her contacts with those mostly older females on a strictly professional basis. She had no doubt that some of the members liked to spread idle talk. She'd seen them clustering together after meetings, casting thinly disguised hate looks at one or another—the kind one of her sisters used to give her when Laura Alice insisted on achieving at the top in school.

For the past three years, Laura Alice had worked on every spring plant sale and had attended a few meetings each year. At the meetings, she'd persistently demanded that they have good content in their programs, so people could learn something. Good programs, *duh!* Wasn't that what she joined the club for in the first place? To find out more about the history and culture of plants, to hear those Latin plant names rolling off the tongues of the lecturers.

The first program she'd attended was on making Christmas wreaths. She'd gotten up at the end and bluntly termed it "inadequate" and not what she'd joined the club for. Although the other members hadn't loved her for her frankness—the frozen looks she got could have chilled a polar bear—she noticed they never repeated "Wreath Making 101."

It was easy to figure out that Emily, Dorothy, and Louise had been talking about the murder. What else could cause such nervous excitement in their little klatches? She'd heard that Louise had solved a couple of crimes for the cops down in northern Virginia. Maybe she'd be good at figuring out what had happened to the overweight dowager president of the garden club.

Frankly, Catherine Freeman's charms had eluded Laura Alice, who had seen her as one of those gracious control freaks who made a career out of getting others to do their bidding. On the other hand, the woman had hybridized some great azaleas—several grew in Laura Alice's front garden. Too bad the woman had become so grossly overweight. Laura Alice believed one's physical size somehow had a part in one's ultimate destiny.

Today she'd agreed to come for lunch at Emily's to satisfy her curiosity and find out what Emily and Louise were up to. Maybe she could toss them a bone, too, for she knew one person in Walter Freeman's life who she bet *they* had no idea even existed.

Reese Janning. Though Laura Alice could hardly imagine the homely, bony Reese having anything to do with a crime. After all, it would interfere with her career, which came first with her, and was flourishing since she'd hit pay dirt by becoming Freeman's top aide. Laura Alice herself would give a lot to have such a job with that kind of connections.

Now, happily, Emily had fetched a plate of little tarts for dessert. Laura Alice reached for one, still hungry. She said, "It's nice of you to invite me, Emily—though I'm not accustomed to girl luncheons. And after the way I'm pigging out, you may never ask me again."

Emily smiled at Laura Alice. "Well, then, extra thanks for coming. We 'girls' will try to treat you well. So, what's with that Sherlock Holmes remark? How did you guess Louise and I were snooping around?"

Laura Alice smiled coolly. "I saw you two with Dorothy: a trio of sleuths. What was the name of Agatha Christie's character? Miss something . . ."

"You mean Miss Marple?" said Louise.

"Yes," said Laura Alice. "A trio of Miss Marples, checking out folks in friendly, downtown Bethesda."

"Really," said Louise, in a cool voice.

Oops, thought Laura Alice. It was obvious that the sleek-looking TV garden show hostess wasn't thrilled with being likened to this fictional character, Miss Marple, who must be a lot older than Louise. How was *she* supposed to know? She didn't read Agatha Christie, and only knew the name "Miss Marple" because a series with that character, which she never watched, occasionally appeared in TV listings.

Laura Alice hastily tried to retrench: "I just couldn't think of another woman detective, except for Kinsey Milhone—but somehow you two didn't remind me—" That wasn't going over so well, either.

Louise fortunately changed the subject. "Just what do you mean by 'friendly downtown Bethesda?' "

Laura Alice waved a hand, grateful at the reprieve. "That includes not only our jam-packed business district with its fancy restaurants and businesses, but also our great, close-in neighborhoods—you know, Battery Lane and Ledgebrook. They're all so joined together that I call the whole thing 'friendly downtown Bethesda.' "

"So you decided Emily and I were snooping, hmm?" said Louise, not letting her off the hook.

Laura Alice sat back and let her stomach hang out, which it did obligingly; pregnancy ought to have its privileges. She didn't need this Louise Eldridge to give her a guilt trip. "It was just by the process of elimination. What else would draw garden club members around here like bees to a honey pot? And make your guest"—she nodded graciously at Louise, hoping she would forget those gaffes about Miss Marple and Kinsey Milhone—"the center of conversation most of the time."

Louise looked as sober as a judge as she explained things. "We did a bit of touring about and talking to people. Emily had a lot of ideas as to who we should talk to. I suppose it bothers you, as it does Emily, that there's a unsolved murder in the neighborhood."

"Of course it does. My husband Jim and I feel pretty uncomfortable with it. Jim isn't the worrying type, but he's a little concerned now. He warns me to keep the door locked when I'm home alone, and he brought out his old baseball bat from college days and stuck it in the corner next to the front door." Her mouth softened in a smile. "But that doesn't mean we've gone so far as to try to catch the criminal, like you."

Emily piped up, her voice more irritated than Laura Alice had ever heard it. "You may think we're silly, Laura Alice, but Louise has already given the police at least two useful tips, and all they did was sneer at her—and *that* makes me mad."

Laura Alice realized she had pissed off the normally docile Emily. Good: that was half the reason she'd thrown out the remark, to see if Emily had any backbone at all— and she did. "I can see it's ticked you off. Good for you, Emily. *Go*, girl!"

Emily blushed bright red. "So we just decided to pick up information where we could—you know, around the Freeman neighborhood, among the people we both know in the club. We're, uh, trying very hard not to become gossipmongers. I know you hate gossip, Laura Alice, or anything that smacks of gossip. I don't like it myself. So maybe we shouldn't share some of the tidbits we've learned. They're about garden club members—"

Laura Alice sat back in the patio chair and said, "Oh, go ahead—I can take it, especially since the two of you are not a couple of muckrakers, and are doing it for a reason."

Louise and Emily looked at each other.

"On the other hand," said Laura Alice, pressing her side where the baby was kicking the hell out of her ribs, "you don't have to give me details, unless you think one of these gals is going to repeat the crime. Let me tell you the only thing *I* know that relates to Walter Freeman. It concerns his aide, Reese Janning."

"Oh," said Louise, in a detached voice, but the Eldridge woman's big hazel eyes gave her away. They were alive with excitement. "What do you know about Reese Janning? We've heard she's quite an interesting character."

Laura Alice shrugged, and then had to pull down her shirt, which was riding high on the large mound of her belly. She also realized she had to dash to the lady's room, so she'd make this brief. "I bet you already know the public stuff—the hot books on the economy, the charges of plagiarism, and how Walter Freeman came to bat for her."

"Yes, we've heard that much."

"The woman has lots of resources, from her job, her book sales, and from her wealthy family. She's moved from a Bethesda apartment to a condo in Georgetown, and drives an expensive car."

"You know all about this," said Louise. "Aides are always super-close with their bosses, aren't they?"

"Often they are. That's certainly true of Reese," said Laura Alice. "She has become indispensable to Freeman, everybody agrees to that. I'm in the same area, finance, so I hear the talk. Apparently, not only is she a good, creative thinker on his topic, the global economy, but she's terrific at handling all the bigwigs who blow in to pick Freeman's brain and give him advice."

Louise leaned forward in her chair toward Laura Alice. "Could it be more than a close business arrangement?"

Laura Alice shrugged. "Who knows? Certainly not me. I'm inclined to doubt it, because, quite frankly, Reese is . . . exceptionally homely. You know, thin face, hawk nose,

overly prominent chin. These boss-aide romances usually
spring up when they have a dishy-looking aide. Walter's
wife, even with sixty extra pounds on her, was lots more
handsome."

"But they spend lots of time together, Walter and Reese,"
pressed Louise.

"Naturally. They need to, Louise. Do you know anything at all about the pressure of Walter Freeman's job?
It's enormous. It takes great know-how, combined with
great political skill. His is in a class by itself, because although he thinks he's in a world above politics, Walter
Freeman is *highly* political. Every word he speaks and
every move he makes has a political effect."

"Well spoken, Laura Alice," said Louise. "Actually, I've
had some acquaintance with Washington politics." Now it
was Laura Alice's turn to blush. Louise had been around
for a while; hadn't she even helped to uncover that murder committed by an aide to the president? Maybe Laura
Alice had underestimated her knowledge of how Washington worked.

Laura Alice decided to quit pontificating and instead
ask a few questions. Louise, she discovered, had lived with
her family in four foreign countries. She was ten years
older than Laura Alice, but had a daughter of twenty.
Probably led the standard life of courtship, early marriage, and childbearing that was prevalent in the eighties.
Louise looked great, curvy and slim and alive and having
fun, the way a woman should. It made Laura Alice wish
she'd done her childbearing in her early twenties, so that
she'd have her later life, as Louise did, for an interesting
career and hobbies. Instead, she might well be changing
diapers when she was forty, since Jim wanted at least two
more children. He was from a family with five boys, brothers who would slap each other on the back upon meeting,
then embrace, then set out to have as much fun together
as time allowed. At the drop of a hat, they would go off on

a hunting or fishing trip, or gather up the entire family for a raucous bowling game at the local alley, or turn a family backyard into a baseball or badminton arena where young and old would fiercely but good-naturedly compete. Their parents' anniversaries were always remembered with a celebration; children in the family were treated as beloved objects. It was not surprising that her husband wanted more than one.

Laura Alice's own family experience was different. Love was exhibited in a more restrained way, and parceled out with dry humor. And though she loved her sometimes contentious sisters, she'd never experienced the kind of camaraderie that Jim had with his brothers. Having undergone amniocentesis to discover this baby was a boy, at least she knew she wouldn't be facing the task of raising all girls.

Now that personal lives had been discussed sufficiently, Laura Alice honed in on the topic of Reese Janning once again. "I'll tell you another way that Reese is invaluable," she said. "It's common knowledge that Freeman and Reese, along with members of Congress or other officials, take visiting bigshots out to eat. Then, over a good lunch and some good wine, the two of them do something— maybe play good cop–bad cop, who knows?—and get their way with the visiting economic minister, or whoever the visiting dignitary is. You know—'Lower those trade barriers or you don't get your crème brûlée for dessert.' "

They all laughed at that.

"Which restaurant do they like best?" asked Emily.

"Correlli's, just off Pennsylvania. Freeman must love that place as much as I do. I've seen him there three or four times in the past month. He arrives on the dot of noon, and gets the best table in the place, of course."

"I suppose he comes in a chauffeur-driven car," said Louise.

"No, he doesn't. I guess he'd have one if he wanted one, but I've seen him getting out of Reese's fancy SUV."

"She has an SUV?" said Louise. "Um, what color is it?"

Laura Alice shrugged. "Dark green. Despite all the negative talk about SUVs it's still the car of choice for the prosperous Washington suburbanite. Reese has one because she has to ferry VIPs around town."

Louise said, "You certainly know the Washington scene. You make the scene yourself, or you wouldn't know about Walter Freeman's lunch habits."

"Obviously," said Laura Alice with a grin. "I couldn't have seen them if I hadn't been dragging *my* visiting firemen there, hoping to impress them." She pulled herself laboriously up from her chair, the weight of the child in her belly suddenly seeming to keep her grounded.

She had a moment of panic. Was this the way the child would be after it was born, a drag on her? "Excuse me for a minute while I make a powder-room run. And when I get back, you two had better give me details on what you've learned. I have to go in to work tomorrow, but then I'll be home for the rest of the week. If I'm to be part of this detecting team, I need to hear all the skinny."

Then she sprinted inside. The dog bounded after her, as if she might need assistance.

28

L ouise and Emily exchanged looks. A smile spread across Louise's face, and she said, "That wasn't an easy sell."

"No," agreed Emily, stacking the dessert plates. "Laura Alice is very . . . private. I can't believe she finally opened up like that. I'm sure it's because she likes you, Louise."

"She likes you, too."

Emily shook her head. "That's not necessarily true. She's never warmed up to me, and I know why. She doesn't *admire* me for anything—or, rather, she has nothing to admire me for. Laura Alice is one of those achievers who can't stop working at it, so why should she respect women who don't *try?*"

Suddenly, tears pooled in her eyes, and she couldn't go on.

"Emily, you're a worthwhile person. You were an absolute whiz of a student in grad school. What makes you think so poorly of yourself now?"

"Oh, grad school was an eternity ago. Since then it's as if I've been walking into the distance, like a figure in a Renaissance painting, so that soon I will be only a dot on the horizon."

"Emily!" Louise was appalled at this image. It scared her,

to think of what a person with such a bad self-image might do.

Emily went on. "I can always read what Laura Alice is thinking, Louise. She sees me moping around here, with no children, answering the call of my authoritarian husband. I know she thinks I'm a complete sap."

Realizing that some of this was true—at least the moping and the responding to husbandly commands—Louise lapsed into silence. Then Laura Alice strode back out onto the patio and said, in her quiet voice, "Now give me the skinny."

They told her what they'd learned in their travels around Bethesda and from the invaluable Dorothy. Laura Alice chortled when she heard the way the Montgomery police responded. "They don't think they need you—and maybe they don't. Emily, I have to go now, but this has been lots of fun. Furthermore, I admire you for plunging into this matter even if it took encouragement from Louise. When Louise goes home, you can continue to keep your eyes open. You're doing a good job at it."

Emily seemed shocked by the praise. "You think so?"

"I really do," said Laura Alice, grinning. She turned to Louise. "Why, if you guys should help find the killer, think what a local reputation Emily will have—about as good as yours is down there in Virginny."

The look on Emily's face made Louise feel better about her friend. Their investigative forays had put some fire in her friend's eye, but then her self-doubts had come raging back. Now, simple praise from a detached observer like Laura Alice Shea gave Emily a look she hadn't had before. Maybe as time went on she would come to feel like a strong independent woman, not one who lived only to please others.

Laura Alice left, promising to check back with Louise and Emily on Wednesday to see how things were going, and at any rate to accompany the two to Catherine's funeral on Thursday.

Emily and Louise gathered up the dessert dishes. "All the little details Laura Alice gave us—it's like a pointillist painting," said Louise. "A picture is beginning to emerge of a man who leans heavily on his administrative aide, and has something romantic going on with his attractive blond neighbor."

"You aren't implying he's romantically involved with both Sophie Chalois and Reese Janning, are you, Louise? I'll never believe that."

"I doubt it. Hard-working men of his age—and we all know Walter Freeman is a hard-working man—don't necessarily have that much strength left for sex with *one* woman, never mind two. But there are exceptions." With a grin that she hoped was not lascivious, she said, "What have we here, Emily? A sex maniac, or just a workaholic with one mistress?"

They both laughed.

"But to change the subject," said Louise, "I wonder how Richard Ralston is doing with the funeral bouquet?"

She found herself now fully involved in Emily's domestic life and responsibilities, and was next about to ask her if she could help with dinner. At home, of course, she'd have given dinner hardly a thought at three in the afternoon, since cooking was one of her least favorite things to do.

"Richard said not to worry about it, but I'll call him anyway," said Emily, pausing to reach for her phone. "Dorothy will never forgive me if something goes wrong with this memorial from the club. He promised to deliver it tomorrow to the funeral home. Viewing begins then."

"Good," said Louise. "That means we're free tomorrow to go downtown and have lunch before we pay our respects at the funeral home."

Emily looked delighted. "You mean we're going to—"

"To have lunch at Correlli's," said Louise with a casual shrug of her shoulders. She couldn't help a smile. "On the dot of noon, of course."

"Great!" exulted Emily. "I'll phone and make a reservation."

By the time they'd cleared the lunch dishes and settled in the living room, Richard Ralston called back. From the little pleasurable remarks Emily made, Louise could tell that he had hit the mark.

"Oh, *wonderful,*" she gushed. "French tulips? Perfect. And the raffia—oh, what a touch! It symbolizes *what?*" Emily crumpled into her overstuffed chair, looking overcome with the perfection of it all. "That is *so*—so *evocative* of Catherine. You're sending a sketch? I can hardly wait."

Switching off the phone, she turned to Louise. In a dramatic voice, she said, "He's going to fax me a rough sketch of it. It will be a huge bouquet of palest pink French tulips—*very* tall—in a huge, round, crystal vase. With a cloud of even paler raffia, as Richard described it, 'swirling above the flowers, as if the bouquet itself existed in some supernatural, heavenly state.' It will stand in the funeral home, and later, at the head of her casket. Can you *believe* it, Louise? It will be *fabulous!*"

Louise shook her head. "Oh, yes, I can believe it. If it's Richard Ralston, it has to be fabulous."

Sketch of Catherine Freeman's funeral bouquet

29

Detective Kovach sat back in his desk chair and tried to get comfortable. He needed one that was about fifty percent bigger than the general-issue gray vinyl job he was now sitting in. Across the desk sat his partner, Peter Girard. Kovach had a keen sense of discomfort. He hated it when he was forced to divide his pool of detectives up on multiple cases, but another homicide had just intruded, taking resources away from the Catherine Freeman murder.

"Do you think we're barking up the wrong tree on Freeman?" asked Kovach, chewing on a wooden toothpick resurrected from his club sandwich from lunch.

"It's an expensive tree we're barking up," noted Girard. "Maybe we're putting too much credence in those threatening letters Freeman received ... maybe turned too many resources in the direction of a hit on our famous Walter. It's taking most of our manpower."

"That Eldridge woman bothers me." Kovach had no malice in his voice, just a kind of lingering disdain. He never held a personal grudge against nosy citizens, the nosiest of which were usually middle-aged women. "She gives us these fluffy scenarios, as to why a garden club colleague might have killed Catherine Freeman. And specific knowledge about an affair Freeman's alleged to be having with one of the good-looking old gals. Now, you come up with this."

Kovach referred to a sheet Girard had plucked from the computer, a report from Princeton, New Jersey. "So this Sophie Chalois was once charged with attempted assault and battery on her professor husband. Charges were dropped at his request. Whaddaya think? Can we make a case that she'd commit a cold-blooded murder so she could become Walter Freeman's new wife?"

Girard shook his head. "I don't know; I kind of doubt it. I talked to the chief who ran the department back when the Chalois woman was charged. It was definitely a crime of passion. She apparently went berserk when she discovered her husband in their bed with his secretary, and came after him with a knife."

Kovach chuckled. "I gather he ran faster than she did. Well, she's pretty well-established in Bethesda, a churchgoer, belongs to the Cultural Women's League and the garden club—all that. Sounds pretty straight to me."

"And from the way I read it, her 'affair' with Walter Freeman is a sporadic thing—just a visit once in a while, maybe not more than once a month. Not something a woman is going to pin her hopes on." Girard spread his hands wide. "Hell, we don't even know if they're going to bed. Maybe they're getting together to study the classics."

"Yeah," snorted Kovach, leaning back and staring at the ceiling, "I wouldn't bet on it. Let's put these garden club cronies of Catherine Freeman a little closer to the top of the list. I'd hate like hell to get caught with my pants down."

Girard's freckled face broke into a grin. "You mean have Louise Eldridge upstage you? I hear she's done that before with the Fairfax police."

"Let's not have that happen here in Montgomery County."

30

That evening, after another wonderful dinner, this one of crab legs, garlic mashed potatoes, and snow peas oriental style, Louise noted that Alex Holley didn't have a clue about what his wife was up to. She helped Emily in the garden with some minor weeding until the light faded while Alex sat on the patio with the paper. Occasionally he read a little story or a story lead to them, in a good-natured way. He seemed to be getting used to Louise's presence around the place. Only occasionally did he give her a dark look, indicating that though her company was a boost to his wife, her tenure in the Holley home had its limits. She explained to him why she continued to stay, even though he was much too well-bred to come out and ask. "Emily and I are having such a good time together, Alex. It's like college days revisited."

"And tomorrow, darling," Emily told him, "we decided to do some shopping in Georgetown. We'll drop by the university, too, to see how much it's changed. I don't suppose you're free for lunch?"

"Tomorrow?" Alex's brow knitted, as he thought it over. "Too bad—I have a lunch date, or I'd take the two of you to my club to eat."

Emily affected a long face, and Louise could see that a

woman living with a man like Alex would have to develop her acting skills. "Oh, then we'll just have to get along on our own."

"'Fraid so," said Alex, burrowing back into his news-paper. "There's no way I can break my business date."

31

Wednesday dawned overcast and cloudy, which everyone welcomed because it could mean rain for parched lawns and gardens. Louise and Emily took Lancelot for a long walk so he wouldn't miss them when they left, for the dog had grown quite used to Louise and Emily's companionship over the past few days. They would wait until ten so that the rush of traffic into the District would have abated.

As they were getting ready to leave, Emily looked in a full-length antique mirror that hung in the big hallway. "He'll recognize me," she said.

"Oh, you mean Walter Freeman."

Emily gave Louise a look. "He's very sharp: he'll remember you, too, even though he's only seen you once or twice. What would we do then? I mean, it would be embarrassing. Alex would simply kill me."

"There's only one thing to do," said Louise matter-of-factly. "Let's go upstairs. I'm sure you have plenty of things we can use."

Emily's eyes sparkled."What do you mean? Disguises?"

"Yes, Double-O-Seven, disguises."

Emily giggled. A half hour later, a pair of very different-looking women left the house. Louise wore a bright head-scarf, with her hair bundled up beneath it, and scarlet lipstick. She had changed into tight tan slacks and a top, which she wore with lots of turquoise jewelry Emily pulled from her plentiful supply. Emily put on what she called her "floozy" outfit, a form-fitting black dress. With it she wore dark hose and high heels. The shoes were unused and like new, since Alex had not approved of them. She clasped her hair back with rhinestone clips and put on big dark glasses. "It's the best I can do," she said. "Do you think I look different?"

"Much different," said Louise, not telling her that the two of them resembled women looking for a noontime pickup. Emily was so innocent that she would never think of this.

Louise drove, and was glad she'd taken her husband's beige Camry when she set out for Bethesda four days ago rather than her car, a black PT Cruiser. The Cruiser was a little conspicuous, and when she drove it, she felt like a character out of a 1930s movie. The Camry was much more anonymous, and she and Emily needed anonymity today if they were going to tail one of the most important men in Washington, D.C.

They went downtown by way of Massachusetts Avenue and Rock Creek Parkway. A little too quickly, in fact, for they reached downtown Washington fifteen minutes early.

"What will we do now?" asked Emily. "Walk about a bit?"

"It will be a zoo near the Federal Reserve Building, but why don't we drive by anyway, on the chance that we might see something?"

"If we see Walter, we could tail him," said Emily enthusiastically.

"If we're that lucky, but I doubt it. We're just getting a feeling for things."

They drove by the building on Constitution Avenue, then went around the block to find the Federal Reserve's parking lot exit. As they approached, Louise crowded the curb as if she were having car trouble.

Emily said, "This may be a wild-goose chase. Maybe Walter isn't even at work. Wouldn't he still be home mourning his wife after only five days?"

"I don't know Walter enough to answer that," said Louise, as she hovered near the exit. Then she saw a uniformed traffic officer approaching. "Oh oh," she said. "Be prepared to act like a couple of dumb females who don't know how to drive in traffic."

"We can pretend we're from southern Virginia and don't know the ways of the big city."

By the time the officer had reached their car, a deep green Lexus wagon had slowly emerged from the parking lot. A gaunt-faced young woman with a prominent nose was at the wheel.

Louise's heartbeat doubled its tempo. "My God, Emily, that's Reese. And that looks like the car I saw."

Emily peered hard at the license plate. "Oh, yeah," she said slowly, "the British rule in India."

"What are you talking about?"

"That license plate. RAJ03. I've seen it somewhere else before today."

Hope grew inside Louise. "Where did you see it?"

"It was parked in an alley, or something—"

"Saturday night when we took our walk?"

"Yes," said Emily. "I would have told the police, but it didn't really register. I could barely see the car, and all I concentrated on was the meaning of that license plate. Remember that great program, *Jewel in the Crown*? It was all about the Raj—"

"RAJ: Reese A. Janning."

"Of *course*," said Emily, eyes widening. "You mean she was in Ledgebrook Saturday night?"

"It's likely. I saw the rear end of her car but didn't notice the plate."

Emily grinned. "See, Louise, it takes the two of us to figure things out. But right now, you'd better concentrate on following that car. We can kick our reservation at Correlli's if they're headed somewhere else."

But first there was the problem of the approaching patrolman. Louise gave him an acquiescent smile. Taking advantage of the fact that she had Virginia license plates, she reinforced the image by laying on a thick accent: "Officer, I was havin' trouble getting myself through this lil' ol' traffic jam, but now I'm doin' just fahn."

Giving them a close look, he shook his head and waved them on. Two hookers out on the town, he probably thought. Washington cops had bigger fish to fry than them, Louise realized.

Louise put on the speed, struggling to keep up with the Lexus. "I guess we're sure that was Reese," she said.

"It matched Laura Alice's description. Don't let them get away, Louise."

They followed, and turned where the Lexus did. What excited Louise was that both she and Emily could now put Reese Janning's car in the neighborhood the night of the murder. What innocent reason could the woman have to be there the night that Catherine was killed?

When they reached the restaurant, Emily hopped out to claim their table while Louise, after circling the block only once, found a parking spot.

Louise sat gratefully at a table in a side alcove, realizing that Emily must have passed silver over the palm of the maître d'. Their seats were situated perfectly to observe at a distance the table at which Walter Freeman sat with three other people. One was Reese Janning.

In a soft voice, Emily said, "Not very cute, is she?" By virtue of her severe hairdo and lack of makeup, Reese had removed all possibility of looking attractive or feminine.

"No wonder Laura Alice Shea couldn't believe that she and Walter were an item," said Louise. "We do tend to think of the 'other woman' as someone more physically appealing than that."

The two other men at the table talked animatedly to Freeman and Janning. They looked like congressmen, and Louise wondered if they were members of the House Finance Committee. There were not many smiles; the luncheon seemed to be all business. The most businesslike of all was Freeman's aide, who also displayed a surprising deferential manner.

When Louise and Emily's poached swordfish arrived, it was delicious. Louise would have liked to slow down and enjoy it, but she told Emily, "We have to eat and run. My car is in a good spot. Then we can follow them when they leave."

Emily looked at Louise in wonder. "I didn't think we'd go that far."

Louise wondered if her friend was losing her nerve. Calmly she told her, "Just sitting here watching them having a business luncheon tells us nothing. Talk about lack of body language: that personifies Walter Freeman."

"Yes," whispered Emily, "but don't forget what we heard about him and Sophie Chalois. Can you picture . . ."

Louise took a small sip of coffee. "I'd prefer not to. First of all, I hate adultery: it's such a dishonest thing. But I know it exists. We might have done better surveilling Sophie's house at midnight than running downtown like this. As it is, we have to continue to follow them."

It wasn't until they'd ordered dessert that Louise realized she was right about her and Emily's sartorial getup. A handsome-looking gray-haired man approached their table and leaned over and peered in their faces in a way that was intimate to the point of being insulting. He said nothing, only smiled at them.

"Did you *want* something?" asked Louise. "Or are you giving us a visual sobriety test?"

"Ah, a clever one, aren't you? Are you ladies available today?"

"*Available?*" repeated Emily, in a horrified tone, not realizing she looked like a 1920s vamp with her short bob and glittering rhinestones. She put a hand to her mouth, suddenly catching on.

Louise quietly told him, "We're not available. We have an appointment at Treasury with the Foreign Trade Commission this afternoon. Forgive us."

The man stood up straight and said, "Oh, so you babes think it's cool to string me on or something. Playing hard to get is going to leave you with exactly nothing. *Forget* about it." And he hurried back to his table.

When he'd left, Emily whispered, "Louise, that man thought—"

"Don't let it bother you. This is all for the sake of our undercover operation, partner." Her words did not remove the shocked expression from her friend's face. "And don't get to thinking you have to confess this stuff to Alex: we've done nothing wrong."

Emily rolled her eyes, which only increased her vampish look. "You're right, we've done nothing wrong."

They ate their dessert quickly and paid the bill, then sprang up to leave. Freeman's party of four looked as if it were finishing quickly, too.

As they hurried to their car, Louise found that Emily's dismay at being viewed as a prostitute had turned to humor. "I never thought that would happen to me in a million years." She giggled. "Wouldn't Alex just die if he knew?"

"Wouldn't he, though?" Louise thought Bill wouldn't like it much either.

Revving her engine, Louise was ready to follow when the green Lexus pulled out of the restaurant parking lot. They watched as the two congressmen were dropped off at the Rayburn Building, and Walter Freeman was deposited at the Federal Reserve. Amid the honking of horns by motorists she'd delayed, Louise followed Reese Janning's car as it continued on its way. The woman appeared to be heading to Georgetown.

"She must be going to her condo," said Emily, sitting forward in excitement. "Why would she go home at one o'clock in the afternoon?"

They approached a neighborhood where most of the buildings were virtually windowless office buildings. Staying well back, they noted Reese's SUV pulling into a parking spot on the street near the entrance to a narrow condo building tucked between the businesses.

Louise stopped her car and turned to her friend. "We both know that Walter Freeman is as shrewd as any man can be. He's not going to walk into the front door of a condo building at one in the afternoon. But he might walk in the *back* door, don't you think?"

"Absolutely," said Emily.

"So I have an idea. Emily, you hurry to the other side of the block and look for a parking garage underneath this place. If he comes, I bet he'll arrive on that side. Meanwhile, I'll keep an eye on this entrance."

With some trepidation, she watched her sexy-looking friend walk quickly around the block and out of sight. Louise slunk down in the front seat and pursued a Washington, D.C., map, willing to pretend that she was a confused tourist in case anyone looked in on her.

After ten minutes, Emily reappeared at the corner of the building, and casually—a little too casually—made her way toward the car.

Louise started the engine. Emily leaned on the driver's-side door, a wide smile lighting her face. "Walter Freeman has come! He entered the parking basement. He's probably inside now."

"Hurry, hop in the car," urged Louise. "We have to move in case she can see us." Only a very oblique view out of Reese's windows would detect them, but Louise didn't put anything past people who were having a clandestine affair.

Louise drove the car forward, out of sight of the windows, then kept on going. "Let's park on the other side. After all, it's Walter Freeman we're most interested in."

"We could park in the next block down, and I'll walk closer and keep an eye on the garage."

Louise circled the block and found a spot far enough away to eliminate suspicion. She said, "I wonder if the police thought about a possible liaison between Freeman and his assistant."

Her friend chuckled. "With our poor relations with the police, we'll never know."

Louise shook her head. "There's also the matter of the garden club members. Never in my wildest dreams did I think a garden club member would be a murderer."

"Hmm," said Emily. "I wouldn't put anything past Meg Durrance."

"The one that I find troublesome is Phyllis Ohlmacher," said Louise. "She's a truly passive-aggressive person."

"Do they make good murderers?"

"I don't pretend to be a profiler, but there are plenty of cases of passive-aggressive women who suffer abuse and suddenly turn around and kill. Phyllis felt she was seriously wronged by Catherine Freeman. She suffered in the pocketbook, where it counts."

"You mean it's more than just an ego thing, as is the case with Meg Durrance. I can see how Phyllis had more reason to kill. And she isn't naive: after that merchant was murdered a year or so ago in his store, businesspeople like the Ohlmachers bought themselves guns and went out and got training in how to use them. I know that for a fact; she told us all about it at one of the garden club meetings."

"Motive, method, opportunity," said Louise, "that's all a person needs. Phyllis Ohlmacher had the motive: Catherine Freeman interfered with her livelihood. She was trained in firearms, so shooting someone through a car window would seem within the realm of possibility. As for opportunity, *I* knew what Catherine Freeman's Saturday night social schedule was, because she talked to all of us about it. The fancy party at the French ambassador's home. I'm sure Phyllis heard her, too. That means she had plenty of time to plan her arrival at the Freemans, where she would simply wait. When they drove up, she'd jump from the bushes and shoot Catherine."

Emily looked at her, her mouth falling open. "My God, Louise, you make it sound so *convincing.* Phyllis, with her prim, gray curls?"

"Yes. But she's just one of several viable suspects." Louise yawned, for she was getting sleepy, after their big lunch. Still, she kept a constant eye on the garage entrance.

"We mustn't forget Sophie," said Emily.

"She had her motives. Jealousy, resentment, maybe even financial need. I imagine she'd like the comfort of having a successful husband support her after years on her own. Does she know how to use a gun?"

Emily, sitting sideways in the seat, looked at Louise as if she were a child with a pocket of ignorance that needed to be filled. "Louise, Bethesda has had carjackings—women pulled out of their fancy cars and taken away and *murdered,* just for their car. Businesspeople have been raided by thieves with handguns. One was killed last year. I haven't asked, but I'd guess both Meg Durrance and Sophie Chalois have guns, just like Phyllis, and know how to fire them. *Alex* has one—though he won't let me touch it. But let's get back to the subject of Reese Janning. If she and Walter are carrying on, then she had every reason to believe he would marry her if Catherine were out of the picture. And now there's the fact that her car was in the neighborhood the night Catherine was killed."

Louise stared at the lack of activity at the garage entrance. She had done surveillance a few times before, and as usual found it supremely boring. She wished they could just go home. "What's Walter doing here? Is it a nooner, or could we be wrong? Maybe it's business."

Rather primly, Emily said, "It doesn't make any sense to conduct business at your aide's condo in the middle of the day. You'd do that in your offices." She shook her bobbed head. "No, Louise, this must be what you call a 'nooner.' No doubt about it." She giggled again. "Imagine Walter. Such an odd-looking man, almost sixty years old, and having affairs with two women. Frankly, I always thought he was boring. How wrong can you be?" With that, she hopped out of the car and started walking casually toward the garage entrance.

The sky had grown darker, with threatening clouds billowing overhead. Louise called to Emily out of her open window. "Be careful—the rain might start. Also, don't walk too close to that entry; you don't want him to see you."

32

Reese Janning was beginning to think she was losing it. When she'd taken off her skirt and blouse and hose, leaving on the bra and the frilly teddy Walter preferred to remove himself, she remembered this rendezvous wasn't all for the sake of romance. She'd forgotten to give him the first draft of a speech she'd worked on far into the night.

It was not like Reese to forget such things, but she was nervous lately.

She tried to ignore the small nut of resentment inside her, and she told herself she'd do positively anything for this man who'd saved her reputation when it was threatened with ruin. She'd stayed up until two working on this speech, and still had to accommodate him with a little nookie this afternoon. She tried not to think about the role she played—always the support person, never the principal player. And the suspicion that there was someone else he was screwing.

While Walter admired her with his eyes, she went to her study at the front of the house, grabbed the speech, and noted a small woman all in black who seemed to linger on the sidewalk across the street as if examining the real estate there. Rhinestones glinted in her hair: she was a cheap whore, Reese decided. Or she could be with that design company, but she didn't look the type. Whatever she was, there was her ride, driving up now, taking her away. Reese frowned. She didn't like the fact that prostitutes worked in her new neighborhood.

She knew she was jumpy and irritable. *Okay, calm down,* she told herself. These forty-five-minute romantic appointments with Walter, packed into an already tightly scheduled day, were frazzling her. And it would look terrible if the police were to discover the affair—though she had that half-finished speech draft right here in her hand to justify Walter's dropping by. A day meeting was all that was possible, since neither of them could afford to be seen at the other's house so soon after Catherine's death. She didn't know when a normal existence would resume, but she hoped it would be soon.

In bare feet, clutching the speech in one hand, she padded back to the bedroom and Walter, her excitement growing, her body throbbing. Though they took all her energy, there was nothing quite as exciting as these clandestine meetings with one of the most powerful and sexy men in the world. Once they could settle in together—whenever that day came—things would be a lot easier.

33

Walter Freeman, still feeling the residual pleasures of the flesh, found it a pleasant drive to his tailor in Georgetown. He always combined a visit to Reese's with an errand, to provide adequate reason for his absence from his office. Today, it was a fitting for his new suit. Yet one thing nagged at him. He could have sworn he recognized the small woman in black who was walking on the sidewalk by Reese's place when he drove away.

It was the first time he'd seen any foot traffic in the neighborhood—which was one of its great attractions to both him and Reese. No nosy neighbors. It was convenient, for he was able to combine business with pleasure with his estimable young aide. She never failed to deliver economic briefs, speeches, or a sensational roll in the hay—and best of all, she was able to switch from one mode to another with nary the twitch of an eyebrow. She just set aside the business at hand, let down her abundant but always thoroughly repressed brown hair, and became a different person. He liked the letting down of the prim bun of hair: his Catherine had had short, wavy curls from the day he met her until the night of her horrible death.

The murder scene flowed unbidden back into his consciousness. He'd had no idea that violent death was so wrenching, so depressing. He couldn't erase the picture from his mind. Catherine, in fact, was shot over and over again in his imagination, her brain matter splattering on him each time, the fetid smell that accompanied sudden death swirling into his nostrils each time, the cold sweat of terror creeping across his back and under his armpits each time.

He knew that the killer hovering at his car window could just as easily have killed him instead, and probably wanted to. This thought only chilled him further.

Visions of his wife's death slowly receded, and he waited for the coldness to leave his body and normality to return. Finally his thoughts reverted to the woman on the street. With a stab of reality, he realized it was someone he knew. What *was* her name? A friend of Catherine's, a little sparrow of a woman. Yes, Emily Holley. But why was she dressed so oddly, like a woman of the night?

His distraction turned to annoyance. And when he was annoyed, people reacted. Or heads rolled. Could her presence in Georgetown have anything to do with the fact that she had as her houseguest that woman known for snooping into police business?

How dare they follow him! And a grieving widower at that. A widower who was still a man, and needed surcease from the strain created by the violent murder of his wife. He didn't dare seek it from a shrink, or from his friend in Ledgebrook, since bodyguards accompanied him home each night and kept an eye on the neighborhood as he slept. He changed course, and headed back to the Federal Reserve Building.

By the time he got back to his office, the thought of an insignificant garden club friend of Catherine's spying on him had sent him into a wordless rage. Striding into his office, he told his secretary, "I have a private call to make. Don't disturb me."

34

On the way back to Bethesda, Louise and Emily debated whether forty minutes comprised a "nooner." Both had witnessed the departure of Walter Freeman's gray Jaguar. Emily was walking dangerously close to the building as he made his speedy exit, and Louise only hoped he hadn't spotted her.

"I wonder if we wasted our time," said Louise. "Walter and Reese might only be using that condo for private business meetings. It wouldn't be the first time an aide and a boss met outside the office to get a little peace and quiet. But then why was Reese parked near Walter's home in Ledgebrook the night of the murder? We both remember seeing that SUV."

"That's what we have to tell police," said Emily, "if they'll only listen to us."

By the time they reached Emily's house, discouragement had set in with Louise. She realized the limits of her investigating ability. She'd already annoyed the Montgomery County homicide detectives. She'd also uncovered too many people with motives to murder poor Catherine Freeman, and found little accompanying evidence. The only way she could think of to get through to the police was by way of her friend Mike Geraghty. He was aware of the fact that she was in Bethesda and wouldn't be surprised that she hadn't been able to curb her meddling ways.

Once upstairs and sprawled on her white linen–bedecked, canopy-covered bed, she consulted her pocket phone book and found his telephone number. By a fluke, Geraghty was at his desk in the Mount Vernon substation on Route One. For a moment she experienced a pang of homesickness.

"So, what have you done now, Louise?" said the detective. "Spill it out." She could picture him sitting in his squeaky chair, probably amused that she was involved in a crime once again. She told him what she and Emily had found, hoping he'd be interested in being an intermediary and relaying the information to the Montgomery County Police Department. He seemed impressed when she told him of how both she and Emily now could identify Reese Janning's SUV near the Freeman house Saturday night. She said, "Someone has to tell the police about Reese Janning. And I have more information about the three suspicious members of the garden club."

Geraghty coughed. Garden club members as prospective murderers? It did test one's credulity.

Patiently, he said, "Louise, you're on slippery ground. That Montgomery County detective who phoned me when you stormed his office—"

"Lordy me, Mike, I just walked in—I didn't storm it."

"Well, walked in and started opinin' about this and that. You've gotta watch your step. Don't you think the people there have enough imagination to do what you're doin'? Let the authorities handle the obvious investigation of Freeman himself, and anyone else out there who might be involved. Catherine Freeman's friends are a natural source of information, even if they're not suspects—they'll get to them eventually. Why can't you leave this one alone?"

She rolled her head sideways on the linen sham to ease her neck muscles. She was so comfortable that in a minute she'd be asleep. "I don't know, Mike. My friend Emily and I didn't like the way the police kissed us off. It was as if we were ignorant, snoopy women. You've never treated me that way—although . . ." She didn't like to mention Geraghty's partner, Detective George Morton, who on occasion had given Louise a hard time: *Can't you mind your own business, Mrs. Eldridge?* he'd asked more than once, only to eat his words when Louise had come up with the crucial evidence to solve a crime.

"Look," said Mike Geraghty, "I'll call Kovach and pass some of this by him. Meanwhile, Louise, I suggest you don't do what you do around here. Those Montgomery County guys don't welcome your efforts."

"I know. Will you let me know what they say?"

"I'll call you right back. Hang tight near that phone."

Louise hung up the phone and snuggled into a better position, and was soon asleep.

It was a half hour later when the phone rang, and after letting Emily pick it up in whatever room she was, Louise came on the line, and found it was Geraghty. "You're right, Louise, in a manner of speakin'. The police there are focused on a professional job that went wrong when Freeman dodged the bullet, so to speak. The poor guy now has bodyguards accompanyin' him home to Bethesda at night, though he insists on bein' free of 'em during the day. He'll probably have to go out and train on a shootin' range, because the police have advised him to carry a weapon, and he doesn't know diddly about weapons. They have their reasons for thinkin' it's a professional hit, Louise, reasons you aren't privy to."

The detective paused, and Louise kept silent, hoping. He said, "If you keep it just between the two of us, I'll tell you one thing they have—"

"Of course I'll keep it to myself."

"Freeman has received threatenin' letters, a batch of 'em. Investigatin' them has sent the police in a definite di-

rection. So, you see, Louise, this thing is bigger than any-
thin' you've been involved in before, and you can't help.
Once again, I advise you to keep out of it."

Thanking him, Louise hung up and started back downstairs, feeling like a lost soul in the big, immaculate house.
She'd been excited about the fact that Reese Janning's car
was in the neighborhood the night of the murder, sure
that it meant something. Perhaps Reese *was* there, but just
as a jealous lover hovering around her sweetheart's home.
It wouldn't be the first time a lovesick person became a
voyeur. But then Reese would have been witness to the
murder . . .

Police had now downplayed everything she had to
offer—the presence of the SUV, the possible significance
of the opened driver-side window on the Freeman car,
Sophie's involvement with Walter, Walter's possible involvement with Reese Janning, and Meg Durrance's and
Phyllis Ohlmacher's motives to kill. With slumped shoulders and drooping chin, she decided she would give up
the investigation. Her old friend Geraghty was right: this
could be Russia, or maybe Iran, hiring a killer to do away
with the country's foremost economic adviser. Who was
she to stick her nose into the matter?

Anyway, she missed her own comfy home. It was just an
hour away.

But now there was Catherine's funeral on Thursday,
which she almost had to attend for the sake of Emily and
Dorothy. Dorothy, in particular, would believe that Louise
had just used her for whatever information she might
have if she hightailed it out of Bethesda and headed for
home now. And Dorothy was a sensitive woman, she realized, who had to be handled carefully.

It also turned out she'd underestimated Emily's dedica-
tion to the hunt for the killer, for Emily had a plan. When
Louise walked downstairs, she found her friend on the
patio. She'd prepared a tray of iced tea and small choco-

late éclairs for their afternoon snack. Louise gratefully dived in.

"Emily, you know the way to people's hearts is through their stomach. I only hope Alex fully appreciates you."

"I think he does—sometimes. Now, Louise, I see disappointment all over your face. Did your detective friend call to tell you to lay off?"

"Actually, I called him first. Then he phoned Detective Kovach and found out that the police definitely think it was a hit on Walter that went wrong. All our work is for nothing. After the funeral tomorrow, I'm out of here."

"No," moaned Emily.

"I have work to do, Emily. I still have a job, you know. Marty Corbin and I are going to have to come up with a program to replace the one we had to junk."

Her friend sipped her tea and took a few moments to recover. Then, slyly, she said, "If you were to stay until Friday, I know another ploy we can try."

Louise didn't smile any more when she heard Emily spouting words like "ploy" that she doubted her friend had used before she had plunged into detecting with Louise. "What ploy is that?"

"How about if I call a special club meeting?"

Louise restrained a laugh. This was such a pathetic idea, to think a garden club meeting could shed light on a murder.

Emily persisted, though she could read Louise's skepticism. "You're the one who said we had to suspect everyone—to leave no one out."

Louise reached for a second éclair. "At least a club meeting would give me a chance to tie up a loose end."

"What loose end is that?"

"A thorough search of the club premises, maybe even a look at Dorothy's apartment—but at the very least those scrapbooks down there that you've talked about."

"Those records go way back," said Emily. "And I hear

Catherine was the organized type who kept lots of notes on everything that went on during her presidency."

Wearily, Louise reflected that she'd set the guidelines herself for a good investigation, and now Emily was holding her to it. Copious notes from Catherine? They could hold a clue. She could picture the overweight but lovely garden club president sitting in the downstairs office and meticulously recording the details of the club's, and her, achievements.

As she stared at a pink crab-apple tree heavy with bloom, her friend's idea began to seem not so silly. "Not bad, Emily. In fact, very good. Going through those scrapbooks may be just what we need to get some closure. Let's be realistic: we couldn't nail Walter Freeman even if he *were* guilty of having his wife killed. But we can check out the garden club angle by doing a little research. Anyway, I've never been to a garden club meeting in my whole life. It's high time I went to one."

Emily smiled her newly confident smile. "And don't forget, Louise, we'll need a record."

"A record? What do you mean?"

"You should turn on that voice-activated recorder I lent you."

"Sure," said Louise. Anything to placate a friend.

35

"You *what?*" said Bill, his voice over the long distance as loud as if he were yelling at her in the same room.

Louise said, "We did it very tactfully. We simply ate at the same place he did, then followed Reese, and he came, like a bear to a honey pot."

Her husband groaned on the other end of the line. "Damn, Louise, I wish you wouldn't—"

"Bill, think about it: he's fooling around with *two women.*"

"Darling, you know you're somewhat of a prude about these things."

"Two? Isn't that impressive?"

"It could have been innocent, you know," said her husband. "He goes to her condo to work on a speech. Hell, he has a huge one coming up—I've even heard about this on CNBC. It's his big counterproposal to the Federal Reserve chairman. The man has a lot on his plate right now, Louise. Having to deal with this kind of trauma is not what he needs or wants, I'm sure."

"You like him. Actually, I liked him, too, when I talked to him. But with you it's more than that. You view him as if he's a national institution, don't you?"

"Give the man some credit: he's an impressive thinker.

And he's about to save this country's economic ass, if you'll pardon the expression. Anyway, if he does have two women on the side, the man's only fifty-eight."

"He looks sixty-eight."

"From what you say, Catherine Freeman was in her sixties. He just married a woman who was eight or ten years older than he was—maybe one who wasn't as interested in sex as he was. These things happen."

Bill's voice was quiet and analytical to the point where it was annoying.

"I call that philandering," Louise said.

"Louise, there are frigid women; believe it. That's sometimes the reason men run around on their wives."

"Hmm. It makes me glad I didn't turn you down in the middle of the night last week. Think what that might have done to our marriage—"

He laughed. "Me too. You never know what a man's liable to do."

"Bill!"

"Honey, I'm kidding, and you know it. If anything, your sexual demands can be overwhelming for me sometimes—"

Now she chuckled, and the phone made a clicking noise. "Oh no," said Louise. "Do you think someone was on the line?"

"Serves him right if he was." They both knew it would be Alex, and not Emily, who was listening in. "And who knows? Maybe he'll learn something."

36

Louise hurried downstairs to help with dinner and was given the job of sautéing the mushrooms. Emily sat at the kitchen table and finished phoning members of the garden club's board of directors. Both were pressured by the fact that a hungry, grumpy man awaited his dinner in the other room.

After consulting earlier with Dorothy Cranshaw, Emily had decided that a meeting of the twelve-member board was more appropriate than a confab with all fifty club members. "Dorothy says that if I invite all fifty members, people might get a little upset. But the board has a legitimate reason for getting together, because we have to decide what kind of memorial to propose in Catherine's memory."

Louise flipped the mushrooms about in the frying pan, impatient for them to brown, distressed because for some reason they were releasing too much water. She turned up the heat. "A board meeting. How convenient. The board includes just the people we've been targeting. Meg Durrance, Phyllis Ohlmacher, Sophie Chalois. And Dorothy's on the board, too, isn't she?"

"She's like a permanent member. Dorothy is as responsible as Catherine was for keeping this club going strong over the years—that important person in the wings who keeps the wheels rolling—" She stopped in confusion, groping for a better metaphor.

Louise laughed. "Or keeps the flowers blooming. I was quite impressed with the way she'd planted that garden at the Davis Library."

"That's Dorothy," said Emily, consulting her club directory for the next number to call. "Impressive."

Louise had finally managed to brown the mushrooms and was about to add them to the winy-smelling coq au vin in the black iron pot on the stove. She said, "Wonder if the board meeting draws more than garden club members?"

Emily looked over at her in puzzlement. "Why would outsiders come to our meeting?"

"Just a stray thought. And here's another: if we throw a little gasoline in the fire, we might get a little explosion."

"You mean, get a rise out of people?"

"Yes. Something to keep them off balance. People reveal more when they're thrown off balance." Then she turned to her job at the stove and folded the mushrooms into the light gravy of the coq au vin. The baby bok choy was cooked al dente and resting on a plate, and the fresh-baked buns nestled in a napkin to keep them warm.

Emily's husband had arrived home half an hour ago, looking as dangerous as a nor'easter. He was furious about something, he informed his wife, then poured himself a drink and holed up in the study. Emily in turn had warned Louise. "I don't know just what's the matter with Alex, but he said he had to eat first before he talked about it, or he'd ruin his digestion." A deep sigh. "His pyloric valve, you know. It doesn't open and shut just right, and getting upset only makes it worse. Now, I don't think it's anything *we've* done, but he wouldn't tell me."

They ate dinner in virtual silence, Louise and Emily only exchanging a few remarks about the garden, Emily asking what might be planted in the bare shady spot near the garage "besides boring old impatiens."

"Ligularia," suggested Louise. "Or maybe cimicifuga." Alex rolled his eyes and remained silent.

Finally, after two helpings of the coq au vin, three glasses of wine, and a salad, the master of the house wiped his mouth and sat back in his chair. He looked first at Emily, then at Louise, as if he expected them to stop eating, too. Louise was sloshing a piece of French bread through the gravy and didn't intend to stop just because Alex had a stitch in his knickers.

"Ladies," he said starchily, and Louise noted the now-familiar frown that came down on his brow like a crumpled umbrella. "I was so furious and disappointed when I received a call from Walter Freeman this afternoon that I nearly called to talk to you immediately, Emily. Then I decided to be reasonable, and wait until we'd eaten."

Louise kept on sopping up her gravy, but noted Emily had both hands in her lap and was at full attention. She looked at Alex, and he shook his head, as if she was hopeless. "I'll be done in a minute," said Louise. "Is this something that requires that we hold *hands,* or something?"

Alex's head reared back and he sniffed. "Louise, I don't really know how Bill—"

Sensing a social meltdown, Emily quickly intervened. "Alex, don't you *dare*—how could you say something like that? Louise and Bill are as simpatico as two peas in a pod."

"Nevertheless," he said, turning ponderously to his wife, "she's the one who's gotten you involved here, Emily. She's the one who's responsible for having the man who heads the president's task force on monetary reform call me and chew *me* out because my wife is going around with a snoopy friend and intimating that Walter killed his own wife!"

Louise often wondered about pale redheads like Alex, for their color changed so radically when excited that they looked as if they were having apoplexy. And when sick or tired, they took on the pallor of one dying of consumption.

Alex's face was now deep, deep red. She hoped he had a good, strong heart. She wondered just how much he knew. Looking over at her friend, she sent a silent signal: *Don't tip any more information than necessary.*

Louise cleared her throat and said, "It's all my doing, Alex. You are so right. I contacted the police twice and mentioned a few details to them. Mind you, Walter Freeman, in my opinion, is only one of a number of potential suspects, and I made that quite clear to the police. I assure you that they didn't take me seriously."

Alex leaned ominously toward her, then turned back to his wife as if he'd forgotten something important. "Emily, while Louise and I have this out, kindly serve dessert and coffee."

"No, dear," said Emily in a chilly voice. "I'd rather stay, if you don't mind."

He gave her an annoyed look and turned back to Louise. "Bad enough you gossiped to the police. But you also had the audacity to visit Walter's housekeeper. The woman told on you, did you know that?"

Louise shrugged. "We only paid a condolence call on Martina. Emily knew she was heartbroken, from our visit to Walter on Sunday."

"But Martina is an Island woman, a simple creature. Walter said she nearly swooned, because she felt you, Louise, have some intimation of the murderer, just like she does. Spooky *spooky,* but spooky is not what Walter Freeman likes."

"Then he should probably hire a Polish maid," said Louise, "who wouldn't believe in voodoo, but in the Catholic Church. Or, perhaps, a Norwegian maid, who worships Wotan . . ."

These were snotty, waspish words, but she'd lost Alex's affections anyway—or rather, never had them. She was tired of trying to please him.

"Now let's not get racist," he snarled. "I take your point."

"Emily and I did no harm to the woman. We didn't suggest any guilt on the part of Walter, and neither did she—she highly respects her employer. So I don't understand why Walter Freeman was so upset to have us visit in his kitchen."

"He feels it was underhanded—especially your calls to that detective, Koski, or whatever."

"Kovach, Tom Kovach," said Emily. "What's wrong with a citizen trying to help the police? I was disappointed at how rude that detective was to Louise. She was trying to help."

"Tell me, Alex," said Louise, "did the police hurry right to Freeman and report my phone calls? If that's true, it's very informative, don't you think?"

Looking alarmed, perhaps realizing the import of her question, he said, "No, no, the police are not spilling these things to Walter. I think he learned via the grapevine in the Criminal Division, quite frankly. Someone overheard your conversation with Kovach."

"I see," said Louise.

Alex opened his hands in a gesture of magnanimity. "Now, Louise, now Emily, I can see that your intentions were good. But you mustn't get involved in things that are not your business."

Emily answered pertly. "I thought crime fighting was everyone's business. How about 'The Most Wanted,' and programs like that? They *depend* on the public to help catch criminals."

Alex snapped. "Emily, dammit, *go get dessert*. It must be nine o'clock and I'm still famished."

She sat back in her chair. "Not until this conversation is over, Alex."

He waved his hands in the air. He'd seen that fluffy, homemade yellow sponge cake mixed with fruit and whipped cream that Emily had concocted into an English trifle, and he couldn't wait a moment longer. If their sex wasn't good, thought Louise, maybe their excellent meals were a more than adequate substitute. "O-*kay*. I declare this conversation over. Just *please* don't mention Walter Freeman's name again to the police."

Louise looked at Emily. "I'm good with that. Are you good with that, Emily?"

"I'm good with that, too. And now I'll get dessert."

No apologies asked, and none given. Alex crossed his arms and closed his eyes. Louise got up and finished clearing the table.

A couple of helpings of trifle and the man of the house was almost civil again. His good humor only increased when Louise offered to take the dog for a walk; this, she knew, would give the couple some private time, during which he would berate his wife for all her failings of the day.

And yet Louise wondered if he'd succeed, for Emily had acquired some backbone in the past couple of days. She was hardly the same person who had greeted her four days ago at the Farm Women's Market.

37

"Be careful," Emily warned as Louise went out the front door with the dog. "It's windy, and it still might storm. Lancelot goes absolutely crazy when it thunders. So be prepared for a quick return to home in case the deluge finally comes."

Thinking of the weeks and weeks without any rainfall, Louise laughed. "Rain? I'll only believe it when I see it."

She couldn't resist taking Lancelot on the same route that she, Emily, and Alex had taken the night of Catherine Freeman's murder. With intensified police presence in the "crime" neighborhood, she had no fears—in fact, a police car at that very moment was making what would be for ordinary mortals an illegal left turn off Wilson Lane into the sacrosanct Ledgebrook neighborhood where she was heading, and slowly crawled down the street.

She crossed Wilson Lane, pulling the dog quickly with her to avoid a fast-moving red sports car that showed up from seemingly nowhere. Louise had a theory that drivers became wilder before the onset of a storm. She also believed drivers of red sports cars drove more recklessly than other people. Perhaps this driver had decided that since it was ten o'clock, he or she could put on the gas and exceed the speed limit by twenty miles. Too bad the cops didn't have eyes in the back of their heads, Louise thought, or they could have given the driver a ticket.

As the wind helped push her down the slight hill, her thoughts wandered back to the previous Saturday. Where were the police then, when the Freemans could have used their help? She knew the answer. No community had enough resources to blanket a single neighborhood, not unless it was Podunk, with a population under 1,000. Even in Podunk, bad things happened under the nose of the police. In Bethesda, there was plenty of ground to cover, the far-reaching expanses of suburban homes, and the commercial areas and outlying shopping centers where most of the carjackings took place.

Now she passed that leafy alley where she'd seen the SUV parked crookedly on the night of the murder. As the Freemans' white French-style house came into view, she realized with a start that this was the house that *Catherine* Freeman had built, with money she'd made by investing in the rich commerce of Bethesda. Not that the famous Walter Freeman didn't have money, of course. He'd probably made plenty in those years as a financial consultant. Yet he'd turned to public life early on, and public servants only received so much, no matter how illustrious their reputations. Catherine's fortune must have meant something to him.

All quiet here tonight, except for the whistling wind. The police car disappeared, but probably was still cruising nearby. It was then that she heard something crashing about in the nearby bushes. Quickly, she turned around, pulling the dog closer. She saw nothing. But Lancelot whined, as if he'd heard the sound, too. Her heart, which had begun to beat double time, slowed, and she realized this was nothing more than her imagination.

Nevertheless . . .

"Come on, boy, let's pick up the pace," she told the dog,

and went into a slow jog down the road, straight toward the Freemans. As if trying to avoid the bright lights to do his toilet, Lancelot headed for the farthest edge of the property, which was overhung with huge hemlocks. The dog stopped in the parkway. Louise stood by to pick up his deposit in a blue plastic newspaper sleeve that Emily had given her before departing.

As she bent down to scoop up Lancelot's leavings, she heard the shot go by her head. The sound was blown by the rushing wind so that it might have been a door slamming. But there were no doors out here on the streets of Ledgebrook.

Someone out there in the darkness was taking a potshot at her. Leaving plastic bag and dog deposit behind, she yanked Lancelot around and ran at full speed up the slight rise of Glenbrook Road until she reached the relative brilliance of the streetlights of Wilson Lane. A slow-moving vehicle was approaching from the west, but with the adrenaline now pumping through her body, she knew she could beat it hands down. She sprinted across the street, then took a second to look behind her. Now whoever was taking that shot at her was across the road. Still, having learned from an expert that handguns can shoot much farther than people thought, she stayed well behind the DO NOT ENTER sign on the corner.

There was not a person in sight, not a movement. The wind had abated, so that even the trees had ceased their rustling.

Louise jogged another block, into the safety of Battery Park. Only then did she dare to stop and rest, her body bent at the waist, her hands on her knees, in the stance of a tired sprinter. She wondered if her imagination had simply run away with her. Could it have been something else besides a pistol? She straightened up and walked the brief remaining block to the Holleys as a new burst of wind and a few scattered raindrops cut across her face.

It was definitely time to get out of this place: she was beginning to imagine things, for how could a shooter hide in that posh neighborhood with police cars cruising by every five minutes?

38

Louise came in the front door, and the wind whipped it shut behind her so that it closed with a bang.

"Everything all right?" called a startled Emily from the living room.

"Everything's all right," she answered. She wouldn't tell her hosts about her experience walking the dog. She was sure Alex wouldn't believe her, and Emily would. Then Emily would become so nervous that she might just cancel Friday's meeting of the board of the Old Georgetown Garden Club.

She went in and sat down in the living room, picking up the newspaper that Alex had discarded. Her hands were trembling so much that Emily noticed.

"Louise—are you all right? What is it?"

She set the paper down in her lap and folded her hands. "I'm fine, just a little tired, I guess. I may go to bed in a minute, and not wait for the eleven o'clock news."

It was just as well that she had kept her suspicions to herself, for a few minutes later, Alex got a chance to become upset once more. He seemed to enjoy getting upset, as if it proved what idiots the rest of them were. The doorbell rang, in three consecutive, impatient sets of musical clangs. Alex answered.

"That's strange," he called back to them from the front

hall, "there's no one here. Oh, oh, here's something." He strolled back into the living room, holding a piece of folded white paper. As he read, his voice rose until it edged on hysteria. "Listen to this, if you think you two have done no harm: 'Keep your nose out of this thing if you know what's good for you.' "

He glared down at Louise with pure hatred. "Mrs. Eldridge, you come into this house, and not only do you jeopardize my wife's health with all this silly running around—why, her face has been flushed for three days—but now it's obvious you are jeopardizing her very life as well."

"Let's see that," demanded Emily, reaching out for the note.

Alex pulled it away from her, and held it delicately by its edges. "No, we must call the police. It may have finger-prints." His wary eyes widened. "This was probably written by the murderer himself!"

Emily exhaled sharply. "This could be a joke. It sounds silly to me."

"How do you know it's a joke? We need to call the police."

Louise reached into her shirt pocket. "I have the number right here." She handed the card to him.

He tapped in the numbers, pacing as he did. He muttered, "The best thing you could do, Louise, would be to just disappear from our lives."

She stood speechless, and her face reddened with embarrassment.

Emily was not going to hear this. "She's not going to do that, Alex," she said. "And your remark about the state of my health is totally *wrong*. Since Louise has been here, I've never felt better in my life."

Alex glared at his spouse. Before he could think of an angry rejoinder, Louise told him, "I'll be gone by Friday afternoon. And that will be the end of it, as far as I'm concerned. I'm perfectly willing to let the Montgomery County Police do the work. I have my own to do."

"Is that a promise?"

"Yes."

"But why not leave tomorrow, after the funeral?"

She shrugged, while Emily's face remained closed. Neither one of them was going to tell him about the special garden club board meeting that had been called for eleven o'clock on Friday.

"Oh, that's easy to explain," said Emily. "Louise and I have a little social thing at midday."

The police arrived and stayed more than an hour, trying to understand the situation and the reason why someone would put a warning note on the Holley's doorstep. Since the two patrolmen who stopped in had meager background on the case, they also had to place some calls to headquarters. When they were done with their questions, they warned Alex to lock the house and keep the occupants in for the night.

Alex gave Emily and Louise one of his dark looks, then told the officers, "I certainly will, and I'll throw away the key!"

Emily wasn't going to take that. She stepped up and opened the front door so the uniformed men could leave. She gave them a big wink. "He's just joking, of course. No man in America is going to lock his wife in without a struggle."

39

Thursday

Richard Ralston's bouquet

There it was, looming up at the head of Catherine's now-closed, gold-embossed casket. Louise wished she hadn't overheard Richard Ralston's description of the bouquet as a little piece of heaven—or was it that the bouquet was flying up to heaven, as Catherine Freeman allegedly had done? Without the back story, the flower arrangement would have just taken its place as one of the lovelier ones Louise had ever laid eyes on. But with the spin provided by Richard Ralston, the bouquet took on a life of its own. Despite its charming dishabille, it was grand, much grander than the original sketch that Richard had faxed to Emily. Frilly, almost voluptuous pink tulips soared upward for three feet or more, then curved down like swan's necks, while tiny mauve flowers floated between them like small butterflies. The surrounding swirls of pale raffia, intermixed with subtle twinkles of tiny lights, gave it an otherworldly quality. Louise had no idea how the clever Richard had achieved that effect.

The overflow crowd pouring into the cozy Gothic confines of Bethesda's First Presbyterian Church on this sunny Thursday morning immediately turned their eyes on the unusual floral arrangement. *Dorothy Cranshaw should be well-satisfied,* thought Louise, *and so should Catherine Freeman.*

The dead woman was being memorialized in a church not six blocks from her home. Outside, the traffic on Wilson Lane seemed to have subsided as if in respect for this doyenne of the local garden club. As quiet organ music played in the background, Louise checked out the crowd. In the front row, of course, was Walter Freeman, sitting with some older people who looked to be relatives. Louise noted the stark, homely face of Reese Janning, sitting with government types in back of Walter. In fact, as she looked more closely, she spied many high-level dignitaries including cabinet heads who'd come here out of respect for this revered government official. And at the last moment, in came the vice-president himself, flanked by Secret Service men. The crowd momentarily murmured, then hushed again: it was used to bigshots in church. The vice-president took his place near the widower, and reached over and gave him a warm handshake. Surprisingly, Alex Holley streamed in with these important latecomers and sat on the frontmost pew with Walter. *Don't forget that,* Louise told herself. *Alex Holley is much closer to Walter Freeman than he has ever admitted.*

As the smell of burning candles enveloped them, the majestic Brahms *German Requiem* began, and the dignified, white-haired minister came to the altar. It was amazing and comforting to Louise how like other funerals this one was. The clergyman read all the standard Scriptures, the backbone of which was, as in all Christian churches, that *the Lord is my Shepherd, I shall not want . . .*

Louise hoped that Catherine Freeman indeed would lie down in green pastures.

In his homily, the minister became personal, getting right down to the heart of Catherine Freeman. Apparently she not only was a paragon of gardening skill and an elder of her church, but also contributed both her time and money to the Crippled Children's League. The minister confided to the big crowd that Catherine herself had suffered from a certain unnamed condition, and had great empathy for young people suffering from various afflictions. By the time he was through, there were few dry eyes in the church.

Finally done with his peroration, the minister stepped aside with an impassive, almost pained expression on his face. Sophie Chalois, ravishing in a black faille suit, climbed up to the pulpit for her good-bye.

Louise slid a glance at Emily, as if to say, *"Why her?"*

In response, Emily rolled her eyes. "Can you believe that?" she whispered. "What nerve." Other faint murmurs could be heard, and Louise wondered if Walter's midnight visits to Sophie were secret after all. Or maybe the crowd was just surprised to see this blond bombshell giving a eulogy. But why not? She was a friend of the family, and a friend of the deceased, for those who didn't know more.

First, Sophie threw back the black veil to reveal her splendidly coiffed blond hair and tear-streaked blue eyes. Consulting notes on a sheet of white paper with the aid of stylish half-glasses, Sophie gave a stiff little speech about Catherine's contributions to the Old Georgetown Garden Club. She rose to occasional heights of emotion, as when she said, "Catherine's place can *never* be taken in the garden club, try as we might to fill the void, especially those of us with the longest experience. But we will *try.*" Then, amidst much rustling, Sophie descended from the pulpit.

Louise heard the words, "I bet," whispered by Emily.

She shot her a quick glance. "What do you mean?"

"She wants to take over the garden club, that's what that means. I should have known it."

"Oh," whispered Louise. "And what about you? You're the president now, aren't you?"

"I *thought* so. But Sophie wants to get rid of me. That speech laid down the gauntlet."

Louise looked around self-consciously to see if others noticed their whispering, but it was near the end of the service, and people were talking among themselves behind their hands, especially the garden club members sitting in pews near them. Not Dorothy Cranshaw, though, who sat with her son, Jack, and frowned slightly at the disrespect shown by the muffled interruptions at the end of the service.

Just as Louise was turning her head to the front again, she caught a glimpse of Charlie Hurd, hovering in the aisle not twenty feet away. He gave her a thumbs-up signal, and she briefly nodded her head. Then she saw Detectives Kovach and Girard and other detectives lurking in the side aisle and realized they were still hot on the scent—but how strong was the scent?

Charlie Hurd. Why did he always dog her footsteps? Suddenly she had a mere inkling of what genuinely famous people must endure from the papparazzi. Charlie's manners were no better than those of the papparazzi. And yet, she realized, Charlie was here only because a crime had been committed. In a sense, that was the only reason *she* was still hanging around in Bethesda. So maybe they were more birds of a feather than she would like to admit.

Then the somberness of the occasion overcame Louise once more, and she forgot Charlie and his wiles. The congregation marched out to the final melancholy but victorious strains of Brahms's masterpiece. The high, soft voices of the choir released emotions of loss and sadness in her, wrenching tears from her eyes and loosening her cheek muscles so that her lips trembled uncontrollably. Though she'd hardly known the dead woman, in a minute she'd be bawling like a baby.

Louise knew some of the words in the *Requiem,* and hoped the dead Catherine could hear them, too—*Grave, where is thy triumph? Death, O where is thy sting?*

She dabbed at the tears with a handkerchief, trying to pull herself together in case she needed to talk to people. Dying, she thought ruefully, would almost be worthwhile, to have this music played for one. Beside her, Emily was openly sobbing, and the two of them hooked arms to support each other as they left the church. In the corner of her eye, Louise noticed the two detectives moving swiftly down the church aisles, as if on a hunt. They approached first Laura Alice Shea, then Meg Durrance.

As they reached the back of the church, Laura Alice was near the door, patiently waiting for them. She was sober but tearless, looking stylish and healthy in a black dress with a white tailored collar. In contrast, Louise had on a long-sleeved black T-shirt and black skirt she and Emily had found for her in a local shop, since she hadn't expected to be attending a funeral.

Louise wondered why Alex didn't come over to comfort his wife; he must have spied her in the crowd, crying her heart out. Laura Alice filled the void, throwing an arm around Emily's shoulder and gently saying, "It's hard, isn't it? I remember when I lost my mother last year. Death is so difficult to cope with."

"Did you just arrive?" asked Louise.

"Yes," said Laura Alice, as they moved outdoors and stood in a corner of the church porch. "But I didn't want to march up to the front and join you, just in case I went into labor on the way up the aisle." That brought a smile to Emily's face. "And," said Laura, "that way, those detectives could nab me faster and make an appointment to interview me." When Emily turned aside to greet someone else, Laura Alice directed the question at her. "So tell me, Louise—what's the latest? What's new with you two—" She stopped in mid-sentence and grinned.

Laura Alice, young, and bursting with fertility, was about to mention "Miss Marple" again but had restrained herself. Enough, thought Louise, of being associated with that old-hen English country fiction detective. It was a good thing Laura Alice was so engaging: otherwise, someone might take offense at her wisecracks.

Louise said, "We got in a bit of a jam last night." She told Laura Alice about the note Alex Holley found on his front stoop.

With a worldly roll of her eyes, Laura Alice said, "Alex must have flipped his lid. He goes into orbit over lots less than that. I thought I saw a flash of police lights outside, but I was too sleepy to care, and Jim could sleep through a tornado." In a droll voice she added, "So the police grilled you for an hour or so, huh? I bet you are *really* welcome in that house, Louise. You're attracting more trouble than that husband of Emily's has ever seen. Even Jim, who, because he is so nice, never cracks wise about Alex no matter how quirky he acts, had to laugh when I told him what was going on next door. *The Radicalization of Emily*, I call it. Alex probably thinks you're not only bending her mind, Louise, but you're endangering her, as well. And you *are*, of course."

"I see you can read Alex—and me—pretty well. I promised him I'd leave tomorrow. But not until after the garden club board meeting. I guess you're on the board—I heard Emily phoning you."

"I'm head of the long-range planning committee, whatever that means. Just got the job recently, when the former chairman had to step down on account of suddenly, all her bones began to collapse: serious osteoporosis, y'know." The younger woman giggled. "I know that sounds funny, but it's not, of course."

"No," agreed Louise. "I have an elderly aunt who's in a nursing home in a wheelchair. One day she was standing talking to me, erect and seemingly strong, and the next moment she'd crumpled to the ground. One of her hip bones had simply disintegrated like a piece of spent rock. It's excruciatingly painful to be alive with your bones betraying you."

Laura Alice, with the confidence of youth, said, "Good thing we know more about that these days."

"Good thing. So, I guess Emily and I will see you at the meeting tomorrow morning."

Laura Alice moved closer to Louise and quietly said, "I want to go over to the clubhouse with you."

"Well, sure, we'd like to have you."

"I know Emily called this meeting on the chance of finding out something more about Catherine's death. Isn't that true?"

"Yes," said Louise. "It's my last shot at this thing. Then I have to go home. My husband and daughter will be back from their trip, and I want to be there when they arrive."

She smiled. "No more lingering around friendly down-town Bethesda."

"Okay," said Laura Alice, beaming. "Then one more go at the mystery." She raised a finger, as if alerting the already alert Louise. "Tomorrow. I'll be ready at ten sharp."

As Louise turned to look for Emily, she nearly ran into Walter Freeman. He'd left behind his entourage of family, friends, and important government figures, and made a point of coming over to where she was standing. Taking her firmly by the arm, he pulled her into the far corner of the stone porch.

"I want to talk to you, Mrs. Eldridge," he murmured. "I now have you pegged more clearly—an amateur sleuth with some sort of a reputation as a PBS garden show host, who lives in *northern* Virginia." He enunciated "northern Virginia" in a way that made it sound like Tobacco Road in the thirties.

Louise had liked this man the last time they'd met, had broken through his aloof wall and found him a real human being. She wasn't so sure she felt that way anymore. She wriggled her arm free of the insistent pressure of Freeman's fingers.

He looked down at his hand, as if he hadn't been aware that he'd been holding her in an iron grip. "Sorry, Louise. I didn't mean to hurt you. What distresses me is that you have been going around Bethesda intimating that I put a contract out on my beloved wife."

"Mr. Freeman, I have done no such thing. I heard from Alex that you were upset. I think you have it all wrong."

"I don't think so, Mrs. Eldridge," he said, in his finest, level, *I-have-to-keep-this-economy-from-going-south* tone, the one he used when he testified in front of important congressional committees. "I've pursued the matter and found out that you've been seen and heard in the offices of the Criminal Division, and, of all inopportune things, proposing some bumbling, amateurish detective theory to the police."

She stared up into his pale green eyes. "It was just a few unanswered questions—about your rolled-down window, for one thing. I would have thought Detective Kovach would keep our discussion to himself."

"He did," said Freeman, in a voice that gave Louise a chill, "but I learned it from someone who is, shall we say, 'close to the investigation.' You may not like that, but I have many, many sources for no end of information." His expression told her just how important he was.

"Oh, I'm sure," she said. "I'm surprised that you'd even be interested in my bumbling, amateurish detecting."

"Don't try to twist my words, Mrs. Eldridge. I've heard, even from my inestimable Martina, that you've been tramping around our neighborhood, no doubt asking people about me, and even breached the sanctity of my house. I can't tell you how insulting that was." He looked around, noting people beginning to watch him. "Well, this isn't the time," he said. "I must let it go. Just remember who you're gossiping about, my dear. I do not brook gossip lightly. It is a dishonor to my dead wife." With a final glare, which was as stinging as a slap in the face, he said, "Do you now understand the depths of my feelings?"

"I think I do," said Louise.

Another hard look, and he turned and walked back to his friends and relatives. Louise could feel her face burning. Her gaze frantically searched for Emily. Instead, she ran into Charlie Hurd. He was the last person she'd turn to for solace.

He stood there in the sunshine, cocky as ever, a mocking look on his thin face. "I heard that. What was that all about, anyway? You been doing a little snooping, huh? Been stayin' with some friend near here? What's her name, anyway?"

Louise gave a deep sigh. Nothing like the truth. "It's true my friend and I have done a little talking around the neighborhood. No more than any normal, red-blooded, curious American would do if there was a murder in their neighborhood. Quit making it sound so criminal."

Charlie laughed. "With you, Louise, nothing like that is innocent. No wonder Walter Freeman is pissed at you." He was digging out his handheld computer and scratching down notes. "Now, lessee, I wonder just how I can use this, especially since Freeman won't talk to us."

Louise had a strong urge to rip the electronic device out of his hands. Instead, she stood stiff as stone and said quietly, "If I were you, I wouldn't use it until you find out more of what's really going on." She felt it necessary to dangle a little raw meat in front of this press person to keep him from doing something foolish by dragging her name into a *Post* story.

Charlie rose to the bait. His pale eyebrows gathered in the middle of his brow. "I knew it: you *know* something. *Damn*, Louise, *give.*" He leaned in confidentially and looked up at her. "Matter of fact, I picked up something, too, in Walter's 'hood: did you know he was having a little affair with a neighbor? It's that blond woman named Sophie Chalois who got up and gave a speech honoring her 'friend' Catherine. Man, what chutzpa! I betcha you know Sophie, don'tcha? Whaddaya think of her? Is she a bitch-goddess, or just a goddess?" He looked around in the crowd, trying to spy her. "She's some dish, but I haven't been able to find her since she did her thing on the altar."

"I don't know her, Charlie." That was almost but not quite true. Louise now had the problem of getting loose of Charlie, if she didn't want him following her right home to the Holleys'. "And now excuse me." She smiled. "When you gotta go, you gotta go."

As she passed Emily, she murmured, "I'll walk back to your house on my own. I need to get rid of that reporter, or he'll be clinging to us like a burr." She would duck inside to the women's lavatory, to hide out until Charlie's interest waned.

"But Louise," protested Emily, "first tell me what made Walter so angry at you."

"You noticed?"

"Are you serious?" moaned Emily. "Everyone noticed. Alex wanted to know what the two of us had done. I told him nothing more than what he already knows about." She reached out and clasped her hand. "Louise, don't be surprised if he wants to kick you out of the house when we get home. But don't worry: I won't let him!"

40

Friday

It was almost ten, and Emily and Louise were loading Emily's car with business records and a cherry cobbler they'd prepared for the garden club board meeting. Louise was surprised she was still in Bethesda.

The confrontation with Alex hadn't taken place yesterday after the funeral; it had been called off because of Alex's urgent need to be at a State Department meeting. Then, when he'd come home Thursday night, he'd had dinner and gone straight to his study to work, too distracted with the affairs of the country to remember that their houseguest Louise was corrupting his wife and alienating his important friends in the neighborhood. It was a bittersweet, no-contest victory over the male tyrant of the house. But Louise was sick and tired living in a house with a male tyrant in charge.

The good thing was that Alex's retiring from the ring left Louise free to stay another night and take part in Emily's carefully planned special board meeting. It seemed so innocent: a meeting of the board of a garden club. But Louise felt a sense of unease that manifested itself in a few sharp pains in her chest. This meeting could become very unpleasant, and she felt guilty for encouraging Emily to hold it.

One thing board members would surely discuss were

the visits they had from the Montgomery County detectives yesterday afternoon. They might even ask the question of "who sicced these detectives on us?" Some would be distressed by the daring proposal Emily was going to make to the group—but that was Louise's plan, to get people upset and see what would happen. She knew from experience that truths sometimes emerged when groups of suspects were gathered together, aggravated, and then allowed to sound off. A board meeting was the ideal time for this ploy. Who knew what Sophie, or Meg, or Phyllis, or even others would spill out?

At the same time, she was alarmed at Emily's increasing appetite for detecting. As she packed the last of her big notebooks in the car, her friend said, "Just think, this meeting is an entrapment, Louise. We're going to find our murderer!"

Emily was on a high—almost like a junkie's high—and Louise didn't want her to come off it with hopes dashed. What would Emily do with herself when Louise went home this afternoon if the murder was still unsolved?

"I hate to squelch you, Emily, but don't be too surprised if nothing at all happens."

Emily waved her hand, as if dismissing this thought. She had dressed carefully for the meeting, wearing heels and a highly tailored, beige linen outfit that she called her power suit. "I'll need the security this gives me," she told Louise, "if either the murderer shows up, or if Sophie Chalois starts to cut in on my territory."

"Of those two things," said Louise wryly, "the second is what is more apt to happen." Louise had on the checkered cotton blouse, flared denim skirt, and flats that she'd worn for the TV shoot six days before, not minding that she looked like a bucolic milkmaid. In her shoulder bag she had tucked Emily's voice-activated recorder.

Then Laura Alice Shea arrived, wearing a ruffly, orchid-colored voile dress that made her resemble a pretty, round flower, a lisianthus, perhaps. Her feet were shod in sexy, high-heeled black leather St. John pumps; Louise recognized them, because she had a pair of Manolo Blahniks that resembled them. Laura Alice obviously was not willing to give in completely to the maternal image.

In her hands she carried a covered, rectangular silver dish. She grinned. "I did it right, Emily—I followed the recipe."

Emily explained to Louise. "Laura Alice made the Jell-O salad. Back in the old days of the club, you were supposed to follow a given recipe—lime Jell-O, with finely chopped celery and carrot. If you didn't, or, heaven forbid, if you put it in a mold that wasn't *rectangular,* you would catch it." She shrugged. "These days people don't care that much, as long as it's a salad."

"Tradition, tradition: it's wonderful," said Laura Alice with a wry smile. "And Louise, we're also getting to taste the club's traditional corned-beef *molded* salad. Emily asked Dorothy Cranshaw to make one. Talk about *retro*—"

"Sounds . . . delicious," said Louise, with an effort. Corned beef wasn't her favorite food.

Emily looked embarrassed. "Maybe I'm just being a sentimental fool," she explained, "but I just thought that in memory of Catherine we should turn to the old luncheon recipes." She blinked her eyes to keep a tear back.

"Perfectly understandable," said Louise. "And yet Catherine wasn't grounded in the past, was she? She was the one engineering all the changes in the club."

Emily nodded. "Yes, changes that I guess I'll have to manage now."

The clubhouse was a charming building circa 1925, with gray shingles and a sharply slanted roof, like the witch's house out of *Hansel and Gretel*. The door squeaked when they entered. Emily took Louise on a quick tour of the lobby, meeting room, sunroom, tiny kitchen, and storeroom.

"This place is being modernized?" said Louise, a note of incredulity in her voice.

"Yes," said Emily. "Catherine found a very clever architect to do the work." Her friend wasn't interested in talking about renovations, but rather about their investigations. Giving Louise a meaningful look, she opened a door in the front hall and pointed to the stairway leading to the basement. "Everything's down there," she said. "It's cinchy to find."

Laura Alice said, "Why don't I go and help you?"

They agreed that Emily would call down to them if she needed help with the meeting setup, or else just before the people began to arrive.

The narrow set of stairs led them down into an ancient, Washington, D.C.–style basement, complete with a faint, moldy smell that even constant cleaning and polishing could not remove. Louise thought it would have to be a very clever architect indeed to rid this building of its vestiges of age and fatigue.

Laura Alice turned her face up to Louise, who was following, and wrinkled her nose. "I must say it's clean here, but I don't like that smell much," she said.

"I don't, either. This old place hasn't been changed much over the years."

"They put in a sump pump a few years ago to take care of the flooding problems," said Laura Alice. "But the whole place will be renovated pretty soon now, and that smell's probably going to go."

Louise thought of all of the thousands of basements in the damp, Washington, D.C., area, with the same faint moldy odor—and the contrast with Emily's house. Even though Emily and Alex owned a place just as old as this clubhouse, a smell like this would never have been permitted to exist in its pristine environs. They would have painted it, sealed it, and renovated it out of existence.

Her thoughts immediately turned to Dorothy Cranshaw.

Was this the only entry to her home? Louise hoped not. Bad enough that it faintly smelled, but the very fact of having to descend fourteen steep stairs to get to one's abode must be troubling. She remembered reading and even hearing stories of people who in the Depression had dug themselves a basement home and lived there until they had enough money to complete above-ground stories. It had always spooked Louise to think of living underground, like an animal, and having to go down into the earth to reach the comforts of home.

Yet the heavy oak door at one side of the big downstairs room was cheery enough, with the small nameplate on it reading DOROTHY CRANSHAW. The sign hung above a bright little wreath with dried flowers. Dorothy's home appeared to occupy most of the space, with the club's office and records crowded into the remainder.

"Here are the scrapbooks," called Laura Alice, who had not lingered on the stairs thinking gloomy thoughts about Dorothy's living conditions. Instead, she'd gotten right to business. She had turned on an overhead light with a green shade that hung over a wooden table and started appraising the two dozen or so thick scrapbooks stuffed into a wooden bookshelf behind it.

"This is a huge job," said Louise, discouraged at the sight of the dusty journals.

"No problem," said Laura Alice. "We'll whip right through them. But the financial records aren't here. That's too bad. I suppose Dorothy Cranshaw keeps them separate, in a less public place. She's the club treasurer." She gave Louise a wise glance. "I always think financial records tell you more than anything else. That's probably because I'm a financial analyst."

They took a half-dozen large volumes off the shelves and arranged them on the table, then sat side by side as they pored over the books, one by one, examining the array of photos and historical notes that told the tale of the club. In the first few books, all the photos were black and white and the script a real throwback to the days when penmanship was one of the most important subjects in the grade-school curriculum.

Occasionally Louise consulted her watch. "I'm not sure we want to be here when people arrive," she warned her companion. "We don't want to arouse suspicions."

"Don't worry," said Laura Alice. Louise wasn't surprised at this reaction, for she'd decided Laura Alice was not about to let any circumstance get her down. "I have a perfect reason for being here—and I'll just say you were helping me. I'm supposed to give a little report on long-range stuff. So what better way than if I came down here and sniffed through the scrapbooks?"

Louise laughed. "You're good, Laura Alice. I like the way you think."

When they reached the scrapbook that recorded events of twenty-six years ago, most of the pictures were in color—faded now, but still evocative of the modern era. They discovered the first picture of Dorothy Cranshaw. She was the elder stateswoman of the club. Then, a year later, Catherine Freeman's picture appeared. Dorothy was club president for five years, then Catherine succeeded her, with Dorothy ensconced as vice president.

Louise gave Laura Alice a look. "The two of them have practically run this club for a quarter of a century, barring the occasional interloper." One of these "interlopers" was Meg Durrance.

"Twenty-five years is forever," said Laura Alice. "I suppose it means they did a darned good job—or something."

The door at the head of the stairs opened, and Emily clattered down the stairs in her heels. She was breathing heavily by the time she reached the bottom. "Louise, Laura Alice," she said, "better come upstairs." Her eyes were round with agitation. "You'll never guess who's here—Walter Freeman!"

Looking thoughtful, Louise got up from the table. "How did *he* hear about this meeting?"

"I'm guessing that Sophie told him. All I know is that he's prowling restlessly around in the outer hall with two other official-looking men. I think they could be bodyguards."

"Maybe they're detectives, to protect him against the Miss Marples," quipped Laura Alice.

Louise gave her a droll look. "Don't forget that you're one of the Miss Marples now, even if you don't look the part."

"Hey, I can live with that," said Laura Alice. "I'll just dye a gray streak in my hair, like the one that's developing in yours."

Louise smiled, appreciating how quickly Laura Alice had dispelled the tension caused by Freeman's unexpected arrival. She climbed the stairs behind Laura Alice, who even with her heavy load of child lumbered up as quickly as a small bear up an incline.

The weight of Louise's purse on her shoulder reminded her to click on her tape recorder. She was sure that it was a waste of effort, but she didn't have the heart to reject Emily's unsophisticated investigative methods. Anyway, it would be interesting to have a tape of a garden club meeting, since this was the first one she'd ever attended. She expected it to be a mixture of serious stuff, and perhaps some amusing repartee typical of women's club meetings. On the other hand, this probably was a bit of snobbism on her part, she realized. Men's clubs, the Lions or the Elks, must have their same amount of silliness—especially since she'd heard one of those clubs ended their meetings with the cry, "Tiger, tiger, tiger!" She assumed it was the Lions who did that. Now, a garden club meeting would never end with the cry of "Grow, grow, grow!"—would it?

Stepping out of the basement darkness into the sunlit front hall of the clubhouse, Louise blinked a few times before she saw Walter Freeman standing near the front door. His hands were shoved in his pants pockets, his face calm. This was not the angry man who'd confronted her at the funeral, so maybe she wouldn't get a scolding today as she had yesterday.

"Ah, Mrs. Eldridge," he said in a soft voice, "I see you're still in town. Perhaps you're the reason for this special board meeting."

Louise nearly said it out loud, for the thought pounded in her head: *What are you doing at a garden club meeting?* But the man's very presence was intimidating; all words stopped in her throat.

To her credit, Emily stepped up, all five feet of her, and confronted Freeman, who not only loomed above her by a foot but was flanked by two even taller, younger men who certainly were big enough to be bodyguards. "Walter," said Emily, "I hope you aren't going to be hard on Louise again. You already chastised her at the funeral. But she has done you no harm, and I think it's quite wrong of you to talk to her this way."

He bent down and touched Emily's arm. "My dear, you knew Catherine well. I trust you, and I apologize: I didn't know your friend from northern Virginia would be here. Just let me stay. Let me listen to the affairs of the garden club. It—it will make me feel better."

His voice actually caught in his throat for a moment, and Louise wondered why she'd been so suspicious of a man who was so obviously grieving for his dead wife. He turned to Louise and bent over her in an almost tender way. "Mrs. Eldridge, I think a *rapprochement* is needed between the two of us. There's a simple explanation for your concerns, as I heard them, second-hand, regarding my car window being open. Perhaps I should have done this after the funeral, but I was too . . . annoyed with you then. May I give you the explanation now?"

"Why, of course."

"I drove home Saturday night with the window half-lowered because it was a beautiful, fresh night." He smiled as if in remembrance. "You may think this as odd as the habit President Nixon had of running fireplaces in air-conditioned rooms. But it was simply a comfortable way to ride home with my wife. Once home, I discovered the re-mote control within the car for opening the garage was malfunctioning, due to a simple disturbance of the secret entrance code. This meant I couldn't open the garage door from within the car, so I reached out of the window and, using the control that's attached to the portico post, manually tapped in the code. It was at that moment, when I was about to put the car in gear to drive into the garage, that the murderer approached us and"—again, his voice broke and tears flooded his eyes—"shot my poor Cath-erine. Once the shooting had occurred, I could hardly breathe. I lowered the window, then, all the way, just to be able to breathe and call out for help."

"Oh, God," moaned Louise. She wished she could be swallowed up by the old pine floor.

"The police know this, and now you know."

Louise looked at Freeman and realized she'd done him an injustice. "I'm so sorry," she said. "I misinterpreted the whole thing." She'd built her many suspicions on a false premise, and she had been wrong. Because of that low-ered window, she realized that Walter had been her most favored suspect. Now it turned out that there was an inno-cent explanation. Detective Kovach could have told her about it but didn't. And why not? Because he took an in-stant dislike to the Virginian interloper who'd invaded a northern state and proceeded to tell the cops how to solve their murder case.

But if Walter Freeman didn't do it, then who did? Louise's suspect list was short and flawed, and included three garden club members, jealous, respectively, over who made better flower arrangements, who had the better azaleas, and who had sexual or outright ownership of Walter Freeman.

And then there was the fourth woman, Reese Janning. Her motive would have been simple: she wanted to marry the boss.

Two more people came to mind. Dorothy Cranshaw was being ousted from her basement apartment. Would losing a good deal like that have angered her enough to kill Catherine? It seemed unlikely. And yet people sometimes silently nurtured resentments: Dorothy was the sort of person who would seethe quietly, without people noticing, if she had resented her affluent friend.

Like the motives of the other three garden club members, the scenarios for Reese and Dorothy both seemed as flimsy as a straw house.

And then she thought of the most far-out scenario of them all: Alex Holley. Could Alex have been involved in a hit on Catherine? He seemed much too uptight about the murder, too protective of Walter Freeman, and too hostile and suspicious of Louise and her attempts to do a little investigating. And he was closer to Walter Freeman than even his wife Emily realized. That was obvious from the way he was ushered into a seat in Freeman's same church pew at the funeral. The trouble was that Alex seemed to have no motive. There seemed no way in which he could profit from Catherine Freeman's death, and Louise was convinced that Alex liked to profit from every exchange with another human being. No, she would have to be content with simply disliking the man, for he didn't add up as a murder suspect—not unless she could find a hidden motive.

Louise's body felt heavy, as if she were being pulled into

the ground. She knew this fatigue was all mental, that Walter Freeman had humbled her and made her think. He had convinced her that he wasn't responsible for killing his wife.

If Louise was down, Emily wasn't: she had lost none of her zest for the hunt. She grabbed Louise and pulled her into the small club kitchen, where trays of buns and desserts were sitting on the counter under big paper napkins and hazelnut coffee was brewing in a pot. Louise knew that in the small refrigerator resided the historic-minded Jell-O and corned-beef molded salads. Emily said, "I hear you went through nearly all the books. What did you find?"

Louise slumped against the tiny counter. "That Catherine Freeman and Dorothy Cranshaw dominated the garden club for a quarter of a century."

Her friend's face fell. "We already knew that. Nothing else?"

Louise sighed. "Not that Laura Alice or I could identify."

"Then that's it?"

"That's it, Emily. Now it's up to you." Louise had earlier suggested to her friend that recent changes in the club might have had something to do with the murder and that Emily might therefore consider throwing out another plan for change and see what happened.

They went to the main room, where the women who held various offices in the organization were clustered in chairs at the front, waiting for the meeting to open. First came a moment of silent prayer in remembrance of their dead president. Board members cast discreet glances at Walter, now seated with his companions at the back of the room. Louise noted how he bowed his head during the prayer, as if totally despondent.

Emily had scarcely time to collect her meeting notes before Sophie Chalois made her move. Sophie rushed up to the podium and whispered to Emily, then stepped in front of her and announced that she wanted to repeat the remarks she'd made yesterday at the funeral. With straight faces, the board members listened, most of them for the second day in a row. Clad in a pale green linen suit, Sophie was a striking figure, as she reprised the emotional little speech. Even some who hadn't cried at the funeral managed tears this time.

Once Sophie resumed her seat in the middle of the front row, the minutes were read, and Emily opened discussion of the only real debate the board had to face each year: how to spend the profits from this year's plant sale.

To Louise's amazement, the treasurer reported a profit of nine thousand dollars. Louise quickly figured it out: six hours of backbreaking labor last Saturday by four dozen women had netted fifteen hundred dollars per hour. It was as if each woman had earned thirty-one dollars per hour. Not bad, she thought.

A few environmentally minded board members apparently had met together before the meeting opened. After a whispered confab, Laura Alice rose to be their spokesperson. They wanted the proceeds to go to a Nature Conservancy land-preservation project in nearby Maryland.

Red-haired Meg Durrance, imposing in an emerald green dress, rose to differ. "Why should we do that?" she argued, brown eyes flashing. "That's just another 'green movement' project, of a thousand 'green movement' projects. I think we should plow the money into another local public garden, with a placard reading 'Old Georgetown Garden Club.' That's what really makes people know we're on the map."

"Oh, sure," said Laura Alice saucily, obviously ready to go head to head with any of the old-timers on the board. "Why don't we cut a garden into the median strip of one of our clogged highways, where metro motorists will drive by so fast they will hardly be able to smell the flowers?"

The tall redhead, who loomed over the smaller Laura Alice, said, "Sarcasm isn't needed, Laura Alice. Lots of people visit our library garden and just love it."

Emily suggested they table that question, and that board members submit all their ideas and take it up again next month. Louise thought it refreshing to hear this debate on what to do with the profits. Because she'd helped earn that nine thousand dollars by heaving pots of flowers to and fro, she felt as if she herself had a stake in how it was spent.

It was obvious to her that the board members repre-sented all sorts of gardening philosophies and ways to manifest their goodwill and community spirit. Garden clubs of America had changed the look of national high-ways and cities, and made gardens a source of healing and pleasure to many people. This little club in Bethesda was doing its part.

"Now for the next item," said Emily. "I want to call for more written suggestions on what kind of memorial we should establish in Catherine Freeman's name. Sugges-tions I have received so far are for horticultural scholar-ships and for a 'Catherine Freeman Garden,' to be located somewhere in downtown Bethesda. So please submit your ideas. And for the final item of the day . . ."

The petite vice-president-just-turned-president glanced around with large gray eyes and nervously cleared her throat.

Louise sat forward, knowing what was coming. Emily said, "I want to pass on a proposal I've received for an-other change in club rules. This is beyond those that have recently been adopted regarding building renovation." Another clearing of her throat. "It has been suggested that the club allow inactive members to stay in the organi-zation even if they don't help with its various projects and even if they miss more than three meetings per year."

The suggestion that club membership rules be relaxed

was the best that she and Emily could come up with last night, when they decided to stir the pot a little.

Emily looked warily around the room, seeking a reaction. She quickly got one. Dorothy Cranshaw raised her hand and then slowly rose to her feet. "Madam President, I can understand how you think this is a good idea, because you've been a club member a mere seven years. You probably don't realize that what you propose is *not* the garden club way."

Dorothy was the picture of a plain, hardworking woman, with faded eyes, age lines undiminished by expensive creams or BOTOX solutions, graying hair fixed in its usual neat bun. Like other board members, she'd taken the time to dress up, in a trim navy blue pantsuit. She continued, in her no-nonsense voice. "The garden club way should reflect tradition and order, not reckless change and disorder. We live by the rules, don't we? By Roberts' Rules of Order? Our club should also live by the *spirit* of the rules: it should be a bulwark of society, not buffeted this way and that, like a ship in a storm. Bethesda's changed, and the garden club has changed—both for the worse. Nothing we can do about our city of Bethesda. But the club should be a bastion of American values. And yet we're undermining its values, weakening its character, by letting laggards remain as club members. Voting for this change will make us just as bad as other institutions in society which have let down their standards. It's the equivalent of condoning bald sex on prime-time TV, permitting dirty lyrics in popular music, allowing kids' access to Internet porn, and failing to remove a president involved in a sex scandal."

Condoning. Permitting. Allowing. Failing. These warning words made Dorothy Cranshaw sound like a veritable Cassandra. Louise had had no idea Dorothy was so hidebound.

Several board members nodded and spoke up in agreement with Dorothy. *They* got it: It was all about laxness, thought Louise, sexual, organizational, and governmental laxness. It was why people thought America was going to the dogs, and why foreigners hated us. The incident confirmed what Louise had suspected, that changes in the venerable garden club weren't going down well with all club members. And Dorothy Cranshaw had a very personal reason to be against modernizing the club—it had caused her to lose her free apartment downstairs.

Another dissenter got to her feet. Sophie Chalois stood at her front-row seat and turned to face her fellow board members. "I agree with Dorothy. Enough is enough. Let's not allow lazy club members to remain in our midst. I oppose *that* kind of change, though many of the changes our dear, deceased president made were good. We need to spruce up this building, for instance, and use it more efficiently. We also need a change in parliamentary rules."

Uh oh, thought Louise. *Here it comes.* Sophie was trying to unseat Emily from the presidency. With a toss of her blond head, which was frizzed up today in a youthful style, Sophie said, "Because of the special circumstances of our president's departure—that is, because she didn't depart of her own free will, or because her term ran out—I ask for a suspension of the rules and call for a special election in September of the full club membership to name a new president."

A murmur went through the room. Emily poised her gavel in the air, looking as vulnerable as a deer in the headlights, but did not have the nerve to pound it down, or to find Sophie out of order.

Obviously basking in the attention she was getting, Sophie focused her gaze not on the dozen female board members, but on the man who hovered at the back of the room. Yet the matter of special elections didn't interest

Freeman; he was back on his feet and pacing to and fro like a caged lion, as if waiting for something *else* to happen.

Louise suddenly understood. The man was here for the same reason Louise was, to watch over the situation and possibly to uncover the person who could have murdered his wife.

41

Laura Alice Shea, who appeared to be the loose-cannon liberal on the garden club board, stood up next to protest. "I'm with whoever proposed to Emily that membership rules should be relaxed. Why make this club resemble the S.S.?" Giving a delightful, rosy glance at fellow board members, she continued. "But I disagree with Sophie on the matter of a special election. Why do we have a constitution if we don't follow it in respect to cut-and-dried things such as ascendancy to the presidency, election procedures, and that sort of thing?"

Phyllis Ohlmacher leaped to her feet. "S.S., indeed, Laura Alice! That's a bit much . . ." And Phyllis went on to disagree with the younger, pregnant woman on both matters.

Seeing that everyone was engaged, to a point just short of fisticuffs, Louise decided it was time to duck downstairs again to complete her search through the old club records. Maybe she could even have a look at Dorothy Cranshaw's quarters. After all, she'd had glimpses of the houses of Meg Durrance, Phyllis Ohlmacher, and Sophie Chalois, but she had no idea of the living conditions of Dorothy.

Quietly, she eased out of her seat, giving Laura Alice a look as she passed her, hoping that the younger woman would understand what she was up to. For some reason, the very pregnant Laura Alice seemed a pillar of strength, and Louise felt vulnerable going down into that basement on her own. It would be nice to have a person like Laura Alice watching her back.

Louise made her way along the edge of the room and into the hall. Walter Freeman was so engrossed in the spirited debate that he didn't apparently notice her pass by, although his two male companions gave her the eye.

She put a businesslike expression on her face, as if to say, *I'm just going downstairs to fetch a jar of pickles.* She passed through the empty lobby and reached the door to the basement. She wouldn't have a need for the tape recorder now, so she gave a hurried flick to the switch and shut it off in order to save tape. Then she opened the door and started to descend.

When she was a few steps down, she heard a click, and the dim light at the bottom of the stairs went out. Just as she looked upward, she saw the face in the dark, haloed with blond hair, and felt the shove that sent her flying downward.

Through some fluke, her body crashed against a wooden rail on the right of the stairs, her big purse cushioning her against the collision and taking the brunt of the hit. She reached out with desperate hands and grabbed the rail. Her torso spun around and she landed unceremoniously on her buttocks at the base of the stairs.

Her body was bruised and bent, one arm feeling as if the tendons had been ripped. She sat on the bottom step, heart pounding, trying to regain her composure. Then she looked up, to see total darkness. Someone had closed the door.

She knew who had done this. Sophie Chalois's frizzy, blond-streaked hairdo had glowed against the daylight in the room above.

Until now, Louise had not considered Sophie a creditable suspect in Catherine Freeman's murder. But now she did. Perhaps she should give up her quest in the clubhouse basement, for that shove was a definite warning. Then the door above her opened, and a shaft of light appeared.

"Don't you want some light down there?" called Laura Alice, in a soft but carrying voice.

"I sure do," said Louise, in a shaky voice.

The younger woman flipped the switch. "Everything all right, Louise?" she asked.

"Almost," said Louise. "I'll be down here a while. Maybe you'd better close that door—but be sure to let me know if anyone else tries to come down." She looked up at Laura Alice's bulky silhouette. "I mean it, Laura Alice: I could be in danger."

"Something happened," said the younger woman. *"What?"*

Louise sighed. "It's too awkward to tell you now. I'll be up in just a few minutes. I might as well be sure there's nothing else to find down here."

"All right," said Laura Alice and quietly shut the door.

Louise looked across the dim basement at the door that led to Dorothy's digs. It practically beckoned to her, but she restrained her curiosity about that. That was not why she had come down here. Right now, she was looking for anything that might explain why Sophie Chalois might have murdered Catherine Freeman.

She turned on the light over the table, seated herself, and quickly went through the last books of records. They represented the last two years. As usual, they were full of records of Catherine Freeman's awards in everything from state flower shows to plant-propagation events. They also had the up-to-the-minute details of changes to be made in the clubhouse, including architect's plans.

One picture did become clear: Catherine Freeman was the kind of woman who knew how to lead an organization the old-fashioned way—by its nose. This meant she was a person one could dislike intensely, and maybe even hate. Sophie may have had more than one reason to hate her, though losing a man to her, especially a distinguished suitor like Walter Freeman, might be motive enough.

Closing the last book, Louise got up, switched off the light over the table, and was about to go upstairs, for she needed a cup of coffee to relieve the pain in her body from her fall. Also, she could smell good food smells, and was curious to try out the corned-beef salad. Maybe she'd even prepare it for her own family if it turned out to be good.

At the last second she turned back. She couldn't resist at least trying the door to Dorothy Cranshaw's apartment.

42

The woman must have nothing to hide, reflected Louise. The apartment door was unlocked and in fact slightly ajar, as good as an invitation to come inside. She entered the comfortable quarters, immediately struck by the amazing order of things. If caught by Dorothy, who as luncheon chairman today was surely busy setting out food or else serving it, she could always say . . . what would she say? *The door was ajar, Dorothy, and it was so delightful looking in here . . .*

She stepped farther into a bright living room where a matching couch and chair made a comfy place to rest. Underfoot was attractive Berber carpeting, like new. Arrays of shelves on the walls kept everything organized, from books, to knickknacks, to scrapbooks arranged in order of height. On one side was an attractive kitchen with sixties-era dishes and pans nestled closely together in perfect order. A quick peek in the refrigerator showed her that the woman ate a good diet of greens and cheeses: two rounded packages of gouda rested on the refrigerator door.

Dorothy kept everything, she discovered, as she opened a kitchen cabinet—jars, jar lids, and little tins of varied sizes. One jar held a mysterious collection of odd-colored balls. She picked up one; it was made of wax, and she finally caught on that these were neatly globalized wax balls made out of the red and yellow wrappings from gouda cheeses eaten in the past. A small box contained pieces of string and twine, carefully secured with rubber bands. There also was a huge collection of rubber bands, which must have included every one that ever arrived on a newspaper or package.

In the bedroom, Louise was struck by the faded chenille bedspread with turquoise and peach-colored flowers that covered the bed. She guessed it was right out of the 1930s, probably a hand-me-down from Dorothy's mother. Dorothy's clothes were sparse but easy to find. One drawer held worn and mended underwear that was folded so neatly that it looked as if it had never been used. Beneath it was a drawer of socks and hosiery regimented like tan soldiers—for there was no other color but tan.

Dorothy Cranshaw never threw anything away. Of this Louise was certain.

Wandering back to the living room, she was captured by the view of a walled garden through oversized French doors. The doors had been cut into the living room in some recent time to allow for maximum sunlight to pour in from the outside. Thus the two spaces became like one, undoubtedly a great joy for a gardener like Dorothy. Roses, forsythia, and wisteria were massed on the high stockade walls, while small flower beds in the foreground held annual starts. Several urns added a dramatic accent to the tiny area.

Returning her gaze to the inside of the house, Louise became engrossed in the pictures on what Dorothy probably thought of as her "picture" wall. It was solid with images, mostly in black and white. Typical of the well-organized Dorothy, the pictures were in chronological order. Photos from the thirties showing Dorothy as a baby, sitting on a cushion of her father's car. Shots of Dorothy as a young woman, not handsome, but always composed, with long, flowing brown hair. A picture of Dorothy with a man, probably her husband, his face in half-shadow, a preteen boy standing between them. They stood in front of an imposing colonial house that Louise guessed had been the family home in Ledgebrook. Thereafter there were pictures only of the mother with the son. The photos spoke of the lonely life of a woman on her own: Dorothy alone, Dorothy with her aloof-looking offspring, Jack. There was even a forlorn photo of the side entrance that led to this basement apartment, with a neat but unembellished yard. It was dated ten years ago, when Dorothy must have first moved in, before the fence and French door renovation. A newer photo showed the tiny garden in all its mature beauty.

A few pictures showed Dorothy doing garden club things, including several of her kneeling while planting seedlings at the Davis Library garden. Usually, Catherine Freeman was in these shots with her. In one, Phyllis Ohlmacher was part of the group. Noticeably absent were any of the newer club members, or in fact anyone but the two, Catherine and Phyllis. They appeared to be her main friends.

What a sad life, thought Louise, feeling a little ashamed of herself for entering Dorothy's private quarters. And yet when she spied an open alphabet file, she had to look. Dorothy kept newspaper articles, everything from gardening pieces to articles about bizarre human interest events, many on crimes. Book reviews made the "B" file cavity bulge. Her tastes were eclectic, at least in reviews: everything from history to mystery, and science fiction. Completely absent were any business files, copies of bills, or the like.

One bookshelf was filled with Penguin Book classics. Here also were two copies of *Roberts' Rules of Order,* one old and dog-eared, the other newer looking. Another bookshelf held more current literature.

Louise continued her search. She was on a roll now and couldn't bring herself to stop; curiosity drove her on.

Unlike the antiseptic Freeman residence in Ledgebrook, Dorothy's little home was a collector's castle, and a clear demonstration of the woman's interior thinking.

She opened the drawer of what turned out to be a Victorian sewing table. Set in its shallow interior were spools of thread, arranged meticulously not only by color but in the order of the colors of the rainbow. Louise thought of her own sewing drawer, and its disarray, for Louise was neat on the surface, but messy below it. In the fat drawer at the bottom of the table she found buttons in boxes, again sorted by color. Some buttons obviously were as ancient as the hills.

She gently touched the possessions of a virtual stranger, and wondered. Was there something behind Dorothy's calm, well-organized exterior? A few minutes ago upstairs, the woman, surprisingly enough, had lost it; she had become like a hysterical tyrant, totally undone when Emily Holley proposed another change in club rules. Had Catherine Freeman's previous changes angered her just as much? Was Dorothy a murder suspect whom she'd totally ignored?

Sheepishly, Louise realized Dorothy suffered from the fact that Louise, the unauthorized amateur snoop, had private access to her house. No such bad luck had befallen Sophie Chalois or Meg Durrance, or even Phyllis Ohlmacher, though she had overheard that searingly personal scene between Phyllis and Al. When she had bridged the ramparts of Walter Freeman's house, she'd learned little more than the fact that Walter and Catherine appeared to have separate bedrooms. And ran a pristine household devoid of the personal touch: none of the family photos or scrapbooks, sports equipment, or even exercise equipment, that littered or graced most other people's homes.

No, Louise was wrong: Catherine Freeman's charming bouquets were personal touches. But bouquets didn't tell the kind of story that Dorothy's possessions did.

Louise slumped down in Dorothy's living room easy-chair, and suddenly the pointillist painting forming in her mind began to fill in—she felt as if she were Seurat, adding the final dots of color. Her dots of color were little pieces of information that brought people out of the shadow of being just strangers and into the light of being known quantities, though certainly not friends.

As she sat there in Dorothy's chair, Louise began stroking in the information about the opened car window that seemed to relieve Walter Freeman of guilt. Dabbing in the color of Sophie Chalois's strong, manipulative personality—that performance upstairs where she was clearly determined to get her way, even if she had to change the constitution of the venerable garden club. Defining what was the vague outline of Dorothy Cranshaw with the true colors of this apartment, with its careful collections of preserved items.

Four characters had come into focus, Walter Freeman, Sophie Chalois, Phyllis Ohlmacher, and Dorothy Cranshaw.

Three of these were partially delineated, not fully realized. Unfortunately for Dorothy, the abundance of detail was right here for Louise to see, and her shadowy figure was coming into full view.

Louise got up and stood perfectly still in the middle of the room as an idea struck her. If Dorothy had shot Catherine Freeman, she was the sort of person who wouldn't throw away the gun. Guns cost money. She wouldn't do the prudent thing and ditch the incriminating weapon in a Bethesda sewer. No, she'd keep it and cherish it, polish it, clean it.

Where would she keep it?

Her gaze traveled back to Dorothy's private little garden. What more symbolic place than her garden to safeguard a weapon? Louise closed her eyes for a moment and realized how outlandish this all was. Could she truly think that just because the woman was a neatnik who hated change that she had gone so far as to kill her best friend?

She went closer to the glass doors. What caught her eye was the large arrangement sitting in one of the three urns in the garden. Not a pennywise starter pot of flowers like the others, but a lush arrangement of plants that had to have been purchased from a nursery in full bloom.

These fancy hanging baskets went for a hundred dollars or more. Why did the frugal Dorothy have one huge, expansive pot of hanging flowers when the rest of her containers held scrawny plant babies? Maybe it had been a gift from someone. But that arrangement of *Helichrysum petiolare, Leguminosae berthelotii,* petunias, lisianthus, zinnias, lobelias, and alyssum could be disguising something.

Louise felt herself compelled outdoors, as if being drawn by a giant magnet. She unlocked the French doors and walked out. A flick of movement behind the stockade fence caught her eye, so she stood and stared at that spot, wishing she could x-ray the fence. Suddenly, a black crow flew up in the air, and she gave a sigh of relief.

Now that she was in the garden, Louise had committed herself to being accused of breaking and entering. Before, when searching Dorothy's apartment, she could have said she came in to be sure that no one was there.

It was a charming May garden. Against the backdrop of lavender wisterea and yellow forsythia bloomed gay patches of tulips, daffodils, and checkered lilies. In the center of the garden were the three urns of flowers. She walked over to the first one. It was planted with geranium and verbena seedlings and small vinca plants. The second held marigold and zinnia seedlings, with a small mound of fountain grass in the center. When she came to the massively blooming third pot, she reached down and felt among the plants, not minding the potting soil being ground into her fingernails.

"Sorry, flowers," she said, probing far down toward their

roots in several places, to prove to herself that she was an utter fool.

Then her forefinger came to a plastic edge. She realized the flowers were in an inset pot, and not planted directly in the urn itself, as the others were. A little strange, and not what an expert gardener would do. She carefully reached down among the flowers and hefted the pot out of the urn and lifted it up. There in the bottom of the urn was a translucent plastic rectangular container, about eight inches by four inches, the kind Louise stored dinner leftovers in. Inside, she could see a pistol-shaped object swathed in a piece of chamois cloth.

She had to admire Dorothy. Only a gardener would have thought up this trick. With trembling hands, Louise carefully set down the plant arrangement on the ground. She couldn't get carried away: finding a gun wouldn't prove it was the one that killed Catherine Freeman. She had been wrong once in suspecting Walter Freeman. And maybe she was wrong in suspecting Sophie Chalois, even if the woman had just shoved her down a flight of stairs. She could be misjudging Dorothy.

On the other hand, she thought, looking nervously at the open doors of the apartment, why would Dorothy hide a gun if it was a legally owned weapon? Her best strategy was to return the plants to the urn where they belonged, and report her find to police. Yet she doubted the police would pay any attention to her: she'd cried wolf once too often.

Instead of returning things to normal, she picked up the plastic box. From what little Detective Kovach had told her, the weapon used to kill Catherine Freeman had been a Glock nine-millimeter semiautomatic. Louise snapped off the top and unwrapped the chamois. She shivered as she realized she probably was holding the weapon that had killed Catherine Freeman.

As she stood in the pleasant, small garden, the sunshine

pouring down on her head, she felt a sense of complete unreality. Why would Dorothy Cranshaw murder her best friend? For that matter, why would she take a potshot at Louise? She wished fervently that she was on the wrong track. Maybe it was just a terrible coincidence that this weapon was hidden so furtively in the garden.

She put the gun to her nose and smelled it. It had been fired recently. Her hopes sank, like a stone in a pool. This plain, smart woman whom she'd grown to like was a murderer. Then she heard the angry sound behind her and realized she'd spent too much time fruitlessly trying to lift the guilt from Dorothy's shoulders. The plastic box parts flipped to the ground, but she gripped the gun tightly.

"Goddamnit!"

The woman had burst through the patio door to the garden, an expression on her face that was as good as a confession. Her voice was kept low purposely because she knew there was a roomful of people above whom she didn't want to alert. "Who do you think you are, you cheap snoop?"

Louise talked fast, ignoring the fact that her heart had gone into overdrive. *Please, God,* she thought, *don't let my heart fail me now!* She blurted out the words: "The apartment door was open. I was afraid someone had broken in. I was trying to *help* you, Dorothy. I was looking around just to be sure there was no burglar—"

"Baloney," said Dorothy. "You're *full* of it, Louise." She frightened Louise, with her bulging eyes and her gray hair pulling loose from its bun. Unkempt hair in this extra-neat woman was a sign of her complete disorientation.

Dorothy didn't waste any more time talking. With strong hands, she reached out and grabbed the pistol from Louise's hands, took a moment to adjust it, and then pointed it straight at Louise's stomach.

She could almost feel the bullet sinking into her gut, and found it a strain to keep from emptying her bowels and bladder. The only thing that would save her would be Dorothy's reluctance to have others hear the sound of gunfire.

"Get in the apartment," Dorothy muttered, grabbing Louise's forearm and twisting it painfully. Louise heard the sound of wood creaking in back of her and for a minute wondered if someone had come to save her. Then there was silence.

She responded quickly to the command, holding her hands up, even though not told to do so. She came in and stood in the middle of the small living room, scanning the place for possible defensive weapons, desperately thinking of a way to escape. Dorothy had hurriedly shut the French doors, but they'd flipped back open a few inches. But the door to the apartment that led out to the basement was tightly closed. That made it useless to scream. As for escape, she was so scared now that her limbs felt paralyzed. If she had a chance to run somewhere, she didn't know whether her legs would obey.

But it turned out not to matter, for there was no escape. Without missing a beat, Dorothy struck out with the gun and hit Louise sharply on the temple. "There," she said, "take that, you snoop—"

"Ooh!" moaned Louise, as she collapsed to the floor. She could feel the blood trickling down her cheek and into her long hair. Toppling her had been as easy as toppling a young sapling. Despite the pain and the blood, she instinctively grabbed out at one of Dorothy's legs, fearing that otherwise she would be shot like a fish in a barrel.

Not expecting this, her opponent was thrown off balance and fell to the floor with a thud. Dorothy's body struck a brass pot sitting on the floor, and it clanged metallically. The gun had fallen from her hand but was lying nearby. She had just picked it up again when the apartment door flew open.

Walter Freeman stood in the doorway, exuding his

usual air of quiet dignity. Then he came in and closed the door.

"Oh," moaned Louise, as relief flooded over her. "Thank God." The nation's economic oracle, the man whose every word was precious to financiers and world leaders alike, surely could save her from this mad Dorothy Cranshaw. She rued the day that she'd ever suspected him of killing the amiable Catherine. She now knew why the man was so revered, for his very presence in the room gave her a feeling of confidence.

Yet her hopes dangled like an acrobat high on a swing as Walter Freeman stood there, silently viewing the scene. Was this not just a matter of displaying his usual poise? Yet why wasn't he unsettled by the sight of Louise with her head dripping blood, and of Dorothy half-sitting, half-lying on her living room floor, a small, black firearm held firmly in her hand? Freeman knew Dorothy, probably better than any of Catherine's garden club buddies. So why didn't the man use his smooth words and his accustomed savoir faire to disarm her? Any moment, Louise expected this to happen.

Instead, Dorothy said something that chilled Louise to the bone. She cried, *"Damn* you, Walter, all this is your fault! You've put all of this on me. Getting me to kill Catherine just so she wouldn't divorce you for adultery. Then, trying to stop this bitch, Louise—"

"Dorothy, shut *up,"* he snapped.

But Dorothy didn't. "You've turned my life into a disorderly *nightmare!* Why don't *you* do something? Why have you left it all to me?"

Freeman gave Louise a nervous glance, then walked quickly over to Dorothy. He said, "You must not talk about this now, I'm cautioning you."

Dorothy turned her red face up to him. "That's a laugh, you cautioning me, after what I've been through. I had to hover in the bushes until you and Catherine drove in, then shoot her, then sprint away to meet Reese. All week long I've had to keep track of *this* woman while she snooped about—why, I could have been hauled in by the police when I took a shot at her the other night. Meanwhile, you and Reese are out there *frolicking* together!"

"I told you to shut up. You've already said much too much."

Stunned, Louise realized the meaning of their exchange. This was why Walter Freeman had crashed the garden club meeting. Dorothy and he were co-conspirators, along with Reese Janning. He'd had the prudish Catherine murdered because she'd discovered his infidelities. She must have threatened to divorce and disinherit him. He'd come today because the alarums were sounding in his brain: he was afraid Dorothy would panic and disclose the truth behind the murder.

She understood her chances for survival had just sunk to practically nothing. If she almost closed her eyes, she reasoned, they might think she was already dead. So, through slitted lids, she watched the drama between the man and woman in the basement room.

Freeman stared down at Dorothy. Her leg apparently had been injured when Louise tumbled her onto the floor. He looked as if he couldn't decide what to do.

The prostrate woman looked back at him with wild eyes. "I know what it is—you're mad because I shot Catherine while she was still inside the car." She gave a feeble laugh. "Her innards splattered all over you, didn't they, and I know how you hated that. I know how the great Walter Freeman hates *messes*. Why, the foul smell alone must have driven you crazy. But I couldn't wait until you told her to leave the car, because I heard people coming."

Freeman shook his head. "My God, even my dead wife was right about you. Catherine had you pegged. She said you were smart but that you had this obtuse quality. You, who act the part of being reliable and intelligent, are actually a miserable screw-up."

It was a throwaway insult, made all the more insulting because it was delivered as normally as if he were palavering with a fellow economist. Louise found she was shocked to hear Freeman speak so coarsely. At least he didn't say "fuck-up." The rest of his manner, his impassive face, his cold eyes, his dapper stance, were as normal-looking as if he were addressing a board meeting. She looked from one to the other, and realized neither Dorothy nor Walter were paying attention to her any longer.

Dorothy retorted, in a cold, hopeless tone, "You call me a screw-up, Walter, but *you're* a monster. You think I mismanaged things with Jack, leaving him around to tell the true story after I killed my husband." She gave a bitter half-laugh. "You would have had me kill my own son. Now, if you hadn't heard that story from your pal, the head of the Maryland State Police, you'd never have been able to get me to do your dirty work."

"But I *did* hear it, didn't I?" said Walter.

"And you can't back out now, you priggish ass, not after all I've done for us, not after you've set up that offshore account for me." Though the woman's voice had a warning tone, Louise could see she was helpless. There was a look of pain on Dorothy's face, and her heart nearly went out to the woman. But then Dorothy's gaze turned on Louise, a gaze so unfeeling that it chilled Louise to the bone. "No, Walter, none of this is my fault—it's *her* fault." Dorothy's finger pointed right at her. "If we get rid of her, we'll be all right."

"But, Dorothy, my dear," said Freeman, with that phony *bonhomie* of his, "how can I ever trust you again?" He pulled a small gun out of his pocket, efficient, Louise knew, for shooting someone at close range. "You are *obsessed*, Dorothy, *obsessed*." He swept an arm around to encompass the scores of little collections of material things that broadcast so clearly that she was a compulsive saver. "You keep things you should get rid of—such as guns. You fixate on a woman"—he cast a brief glance at Louise—"whose only reason for being around is to pry into Catherine's death. Fortunately, as you point out, there's a viable solution at hand. Unfortunately, the solution must factor in *you* as well as Mrs. Eldridge."

He looked at Louise and then at Dorothy, who had agonizingly dragged herself to a sitting position. Dorothy's gray hair had now escaped completely from its strict bun and flowed like a schoolgirl's around her stooped shoulders, as it had in one of the early photos of her on the picture wall.

Dorothy repositioned the gun in her hand, and when she did, Walter Freeman shot her through the heart.

43

Horrified, Louise watched as Freeman now turned his attention to her, and she could practically *see* him turning his great intellect to the knotty problem of what to do with a witness to the execution. Slowly sifting into her consciousness were the angry voices coming from the top of the stairs. Her friends. But would they arrive too late?

Laura Alice Shea's voice, usually soft and low, pealed through the stale air like a drill sergeant's. "You *assholes!* Get out of the way and let me *through!*" If only Laura Alice could get here, thought Louise, she was sure the young woman would get the best of this killer. But the look in Freeman's eyes told her what he had in store for her. She felt the same sickening sensation in her stomach that she'd felt at other times when she was close to death, once when she'd faced another man whose crime she'd uncovered, and who'd been determined to do away with her—

In an instant, she realized Walter Freeman would pick up the gun with Dorothy's prints on it and shoot *her.* Not only had he shot Dorothy in cold blood, but he'd also engineered his wife's murder. Louise was the only living person besides his lover, Reese Janning, who could implicate him. If he killed her now, he could declare it was a bloody triangle: Dorothy first killed Louise—that was the first shot heard in the rooms above, he would claim. Then Freeman stepped up and shot Dorothy, to protect himself—that was the second shot heard.

He made a move toward Dorothy's gun, and something chemical and strange happened to Louise. The adrenaline kicked into her body so powerfully that she forgot the fact that her head was woozy and that she was only half-conscious.

"Don't you dare!" she cried, then sprang into action. She half-stumbled to her feet and kicked Dorothy's gun across the room. It skittered to a stop under the bookcase filled with Dorothy's classics library. Mustering all her remaining strength, she screamed at the top of her lungs, *"Someone,* help me!" Then she crumpled to the floor again.

Suddenly, her adversary looked as if he didn't know what to do. He stood transfixed, staring at the narrow space under the bookcase where the gun had disappeared, then turned toward Louise. She pulled herself up to a sitting position and raised a hand, as if trying to quiet a dangerous beast. "Don't shoot me now, if you know what's good for you. They know I'm alive. It's one thing to claim to have killed Dorothy for some reason, and quite another to kill me now that I've warned my friends." But had her friends heard her cries?

At that moment, a loud crash resounded on the patio in back of him. Her eyes moved from the figure of Walter Freeman to a human shape lying in the garden at the foot of the stockade fence. Someone had climbed up and tumbled onto the other side, and was now slowly rising to a standing position. It was Charlie Hurd.

Charlie pushed open the big double doors and limped into Dorothy Cranshaw's apartment. The reporter, his suit hung with crumbs of garden soil, his usual neat blond hair askew, and his thin face grimacing in pain, was the most welcome person she'd ever seen.

"Charlie!" she cried. "Thank God you're here."

Holding his hip, which apparently had been bruised in the fall, he focused first on Louise, bloody and disheveled, sitting on the Berber carpet. "Holy *shit*, what happened to *you*, Louise? You're a mess." Then he caught sight of the tall, slim man standing in back of him, holding a gun. The reporter immediately threw his hands in the air, as if he'd intruded on a gunfight in a Western bar. "Hey, don't shoot, now," he pleaded. Then he recognized the man. "Walter *Freeman?*"

"Charlie, he shot her—" Louise began.

"Please don't listen to her," interrupted Freeman in his smoothest voice. "This unfortunate-looking scenario can be explained easily." He walked a couple of steps away from Charlie to get both the reporter and Louise in his gun sight. "Mrs. Eldridge has been struck in the head, and is a trifle, uh, disoriented, I fear."

The reporter looked uneasily at Freeman and his pistol. "So," he said, as if trying to buy time, "it *is* you, Mr. Freeman, isn't it?" He slowly lowered his hands. Freeman put the gun back into the pocket of his pinstriped suit, and Louise shuddered with relief. He had no choice but to put it away, she realized. Now that people were here, he could hardly hold her at gunpoint.

"So," said Charlie, in a shaky voice, "exactly what's happened here?"

Freeman turned to the reporter with his usual aplomb. "Let's start at the beginning," he said. "Come closer, first."

"Charlie," she hissed at him, "be careful. He's a killer. The man conspired in his wife's murder. And he just shot the woman you see on the floor."

The reporter stepped back from Freeman. "Jeez, what's she sayin'?"

Freeman moved in closer to Charlie for damage control. "I fear that Mrs. Eldridge is mistaken." He clasped the reporter's elbow. "You're one of those Washington *Post* scribes, aren't you? You've been covering the story of my wife's murder."

"That's right," said Charlie, warily.

"And your name?"

"Uh, Charlie Hurd," said Charlie. The reporter must have felt obliged to extend a hand, since Freeman had extended his. They shook, as if they were in the corridors of Congress, or perhaps meeting at a Washington watering hole. To her horror, this super con man, Walter Freeman, was beginning his con. Would Charlie believe him?

"Oh, wait a *minute,*" Louise said. "This man is a *criminal!*"

"I fear," he interrupted, "that Mrs. Eldridge may be in shock. She certainly will require hospitalization. Let me assure you that I can explain everything, Mr. Hurd. I saved Mrs. Eldridge's life, and I can prove it." He pointed to Dorothy's prone body. "This woman—do you know her? She's Dorothy Cranshaw. She lives down here. Dorothy was about to kill Louise. I believe that to be obvious. I kicked the gun underneath that bookcase over there," he said, nodding to where Louise had landed the gun.

The reporter peeked under the bookcase. "Yeah, the gun is under the bookcase," remarked Charlie, looking from Freeman to Louise.

"No, no, *no,* Charlie!" she cried. "That's not what happened. You have to believe me."

The reporter put his hands up, as if he had just been asked to arbitrate a labor dispute, and circled over to where Louise lay on the floor. He gave her a quick wink. Did this mean Freeman's con job wasn't working? Even if Charlie sensed the economist was lying, the two of them still had to get out of this basement alive. A man who'd already been responsible for two deaths wouldn't stop at killing two more.

Louise played along with Charlie's ruse that he believed

Freeman. "I thought you were a friend, Charlie," she moaned. "But I never could count on you."

They both turned, as sounds outside the apartment reached them. It was the welcome clatter of people descending the stairs. Laura Alice and Emily and her dog piled into the room, followed by the protesting bodyguards.

"Oh my dear!" cried Emily, and rushed over to Louise. "What have they done to you?" Louise found tears coming to her eyes. Almost at the point of sobs, her friend knelt down in front of her and tried to staunch the flow of blood from Louise's head wound with tissues she'd grabbed from her shoulder purse.

Laura Alice stood at the living room door, blocking anyone's exit with her small but bulky body. She took one look at the scene, plucked her cell phone from her purse, and said, "No wonder these assholes didn't want us to come down. Louise, while I phone the police, tell us what's happened here."

As loudly as she could, so no one could misunderstand, Louise announced, "Walter Freeman is a killer. He had Catherine killed. And he murdered Dorothy right in front of my eyes." She could hear Laura Alice relaying this information to the nine-one-one operator.

"What nonsense!" exclaimed Freeman, raising both hands in exasperation. "The poor woman has suffered a blow to the head, and has totally misunderstood what has gone on here. The truth is, I saved Mrs. Eldridge's life—"

Emily paused in her first aid efforts. Her lips trembled as she stared into Louise's eyes. "Walter killed Dorothy and Catherine? Louise, are you *sure?*"

"As God is my witness, Emily, I'm sure. I heard him talk with Dorothy about how he planned Catherine's death. Then I watched him shoot her in cold blood. If Charlie Hurd hadn't tumbled in over the fence, I'd be lying here dead as well." She looked up at Laura Alice. "Don't trust any of them, Laura Alice. The dog can help keep them under control until the police get here."

"Good idea," said Laura Alice. She pursued the Labrador, which, excited by the smells of blood and death, had rounded Dorothy Cranshaw's body and given it a thorough sniffing, then moved over to smell the man who kept backing away from him, Walter Freeman.

"Get this beast away from me," Freeman said to his two bodyguards. "I do not *like* dogs. Would you men step in and do something?"

The taller of the two had pulled a gun from a shoulder holster inside his coat jacket by the time Laura Alice grabbed the dog's leash. She shoved herself in front of the big man, stared up at him, and bumped her protruding belly into his, while telling the dog, "Attack mode, Lancelot." Lancelot snarled, and the bodyguard hurriedly holstered his gun. Laura Alice stepped back from the man, but added, "Remember, folks, this animal looks friendly, but it's very unreliable." Louise would have smiled had she had the energy to do so. She knew Lancelot had not been trained to do anything other than please his owners with a wagging tail and good behavior. But Laura Alice's tone was so confrontational that the animal fell right into her mode.

Catching Laura Alice's tough mood, Emily warned her important neighbor, "Walter, I believe every word Louise has told us."

The economist glared at her but remained silent. Charlie Hurd snapped his phone shut. "Just for good measure, I called nine-one-one again," he reported. "The police are within blocks of here; they ought to arrive any second now." He looked around at the frozen group and sensed an opportunity. Pulling his pocket computer out of his pocket, he said, "So, as I understand it, this Dorothy Cranshaw lyin' on the floor here *lived* down here. Have I got that right?"

Laura Alice Shea looked at him and scowled. "Do you have to ask questions *now?*"

"Of course I do, lady," he argued. "I have a helluva story here. What do you expect me to do? As I said, this Dorothy character"—he pointed a finger at the pale corpse—*"lived* down here in the bowels of the garden club building. And now someone's knocked her off?"

No one answered him. He pursued another tack, asking one of the bodyguards, "So just who are you two guys? Are you with Mr. Freeman?"

One of them nodded. "We're his bodyguards. He's been in jeopardy ever since his wife was murdered last Saturday."

"Oh," groaned Louise, in disgust. "He *engineered* the whole thing." She remembered the voice-activated recorder in her purse. "And I can prove it," she added.

Charlie checked out the dapper economist, in his expensive wool suit, an implacably calm expression now restored to his famous face. "I hope so, Louise. You know I've always liked and admired you, but I find it hard to believe what you're saying about this guy—even if he did have a gun trained on you."

Emily, still crouching beside Louise with makeshift bandage pressed to Louise's brow, fiercely said, "You *should* believe her; she never lies."

Walter Freeman gave Charlie Hurd a sincere look. "Young man, I appreciate the fact that you don't put credence in her account."

"I didn't say that," countered the reporter. "I just said it's a real stretch to believe a bigshot like you would be dumb enough to get involved in a couple of murders."

Louise's adversary stood, aloof now, his gaze somewhere in the distance. She could practically hear his mental tumblers rolling as he established his story of the events of the past few minutes. This would be a harder scenario to come up with than any financial crisis the man had weathered—especially with the proof that Louise had against him in her big, comfy purse.

But then she remembered something that sent a feeling of hopelessness through her whole body. For a moment, she thought she'd faint. She had turned *off* that damned voice recorder to save tape. And she hadn't turned it on again. Now it would be her word against the word of the country's most prominent and believable economist.

44

"So, these men *are* your bodyguards," said Charlie to Walter Freeman. "And it is true they blocked the stairs, wouldn't let anybody else down here. Now, why would they do that?" Charlie had focused on Freeman by default, since he was the only one in the room willing to answer his questions. It must be alluring, Louise thought, for the reporter to have the chance to probe the mind of Walter Freeman, even in these weird conditions. She watched the interchange through a fuzzy veil of pain and regret, mortified that she'd lost the opportunity to prove what had happened down in this dank basement. Emily was right: Louise was too arrogant and sure of her so-called native abilities to respect the use of modern equipment—though voice-activated recorders were nothing very new, just something that would have saved her skin in these circumstances.

Freeman gave Charlie Hurd a critical look, the kind of glance that wilted opponents of his during arguments on big economic issues. But the Washington *Post* reporter was Teflon-coated, Louise knew, brought up by doting, wealthy parents and imbued with a native cunning that made him almost as indifferent as the killer himself. It would take more than a dirty look to squelch Charlie Hurd.

"They had no orders from *me* to block anyone's path," Freeman snapped.

"But, sir—" said the one who'd pulled the gun.

"Yes, go ahead, tell us," Charlie encouraged the man.

"No, don't," retorted Freeman. "Keep your mouth shut." He turned back to Charlie Hurd. "Let me explain things, young man. These two are my safety factor, as I travel from home to my office in downtown Washington, D.C. If they happened to block people from coming down those stairs, it was simply a misunderstanding; they knew I wanted to have a heart-to-heart with Mrs. Cranshaw."

This was too much for Laura Alice, who handed the dog back to Emily and went over to confront Freeman. "You're—how can I phrase it?—just plain lying, Mr. Freeman. They had no right or reason to prevent me from coming downstairs to join Louise. You *planned* to kill Dorothy Cranshaw. That's what I'm telling the police."

Freeman crossed his arms. "Tell them whatever you want, young lady. After I relate my story, they'll probably attribute yours to the fact that you're very pregnant and thus in the category of a hysterical woman."

Whether it was an accident or not, one of the heels of Laura Alice's spike-heeled St. John sling pumps ended on Freeman's toe. The financial genius grabbed his foot and cried out with pain, but people paid him scant attention, for the police were stamping down the stairs, guns drawn.

Relief flooded over Louise, and she lay back on the floor and closed her eyes, finally able to relax. Four uniformed officers crowded into the living room but stood back from the body crumpled near the couch. Upon their arrival, Lancelot had directed his puppy growls at the uniformed men in blue, considering the newcomers highly suspicious.

The patrolman who appeared to be in charge gave a nervous look at the dog and said, "I want everyone out of this room. Go upstairs where you're going to be questioned. First to go is you, lady, and that animal," he said to Emily. Laura Alice lumbered after her.

As the others cleared out, the officer looked sharply at Louise on the floor, peering closely at her bleeding temple. "Can you walk?" he asked her.

"I could use some help in getting up."

The policeman hefted her gently to her feet. "How's that?" He turned to another patrolman and said, "Get her up the stairs, and take it easy. She might have a concussion."

After a slow journey up the basement stairs, Louise emerged into the lobby to see the entire garden club board, plus the visitors, assembled in the main meeting room. Freeman sat diffidently with his two bodyguards, quietly arguing with the policeman in charge, as if he wanted special dispensation to leave. Charlie Hurd was now a witness as well as a reporter, which meant no one could kick him out of here. He took a seat among the garden club members and busily asked questions. She realized he deserved his good story.

Though she was sitting only a couple of rows from Freeman, she didn't bother to look at him. She was conserving her own strength, and thinking hard. From the expression on the economist's face, she could tell he was hardly going to confess. Just as she thought, it was going to be a *he said, she said* situation. And who would the police believe? Louise Eldridge, a visitor in Bethesda, a woman with a bit of stature due to a public television garden show; or the country and the world's most renowned economist? He was a man to whom presidents and premiers listened with respect. Police, especially the likes of Detective Tom Kovach and his partner Peter Girard, were bound to favor his story over hers.

Inside her chest she felt a little knot, and hoped her heart wouldn't start palpitating. She leaned farther back in the metal folding chair and stared at the peeling paint on the old ceiling and tried to think.

45

The detective team arrived about fifteen minutes later. By this time, Louise was groggy with fatigue, even though her buddies, Emily and Laura Alice, sat on either side of her, trying to keep her alert.

Emily's eyes were wide with concern. "Are those pills working?" she asked. She'd given Louise three anonymous, smooth white capsules, which Louise wouldn't take until she learned they were aspirin. "I think they should let you go to the hospital." Medics had come in and cleaned her forehead wound, warning that she should report later to the hospital or a doctor's office.

"The aspirin is making me sleepy, something I can't afford to be," said Louise. "I have to figure this out."

Emily had the recorder in her hand and had listened to the tape over and over. Try as she might, she still couldn't help but look reprovingly at Louise. "If only you'd left it on."

Louise shut her eyes and felt a wave of dizziness. "But I didn't. There has to be another way to make the police believe me. Otherwise, he'll feed them some story about how he shot her in self-defense."

Laura Alice patted Louise's knee. "You'll think of a way, don't worry." Then she put her hand on her stomach.

Louise said, "How about you? You're not—"

With a big smile, Laura Alice said, "I'll have to be among the first questioned, my Misses Marple. The baby's coming."

"Will you call your husband?"

"I don't want to bother him until I'm sure. Ummm . . ." She sat back with a jolt. "Well, maybe I will ring him." She got her cell phone from its pocket on the front of her purse and hit a button and told her spouse it was time to meet her at Sibley Hospital.

Louise turned to Emily. "I hate to see her rush off. You and she have a better sense of what was said downstairs than I do."

Emily gave her a sincere look. "You know the truth: just tell it. They'll have to believe you, or at least investigate."

With a sinking feeling, Louise watched Walter Freeman get up and intercept the two lead detectives. They stood in a confab that must have lasted ten minutes or more while Louise continued to search her brain for a way to prove that the words coming out of Walter Freeman's mouth were a lie.

To her chagrin, she saw Freeman heading for the door, as if free to go. The two bodyguards, she noticed, were still detained. Meanwhile, the big, dark-haired Kovach sauntered over to her, his mouth a grim line, his eyes taking in the big bandage on her forehead. "Now, how's all this we're hearing, Mrs. Eldridge? Mr. Freeman tells us the story of how he saved you from being killed downstairs."

Louise's gaze followed Freeman. He had now reached the lobby and was chatting with the bodyguards as he headed out the door. "If you let him go now, Detective Kovach, you're making a terrible mistake. He's responsible for that body down there, and for his wife's murder."

"Whoa," said Kovach, and crouched down in front of her chair, as Emily and Laura Alice leaned in to listen. "You're accusing Mr. Freeman of two *murders?*" His brow loomed heavily over his eyes, and skeptical lines drew down his mouth. "Do tell me about it."

"I was downstairs, and I'll admit I was rummaging through Dorothy Cranshaw's stuff—I got suspicious of her and thought she might have had something to do with Catherine's murder. I looked around, and found her gun. You can prove that by finding my fingerprints on it. She came downstairs and confronted me, and we, um, exchanged blows. She hit me, and I tripped her—I think she might have broken her leg. At any rate, she fell down and couldn't walk. Then Walter Freeman appeared, and I could tell from what they said to each other that they had planned his wife's murder together. He was afraid Dorothy'd talk, so he shot her." Louise felt tears come to her eyes. "She was a sitting duck."

Kovach's mouth fell slack. Finally he said, "Mr. Freeman has a totally different story, you realize that, don't you? He told us that he came down, saw that you were held at gunpoint by this Dorothy, and saved you by shooting her."

"Ask yourself why he came downstairs in the first place. And ask him why he told his bodyguards to block my friends from following. If he were an innocent man simply wanting to talk to the woman who lived there, why would he prevent others from coming down to the basement?"

Laura Alice and Emily nodded, and Laura Alice said, "They bodily stopped me from going down, when I *knew* she'd be in trouble because Dorothy had gone down and would have caught her looking around."

Kovach looked at the two women with new interest. "Oh. So you knew Mrs. Eldridge might need help."

Emily said, "We were quite aware that the murderer could have been present in the clubhouse today—especially when Walter Freeman arrived on the scene." She smiled disingenuously. "After all, he was among our four or five prospects."

Gruffly, Detective Kovach said, "I think you mean 'suspects.'" He turned to Louise. "Tell me one more time, Mrs. Eldridge."

"I swear, Detective Kovach, that I saw Freeman murder Dorothy in cold blood. And I swear I heard the two of them discuss how Dorothy'd been forced by him to kill his wife, Catherine."

"Forced. How?"

"Blackmailed. He threatened to dredge up the story of how Dorothy 'accidentally' shot her husband twenty-some years ago. Back then, Dorothy's son Jack apparently knew his mother had planned the shooting. Besides that, Freeman also promised her a huge amount of money."

"How do you know that, pray tell?" said Kovach, his voice reflecting his disbelief.

"Dorothy mentioned it just before Freeman shot her. Freeman wanted to tidy things up by picking up the gun with Dorothy's prints and shooting *me.* Then he could have told you Dorothy killed me and threatened him, and that he shot her dead to defend himself. The only reason he didn't is because I kicked Dorothy's gun under the bookcase. And then it sure didn't hurt that Charlie Hurd came along—"

"Charlie Hurd—that reporter?" said the detective.

She nodded over at Charlie, now with a covey of interested garden club members clustered about him. "Yes, he's sitting over there. He climbed Dorothy's garden fence to try to get into the clubhouse, because they wouldn't let him in the front door."

Kovach sat on his haunches, forearms resting on his knees, and shook his big head. At least his dark eyes didn't look quite as hard as they had at the beginning of the interview. "What a story, ma'am. With all due respect, we know Walter Freeman, and we don't know you at all, except for that visit and phone call you made to us."

Louise looked around and saw the garden club members sitting in groups, some around Charlie, some by themselves. Lunchless and no doubt starving just like she was, but with the good food smells still filling the clubhouse. Their voices sounded impatient as they waited their turn to be questioned by the detectives.

Walter Freeman, she noticed, was still at the front door, saying a last word to a couple of patrolmen.

She closed her eyes, about ready to give up hope.

Laura Alice Shea, still rubbing her stomach like someone kneading a magic genie, said, "Detective, I'm going to have to rush off to Sibley, because I'm having labor pains—"

Kovach quickly sprang to his feet, as if the young woman had a deadly, contagious disease. He focused his eyes on her big belly.

She put out a cautionary hand. "Don't worry: I have a minute left. Before I go, this is important. First, I'm an assistant to the undersecretary of the Treasury, so that gives you a little perspective in case you think I'm just a pregnant housewife." She flipped a business card out of her purse and gave it to him, then turned to Emily and grinned, her short-cropped hair falling fetchingly over one eye. "Forgive that crack about housewives, girls." Then she turned back to the detective. "As you can see by the card, Laura Alice Shea's my name. And I'm here to tell you that this woman is not a liar." Louise noted how imposing she was, even in her frilly ruffled dress. "Think about it," argued Laura Alice. "Mrs. Eldridge has absolutely no reason to lie. So my advice to you is to stop that man before he goes anywhere." She pointed a finger at the retreating Walter Freeman, who was going out the front door. Then she got up clumsily and said, "Now how about one of your people helping me to my car? I may have waited too long—"

"Ma'am," said Kovach, taking her arm, "I can do better than that. One of my officers will take you there." He quickly signaled a patrolman, who came over and escorted Laura Alice as she strode away on her high-heeled pumps amid the good wishes from her friends.

"And while you're at it," Kovach called to the officer, "have them intercept Mr. Freeman, will you? Tell him to wait. I have a few questions for him."

Louise watched while the officer conveyed these instructions to another patrolman, who went out on the front porch and laid a big hand on the shoulder of the economist and stopped him in his tracks. As Freeman came back in the lobby with the officer, he gave Louise a look of disgust, then slowly took a seat in the back row of the big room.

Kovach returned and sat beside her in the chair Laura Alice had just vacated. In a low voice he said, "Is there some way you can substantiate this?"

Emily tapped the voice recorder she still held in her lap. "She was supposed to have used this. But she didn't." Her friend looked embarrassed. "Sorry, Louise, I don't mean to criticize."

"It's okay," said Louise. She told Kovach, "I've been thinking hard. When I was down the basement, Dorothy's apartment door was open, so it didn't feel as if I were breaking and entering. One thing led to another"—she blushed in embarrassment—"and I looked through her entire apartment. I saw her collections of things, but I didn't find even a bankbook or a financial record of any kind. Walter Freeman transferred money to Dorothy: she mentioned an offshore bank account. That means he has to have some record of his withdrawals, maybe over a period of months. Dorothy also must have had some record of a bank account number. The information is down there somewhere—just like the gun was there."

"You *hope* it's there," said Kovach. "Why are you so sure?"

"Because of Dorothy's character," said Louise. "She could not bear to throw anything away. She liked to keep things, and keep things in order. In fact, order was what she craved in life, and probably one of the reasons she killed. Money—enough to last her indefinitely—would give order to her life."

"She certainly wanted the garden club to stay in order," said Emily. "She hated change. She always insisted we operate by Roberts' Rules of Order—" Her eyes widened and she turned to Louise. "That's it, Louise—*Roberts' Rules of Order.* Dorothy must have a copy. You know those stories where people hollow out a book to make a hiding place—"

Louise leaned over and gripped her diminutive friend by the shoulder. "Emily, you're a *genius!*"

To the detective she said, "Why don't you look in Dorothy's bookcase—the one nearest the French doors that holds the classics. Bottom shelf. There's not one, but two copies of *Roberts' Rules of Order* sitting on the bottom shelf. I bet you'll find something interesting."

46

Louise was stretched out on the chaise lounge, a light cover over her legs, eating again. She and Emily had made a brief stop at Suburban Hospital, where a doctor assured her that she didn't have a concussion but advised her to take it easy for a few days. While there, Emily had phoned Sibley to check on Laura Alice's progress and learned that the baby had not yet been delivered.

Emily had prepared a late tea, English style, with little meat sandwiches and sweets on a tray, since the two of them had missed lunch during all the excitement at the clubhouse.

As she selected another small sandwich for herself, Emily laughed. "Alex may not like it, but we're having a very late dinner with corned-beef salad as one of the courses. You'll finally get to taste it."

"Once I find out what's happened with the police, I need to go home to my family. They're flying in tomorrow morning, and I want to freshen up the house."

"Louise, you shouldn't be freshening up houses right now."

The doorbell interrupted, and Emily went to answer it and ushered Detective Kovach onto the patio. They looked at the big police officer expectantly. He grinned and said, "You were right, Mrs. Holley. *Roberts' Rules of*

Order contained a lot of valuable information. Walter Freeman is being detained as a material witness in the death of
his wife, as well as in the death of Dorothy Cranshaw."

Louise lay her head back and studied the canopy of green
leaves that fluttered over them in the tall oak trees. "Thank
God." She would not have liked to hear that Freeman was
on the loose.

Kovach told Louise, "You hit it on the nail about Dorothy Cranshaw. She did keep careful records of everything, including the fact that an offshore account had
been opened in her name five months ago, with regular
deposits totaling half a million dollars in it."

"I'm sure Walter told her to keep no such records," said
Louise. "But a woman like Dorothy had to keep records.
But will her records alone implicate Freeman?"

"On the basis of them and your statement, we have
enough to go to a judge and ask permission to investigate
the activity in his private financial accounts. When I told
Freeman that, he indicated he'd be interested in talking
about what happened."

"That's incredible," said Louise. "Why?"

Kovach had a pleased look on his face. "That's because
another part of the puzzle may have just fallen into place.
Reese Janning."

"She's willing to talk?"

"Actually, very anxious to distance herself from her boss,
especially when my partner told her that two persons
could testify that her SUV was near the scene of the crime
last Saturday night. She's told us that she knew a little
about the plot. Said she urged Walter not to 'give in' to
the temptation to get rid of his wife."

Louise frowned. "Let's back up a step: what good will it
do for Walter Freeman to confess he knew about the plan
to murder Catherine?"

"My guess is that he might try to shift blame to Reese
Janning. He might turn the tables and claim that Reese

proposed murdering Catherine, and that he didn't take part in it."

Emily broke into a belly laugh. "That's ridiculous! This great economist who tells the country how to manage its money, interest rates, financial institutions, is going to hide behind a woman to get out of a first-degree murder charge?"

Louise said, "You'd think a man like that would cover his tracks better." She smiled. "Or, as Freeman himself might say in his inimitable, stuffy style, *Underlying trends guiding the future are marked with uncertainty. If calamity is to be avoided, we need a great deal of proactive movement . . .*"

Kovach grinned, signifying he'd caught the humor. But his expression immediately turned solemn again. "What he needed to do, of course, was to silence Dorothy—and that's what he accomplished today. Even if she was supposed to be smart and close-mouthed, she was always going to be a danger to him. He did a splendid job handling us police: he deflected suspicion right off the bat by passing a lie-detector test with flying colors."

"How could he do that?"

"People can, if they're expert in the art of breathing."

Emily said, "Walter was a sportsman type. He played great tennis, he swam, he even scuba dived."

Kovach nodded. "A scuba diver—that explains it. Now, as far as the money trail, we'll look at his pattern of withdrawals, but a lot of this will depend on Dorothy's record-keeping. And then there's Dorothy's son. We had an interesting talk with Jack Cranshaw."

"What did he tell you?"

"Just another nail in Freeman's coffin. He attempted to get close to Jack a few months ago, to worm information out of him about his father's hunting accident. I just began to check on that one, and it seems the case had some suspicious aspects to it."

"*Yes,*" said Louise eagerly, sitting forward. "Dorothy

mentioned this just before she was shot. Walter heard some gossip from the state police chief about the accident. That was why he knew she could be blackmailed."

"So that was how he found Dorothy's Achilles' heel," said Kovach. "Jack was suspicious when Freeman began pumping him, but he didn't tell his mother: they were leading pretty separate lives since the guy lost all her money in some restaurant venture. I sensed two things: that the guy knows more about the hunting accident than he's willing to tell, and that he also knows his mother was involved in Catherine Freeman's death. He did nothing, because we in law enforcement kept viewing it as a mis-hit on Walter Freeman, and maybe because—"

Louise slid a glance at the policeman. "He expected a cut of the proceeds?"

"Possibly." The detective gave Louise a contrite look. "Mrs. Eldridge, I have to apologize for not giving credence to your views."

"I can understand why you were skeptical. I had only the slightest suspicions of Dorothy. Not until today did I take them seriously."

"She wasn't on our radar screen, either." He gave a nervous chuckle. "None of the garden club ladies were on our radar screen at first. Then we heard things that did cause us to look at, um—"

"Sophie, Meg, and Phyllis."

"But not at Dorothy. Now, if we *had* found this weapon and traced it to her—and it's hard to find weapons that are buried in flowerpots—she might have given us a very reasonable story to cover herself. You know: target practice, to account for the gun having been fired recently."

The detective sat back in the lawn chair and looked suddenly weary under his swarthy tan. "The perpetrator isn't here to tell us her exact motives, but it looks as if it was just what you heard, that she was persuaded into becoming a hit woman by the old carrot-and-stick method."

"The carrot being the half-million dollars. And the stick being the threat to disclose how she killed her husband twenty-five years ago."

"Exactly."

Emily said, "Dorothy was terribly short of money—though that alone couldn't have been enough reason to drive her to murder her friend." She bowed her head solemnly. "I thought Dorothy had a lot of good in her. Walter Freeman blackmailed her into it, or she wouldn't have pulled that trigger."

"I'm puzzled about Dorothy and money," said Louise. "Remember how she told us about all the money she was going to make when she went into her own business? What was that all about?"

"When I talked to Dorothy's son," said Kovach, "he said Dorothy felt like a misfit in Bethesda. She sold the family home before values skyrocketed, then turned her nest egg over to him for his fancy restaurant, which failed. She cut back her lifestyle, but recently was about to lose the deal on her free apartment, so she decided she'd start a house-cleaning business. Must have been a bitter pill to contemplate cleaning other people's fancy houses for a living when you used to live in one of them yourself."

Emily said, "She often spoke about what had happened to Bethesda, as if it were a tragedy. It was a farm community in her mother's youth, but in her mind it had become an overgrown mess of traffic and people. She used to rant on about the lovely colonial houses that were being torn down and replaced by showcases for the very rich."

Kovach nodded. "Catherine Freeman was very rich. It must have been easy for Dorothy to resent the woman."

"She did it in typical Dorothy fashion," said Emily, "without fanfare. No one could have guessed she hated Catherine."

"The club records were fascinating, though," said Louise. "Catherine took over the presidency from Dorothy twenty years ago. She probably continued to make Dorothy's life miserable without even being aware of it."

"Catherine annoyed other people, too," said Emily. "She tended to take over the whole show—winning all the garden and design prizes." She spread her hands wide. "But what could the judges do? She was *better* than everyone else."

"The last straw must have been the changes in the club," said Louise. "Under Catherine's leadership, Dorothy thought it was stripped of its old ways and turned into something . . . not so nice." She didn't want to offend the feelings of Emily, who now reigned as president.

But Emily knew this was true. "I think she saw the club as becoming a soulless organization of people who would act like automatons: checking into their burglar-proofed clubhouse with a plastic entry card." She gave a nervous laugh, knowing full well she'd inherited Catherine's cloak, and all Catherine's troubles with it. "Since Catherine also decided Dorothy's apartment had to go," she said, "it was as if Dorothy herself were an anachronism, as useless as the club's gray-shingled, rundown building and worn-out rules."

Detective Kovach shook his head. "That was one crafty, pathetic lady." He got up to go, promising to keep them informed.

As Emily escorted him out, the phone rang. "It's the club members," said Emily. "They'll be dying to know what happened."

47

"It was Phyllis Ohlmacher," said Emily later. "She wanted to hear the latest news. But get this, Louise: she said she couldn't talk long because she and Al are overwhelmed. They're swamped with new orders for azalea plants. Apparently, retail outlets are rejecting Catherine Freeman's nursery stock as being of inferior quality. Can you believe that? Once I told Phyllis the story about Walter Freeman, she had to go and get back to work."

"What's happened to Catherine's azaleas?" said Louise. "Maybe in all the excitement of the murder, they weren't watered."

"Phyllis didn't know, either—just said they appear to be suffering the wilts."

They heard the doorbell, and Emily brought Sophie Chalois onto the patio. Sophie still wore the pale green linen suit she'd had on for the club meeting. She sailed directly over to Louise, like a handsome clothes model, and unceremoniously dragged a chair into place next to where Louise lay on the chaise lounge. In a low, urgent voice, she told Louise, "We have to talk."

"Yes, I think we should," said Louise. She didn't even attempt a smile.

Sophie's head was bent. She seemed to have trouble

making eye contact. "I don't know what you've told the police."

"Nothing." This was the cruel woman who had shoved her down a flight of dark stairs.

Sophie hadn't suffered enough: she could just twist slowly in the wind for a moment longer.

Louise amended her statement. "I've told the police nothing—yet. But I'm thinking I will, Sophie, that it's my duty to tell them. After all, you committed a felony. I saw you at the head of the stairs, plain as day."

"Oh my *God,*" said Sophie throatily, finally staring into Louise's eyes, "I *so* regret what I did, but it seemed as if you were snooping into just everything—those books down there, talking to everyone, pushing at the police with your theories. . . ."

Louise was surprised to hear the woman chattering on, as if she couldn't stop if she wanted to. "And I knew the way you were going at it that you would soon find out about what Meg and I did to Catherine."

Abruptly, Sophie sat back, and her eyes widened with distrust. She halted her rushed confession. "And as I think about it, I don't even know why I brought up that stairs incident. You can't even prove I did anything, can you?"

Privately, Louise agreed with Sophie. This would be a case of *she said, she said.* Only if the sharp-eyed Laura Alice had noticed Sophie in the stairwell would Louise have any kind of a case against her. Even in all the confusion, Laura Alice would have mentioned if she had seen such a thing.

At the moment Louise was curious about the little slip Sophie had just made. What *had* Meg and Sophie done to Catherine Freeman?

Then two little facts clicked together, like pieces of a jigsaw puzzle. Fact one was that Catherine's azalea nursery plants were suffering from something, to the point where buyers preferred Phyllis Ohlmacher's inferior stock. Fact

two was that "friends" like Sophie Chalois and Meg Durrance, who probably had access to Catherine's backyard
greenhouse, had "done" something to her. They might have
been invited there last Saturday afternoon by Catherine
herself. Louise remembered Sophie and Meg with their
heads together with Catherine; that might have been the
moment when they asked for a tour of the place.

"Sophie, you and Meg sabotaged Catherine Freeman's
azalea plants, didn't you?"

"What?" Sophie reared back in her chair. "Are you quite
mad?"

"No, but we just heard from Phyllis that Catherine's azalea stock has suffered a trauma." Louise lay back, feeling
quite calm in the face of the woman's anger, and made a
wild guess. "It was as if someone had fed the plants salts . . ."

Sophie flounced to her feet, just as Emily escorted another visitor in: Meg Durrance. *"Meg,"* cried Sophie in a
plaintive voice, "Louise is accusing you and me of doing
something terrible to Catherine's plants."

Unprepared, Meg's big brown eyes flashed first toward
Louise, then to Emily, and finally toward Sophie. Louise
could see Meg was ignoring all the warnings in Sophie's
eyes. "I *told* you it would be easy as pie for anyone to discover we'd sabotaged her plants—"

"What are you *saying,* Meg?" snarled Sophie. "You're
talking crazy." And she started to flounce off toward the
house, but Emily put a restraining hand on her arm.

The big redhead stood at the foot of the chaise lounge
and looked down at Louise. "I didn't want to do it, but
Sophie was determined, so I went along. It was not that vicious, Louise. It was just to stop Catherine from winning
every goddamned thing she ever tried." Her words came
out in a nervous tumble. "Just a dilute solution of salt
squirted on the plants, when Catherine was called out of
the room that Saturday. We only meant for her to have a

little setback with one batch of plants and maybe lose first place at the azalea show."

Sophie stood like a prisoner, Emily's hand still restraining her. Emily guided her over to a chair, and she finally sat down, not looking at anything but the fading light in the flowery backyard.

48

"So I see it took about six days for the azaleas to wilt down enough so that no one would buy them," said Louise.

"Oh, God," cried Meg, slumping down in the chair next to her fellow culprit. But she leaned toward Louise, as if she could save her. "Couldn't we just make restitution, and keep this to ourselves?"

Emily, standing tight-lipped nearby, was not in the mood for compromise. Her mouth turned in an ironic smile, and her voice was unnaturally clipped. "Who would you make restitution to? Catherine's dead, and Walter will soon be in jail. No, Meg, that won't do. You and Sophie must at least tell the police. Wonder if it came out otherwise? Why, they might even think you were part of the plot to kill Catherine!"

Meg shoved a hand through her pile of auburn hair. "Damn it all, Sophie, stop just sitting there looking stunned and *do* something. We have to go over to the police station and tell them about it."

Sophie gave her friend a glazed look and made a twisting motion with her hands. Meg pulled out a pack of cigarettes and shook the pack until a cigarette came loose. Sophie reached over and took it, and Meg leaned forward with her lighter to light it for her friend. Then Meg lit one up for herself, setting one of Emily's fine china cups aside so they could drop ashes into the saucer.

Emily slumped into a chair, looking suddenly small and frail. It had been a hard day for all of them, Louise realized, and this was just another blow to her friend's sensibilities. "It's bad enough that one of our garden club members committed murder," said Emily. "And now this— it's incredible. What would you call this, Louise, this sabotaging someone's plants?"

"Vandalism. On the other hand, when people try to shove you down a set of basement stairs—"

Sophie looked over at her with a gasp. Had the woman really expected her to forget the incident?

"When did *that* happen?" cried Emily.

"At the clubhouse today, as I was going down the basement stairs for the second time," said Louise. "That's called assault and battery with the intent to do great bodily harm."

Emily looked from Louise to Sophie. "It seems a lot has gone on today that I don't even know about."

Sophie tried again, her blue eyes big with fright. There was no more bluster and denial left in the woman. "Louise, I'm so sorry—I didn't mean to hurt you, I swear. I just wanted to scare you off."

"I'd like to believe you, Sophie," said Louise. "What I find hard to understand is why an intelligent woman like you would try something as foolish as that. You could have killed me." She leaned forward, so that she was almost in Sophie's face. "In fact, after you did that, I was convinced *you'd* murdered Catherine Freeman."

Sophie shrank back in her chair, her eyes glazed, the cigarette still poised in the fingers of one hand. She didn't know what Louise and Emily knew—the things they had just learned from Detective Kovach. For all she knew, she could still be rounded up and dragged in by police as a suspect. "God, no—I wouldn't go that far! What kind of a person do you think I am?"

Louise gave her a wry look and didn't answer. After a moment of silence she said, "Very reluctantly, Sophie, I'll let it go." Privately, Louise knew it would be almost impossible to prove. Laura Alice would surely have told her if she'd seen Sophie skulking around at the top of the basement stairs. "Even if there may be no one to bring charges against you, you and Meg should go tell the police what you did to Catherine's plants."

"All right," said Sophie in a flat voice. "We'll go and tell them and hope they understand."

Even if someone were there to charge the two of them, thought Louise, they could afford good attorneys and would probably get no more than probation and community service. It was the shame of it all that would be their punishment.

Louise wondered if either woman would have the nerve to show her face at another garden club meeting and concluded that both probably would. What the two of them shared, she decided, was a hard-boiled arrogance. Had it come from some earlier hurt, some deprivation of motherly love, perhaps? Or was it just that they were two spoiled, rich American women with no families to keep their feet bound to the earth? Certainly, the two of them—and the unfortunate Dorothy Cranshaw—cast a shadow on the other upstanding members of the Old Georgetown Garden Club.

Then they heard car tires squealing, as someone turned sharply into the driveway next door.

"It must be Jim Shea," said Emily, getting up to peek over the fence. "I wonder how Laura Alice is."

Through the gate in the fence strode a tall, muscular

man with light curly hair, his fashionable suit jacket slung over one shoulder, the sleeves of his white dress shirt rolled up as if he'd been engaged in physical labor. So this was Laura Alice's husband.

He made his way across the grass in huge strides and vaulted up the three steps to the patio. "Does it look like I'm walking on air?" he said, laughing, as he gracefully slouched in their midst. "That's because I am. Laura Alice is okay," he told them, "and we have a healthy boy, a seven-pound, fourteen-ounce boy." Then he flung his jacket on an empty chair and went around the circle of women, introducing himself to those he didn't know, and leaning over to kiss each of them on the cheek. When he kissed her, Louise could smell his fresh sweat, and guessed he'd been at his wife's side through the entire labor. Looking around, she noticed there were tears in several people's eyes, including Sophie's. "Oh, and nearly forgot," added the new father. "We're naming him Christopher Shea. Like that name, Christopher? Kind of rolls off the tongue, doesn't it? It's my dad's name."

They agreed that they liked the name. Then Jim regained his jacket and said, "I have to hurry off now. Laura Alice needs a nightgown and some personal things."

The four women looked from one to the other and smiled. For a brief moment it didn't matter that they had such differing scruples. This was a unifying thing that made them forget their differences: a new baby.

Emily's phone interrupted the moment. When she answered, her alarmed eyes told them it wasn't a pleasant call. She turned away and had a conversation in a low voice. When she rang off, she explained.

"That was Alex. He just heard the news—the bare bones has been put on the TV news: 'A murder in Bethesda at the Old Georgetown Garden Club—with prominent economist Walter Freeman held by police as a material witness.' " She looked almost embarrassed. "Alex is terribly upset that my name—and then his, of course, just because we're married—could get in the press. He's hurrying home."

49

The women soon left, and Emily went to the kitchen to prepare dinner. Louise promptly fell asleep and didn't wake until she heard an angry male voice ringing through the house. Her heart caught in her throat, and for an instant, she thought she was back in that scene of violence in the musty clubhouse basement. With a shudder, she pulled herself fully awake and touched the bandage on her forehead. No, she was quite safe, here in the serene home of her friend Emily. But a ranting husband had destroyed its peace and quiet.

Emily's replies to Alex were so quiet-spoken that Louise couldn't hear them at all, so she pulled herself out of the chaise lounge and went to the kitchen, anxious to deflect his abuse. As she entered the kitchen, Emily was at the stove, casually stirring a pot of soup and saying, "*You* may not like what has happened, Alex, but Detective Kovach thinks we're a couple of heroines." She grinned at Louise. "Isn't that so, Louise?"

Louise smiled and nodded, and slumped onto a kitchen stool, still feeling woozy. Alex gave her a long look, taking in her bandaged head without comment. He strode over and flipped on the kitchen TV. "I just hope our name isn't mentioned in the news." The story of the garden club "murders" focused almost entirely on the involvement of

Washington's top economist. There was no mention of the Holleys. Alex sighed and said, "Thank God for small favors. But this isn't the end of it. Our name will probably come up tomorrow. After all, you're the president now of that infernal garden club."

When the three sat down to dinner, Louise didn't know how Emily had done it. While she had dozed in her chaise, her hostess had produced another elegant dinner: bouill-abaisse; freshly baked rolls; the corned beef dish not eaten at lunch; salad with cheese; and finally, a mouth-watering strawberry shortcake, flavored with kirsch.

As usual, Alex's civility returned once he had eaten. "Well done, my dear," he told his wife. "And after the day you've both had. Louise, Emily tells me you're lucky to be alive—you could have been killed by Walter Freeman. I gather that's why you're bandaged. Give me a rundown of what happened." His glance warily intercepted Emily's dis-approving look. "That is, if you feel up to it."

She told him of how Walter Freeman killed Dorothy, right in front of her eyes. "He didn't dare shoot me with the same gun, or he wouldn't have a logical story to tell police. He needed Dorothy's gun, and that meant I had to kick it away from him. If he'd got hold of it—"

"With Dorothy's fingerprints on it, I suppose," said Alex.

"Yes. He could have shot me with it, and his whole scheme would have succeeded better than a tidy govern-ment bailout."

Emily slowly shook her head. "It's amazing what hap-pened today. I don't think it's all sunk in." She looked cau-tiously at her husband, then back at Louise. "I want you to stay the night, Louise. Don't argue. You know you've suf-fered a blow to the head, and an hour's drive around the Beltway is not what you need right now."

Louise thought longingly of that cozy, antique bed in

the guest room. On the other hand, she realized Alex had wanted her to go home since Sunday. Now it was Friday.

Smoothly, he said, "Maybe she'd rather be home, Emily. Did you ever think that?"

But the dinner and the coffee combined to make Louise not care any more about Alex's feelings. "I'd love to stay. Then I'll leave first thing in the morning. Bill and Janie arrive on a two o'clock plane."

"Great," said Emily. "I'll tuck you in bed early, Louise. And maybe we can talk a little—especially, you know"— she cast another glance at her husband—"about those two club members."

Louise realized Sophie and Meg's plant mischief was no joke to Emily, any more than it was going to be to the Montgomery County Police. Emily probably wanted to drum them right out of the Old Georgetown Garden Club. Louise shared her feelings. And yet Sophie and Meg were pathetic, a couple of lonely misfits without mates or families.

Alex had perked up his ears. "Who are you talking about now, Emily? Have you told me everything that happened today?" He frowned at his wife. "I need to know *everything*. After all, I must go to work on Monday and talk to many people who will be, like I am, *shocked* at this turn of events. To have a man of Walter Freeman's stature taken in and questioned about his wife's murder—"

"I think it's more than just questions," said Louise, "from what Detective Kovach told us. I have a feeling he'll be charged with two murders, and pretty soon."

"Oh my *God*," said Alex and bowed his head a little. "How will we get along without him? How will this affect the markets?"

Emily got up from her chair and came over and patted her spouse's thinning red hair. "Take it easy, Alex. The markets will survive. I haven't told you all the details, but I will. There's just no time right now, because I have to do the dishes before I collapse. I don't need you or Louise to help. The two of you just have a nice chat."

With hands full of piled plates, Emily walked through the swinging door to the kitchen, leaving Louise alone with the imperious Alex. Except he wasn't imperious tonight. He seemed anxious to mend fences.

"You know, Louise, Bill and I work together on occasion."

"I know, Alex."

"And I wouldn't want you to go home with the thought that I didn't thoroughly welcome you here."

"Oh no," she protested, "I felt quite welcome. You did get angry with me once or twice, but I understand why."

Alex looked down and scratched a fingernail idly across the linen cloth. "It's Emily's health. Maybe I worry too much about her. But she's had some really bad days, and though she mightn't have told you, she has some tough years to look forward to."

"You mean the illness grows worse the older you get?"

His pale eyes looked appreciative of the fact that she understood. "That's exactly what happens. She'll just have to be more and more careful, in order to manage the pain. More hot-wax baths, more pain pills. And that means she shouldn't have any undue stress, the kind that comes from the sort of activities the two of you engaged in this week."

She gave him a careful look. How could the man be so blind? Emily had more energy and sparkle in her eye today than she'd had when Louise arrived. Detecting had been good for her. Mildly, she said, "I thought your wife did splendidly this week. She handled the trauma of Catherine's murder very well, because instead of sorrowing, she tried to do something about it."

Alex shoved his face forward. "And yet you put her in jeopardy, Louise."

"Oh, I don't think so," insisted Louise. "A warning note on your front doorstep didn't exactly put anyone in jeopardy."

Bill had told her to watch out for Alex when she visited Emily in Bethesda, because he had "hidden depths." She wasn't sure "depths" was the right word. What Louise was finding was a very shallow, chauvinistic man who was attempting to smother his wife's every creative move. She feared for Emily's future, and made a vow to stay in contact with her to encourage her to escape from this repressive web of husbandly concern.

"What if the murderer hadn't been caught," said Alex, "and was still out there?"

She shrugged philosophically. "We were pretty realistic about the limits of what we could do—a little questioning, a talk with Walter's maid, a little snooping downtown to find out more about Reese Janning. . . ."

"Louise, I respect you, and Bill, and the right for you to live your life as you wish. But these are not things my wife should have done. They are very *brash* things to do, for just a couple of housewives."

Since Louise had held a stressful full-time job for three years now, she hadn't been labeled "just" a housewife in some time. Alex seemed to read her expression.

"The last trick in our housewifely bag of tricks," she said, "was that garden club board meeting. We knew we could do no more than that, and if it hadn't worked, we would have ceased and desisted our detecting efforts."

He leaned back. "It's just that I don't want her to do that again. I don't want Emily thinking she's something she isn't."

"You don't want her to change. But, Alex, suppose she's already changed?"

50

Louise backed the Camry out of the driveway and into Battery Lane, with Emily slowly walking alongside the car.

Emily stopped at the curb, looking as though she'd lost her last friend. "I'll call you soon," she said. Louise wondered how many close pals Alex permitted her to have. At least Laura Alice was now a friend, and comfortingly close, along with her engaging husband, Jim. A new baby would guarantee that Laura Alice remained home for six weeks at least, which would give Emily a chance to cement the relationship. Louise allowed her imagination to roam, and wondered how it would work out if the childless Emily provided day care for baby Christopher.

"And don't forget, Louise," called Emily, "you still owe us one."

"Owe who?"

"The garden clubs. You still need to do a show on them."

"I'll talk to my producer. Maybe we'll have better luck next time."

Just as she was about to accelerate, a car that had zoomed down Battery Lane beeped its horn and pulled in directly behind her. She looked in the rearview mirror and saw a red Porsche and a cocky face behind sunglasses. She knew

at a glance it was Charlie Hurd. Louise didn't feel like talking to anyone. Her instinct was to speed away and see if he
could catch her. But Charlie, with that souped-up engine
of his, would chase her all the way around the Beltway and
back to Sylvan Valley. No, she'd deal with him here. She
pulled her car up to the curb in front of Emily's house and
put it in park. This surely wouldn't take long.

He walked up to her car. "Louise! I been lookin' for
you."

"Charlie. I bet you have. I'm glad to see you. Thank you
for showing up when you did yesterday."

He gave an "Aw, shucks" shrug of his shoulders, as embarrassed as a country boy. "I was just afraid you didn't
think I believed what you'd said about Freeman."

"But I knew you were on to him," she said, while realizing Charlie hadn't believed her one hundred percent.
"Anyway, just your being there was enough."

He smiled, willing to take the praise. He poked her arm
with a finger. "Louise, the cops have been protecting you
from me and the rest of the press."

"That's nice of them."

"But we've found you now. I've discovered where the
Holleys live, and the rest of the media's right behind me.
Emily Holley is the new garden club president, isn't she?"

Louise opened her mouth to answer, but Charlie just
rattled on: "Walter Freeman is in custody for this—did you
know that?"

"I heard. What a story for you. This ought to make you
famous."

He leaned his head in closer to her. "Yep. I was there,
Louise—and I know what you did. Pardon the expression,
but you've got *cojones*. I must admit that for a few brief moments, I almost bought Freeman's line that he killed that
old gal to protect *you*. That was because you were so woozy
I wasn't sure if you were talking straight. But now the guy's
in for questioning, and I can't get anything out of the po-

lice. So I thought why not go right to you? Of course, I can take anything I saw down there in Dorothy Cranshaw's apartment and put it in a story."

"I can't add more right now, Charlie. Detective Kovach warned me it might jeopardize the investigation. I'd hate to have Walter Freeman go free because of anything I might say before he's charged."

He tapped impatient fingers on her car door. "Just confirm one thing: you said yesterday that you saw Freeman kill Dorothy Cranshaw."

"I did. As for the rest of the story, it's complicated." She looked up at the gaunt-faced reporter. She'd protected herself by kicking Dorothy's gun away from Walter Freeman. But who knows what he would have done to her if Charlie hadn't stumbled into Dorothy's apartment? She owed this man something.

"I'll tell you what," she said. "As soon as the police say its okay, I'll give you an exclusive interview."

"Great!"

"Maybe we can meet at the Dixie Pig. We'll do lunch." The restaurant was a down-home place on Route One not too far from Louise's house.

He grinned. "I love that place. It's a deal."

"But right now I'm dying to get home to my family." With that she put the car in gear. Charlie took the hint. He removed his hand from the door and gave her a thumbs-up, and she drove away.

At the corner of Battery Lane and Exeter, she had a sudden urge for a last look at Bethesda before she returned home. Pulling into a driveway, she turned the car around, passing Charlie as he started up Emily's walk, noting that Emily stood inside her front screen, looking forlornly out at the world. Her friend would not be lonesome for long, for she would soon be besieged by Charlie and the rest of the reporters. And Emily would handle the press just fine.

Louise drove down the curved residential streets, past the old houses, some grandly refurbished, some unchanged from the day they were built eighty or so years ago. Past the masses of azaleas and tulips and late daffodils, the flowering crabs and magnolias, a virtual world of spring blossoms.

Sadly, the flowers gave a funereal quality to the morning.

It had taken a combination of motives to drive Dorothy Cranshaw to murder, she realized. Walter blackmailed her into it at first, then offered money to strengthen his hand. But he knew who he was dealing with from the beginning—a woman with a grievance: a woman who, like several others in Catherine's social circle, already felt wronged by the invincible Catherine. Not even the powerful, reflected Louise, could protect themselves against the envy and resentment of others.

She drove by the Old Georgetown Garden Club's clubhouse, which looked shabby in the morning sunshine, a disrespected relic of the 1920s. A couple of trucks with television dishes on top were parked in front, and she could hear the blond on-air newswoman talking into her mike as the camera rolled.

"This neighborhood is considered one of the finest in the entire metropolitan Washington area. It's located in Bethesda, a city with a higher percentage of college graduates than any other city in the nation. It is here, in nearby Ledgebrook, that one of the world's top economists lives, Walter Freeman. But Freeman is at this very moment being questioned in connection with two murders—the drive-by shooting last Saturday night of his successful wife, Catherine, president of the very garden club whose clubhouse stands behind me—and of a second murder that took place yesterday afternoon in the basement of this old building. . . ."

Louise sped up to get by lest the newshounds discover

she was involved in the story. Safe in the next block, her thoughts returned to the garden club and its future after this traumatic incident. Garden club members had given good service to their community for generations. These murders would not stop them from their mission. Under Emily's guidance, though, they might pull back on some of their modernization ideas. At the very least, Emily had told Louise she wanted to drop the card-key entry system and to continue instead to house some needy person as caretaker in a remodeled basement apartment.

The spring plant sale, of course, would go on next year as usual.

Having completed a big half-circle through the neighborhood, Louise had arrived back at Wilson Lane. She turned right, heading west, and pressed her foot hard down on the accelerator—daring a little by going nine miles over the speed limit because of her desperate need to get home.

GARDENING IN A TIME OF DROUGHT

A GARDENING ESSAY

People in half of the contiguous states of the United States are living in drought conditions, with farmers and ranchers suffering and fires raging in the dry American forests, affecting tourism in some parts of the country. Nurserymen, with a multibillion-dollar industry at stake, worry about the drying up of that constant flow of customers normally eager to buy flowers and trees. Some sages tell us that this isn't the first nor will it be the last drought. But living in a time when months may go by without rain or snow causes us home gardeners to rethink our reasons for gardening in the first place.

Some people garden to raise food. Many others do it for the sheer pleasure of it. As America's favorite hobby, and a huge and growing industry, it has become a major wellspring of creativity. Where else can we have this much fun, getting our hands dirty, moving and planting things, then watching them grow and flourish? The garden is a place where we are king. We do what we want—plant, prune, transplant, divide—in other words, tinker around and play God. There is Nature, with all its power, and here are we, with our trowels and shovels, rototillers, bags of soil, seed packets, plant divisions, and promising nursery plants in square black plastic pots. We tweak Nature, shape it, often cooperate with it—and sometimes collide with it. And what is it that we want to achieve?

The goal of gardening. Gardeners look for beauty, symmetry, originality, productivity. We may have any of these goals, or all of them, or perhaps only a simple desire to engage in plant science. For when we root slips, grow seeds, divide roots, hybridize iris, or even do so simple a thing as to shove an African violet leaf into the soil of a windowsill pot, we're indulging in plant science—and rewarding work it is. Philosophers and kings, fools and knaves all are inspired by cultivating flowers, trees, and vegetables, and express it in different ways.

The mighty Colorado and the mighty Euphrates. But as we garden, there are harsh realities to deal with—not only the drought, but world population growth, erratic weather patterns such as El Niño, and the melting of the glacial ice caps. These forces eventually will affect all of us, in ways we don't yet fully understand. But one problem is clear: there is a serious worldwide shortage of pure water. Not only are rainfall supplies precarious, but underground aquifers are being drained and mighty rivers are overcommitted—from the mighty Colorado to the mighty Euphrates. Water supplies cause clashes between nations, between the states of the United States, and between neighbors, some of whose wells are running dry. These water fights are an echo of the water wars in the West in the late 1800s, now occurring on a global scale. Governments are threatened with populist protests against private firms that have bought water rights and jacked up the price of water for poor, indigenous farmers. In an attempt to solve some of these problems, a 1996 United Nations conference was called on water use, but it yielded little cooperation among countries vying for the same water source.

Water-supply problems affect human beings, some more than others. Consider an individual farmer in Bangladesh who struggles to obtain enough potable water to stay alive and sustain a tiny vegetable plot for his family. Meanwhile, in the United States, home construction goes on unabated, putting more and more strain on a finite water supply. Then comes an almost nationwide drought, to give people a taste of the Dust Bowl days of the 1930s. Some concerns—"Can I continue to grow my bluegrass lawn?"—or "Will there be enough water to make man-made snow for skiing?"—seem trivial in comparison to the plight of that Bangladesh farmer. But lots of people don't consider bluegrass lawns mundane, since they are part of America's historical past.

A new way of looking at things. If American gardeners are to deal with water shortages, it will take a new conservation mentality. For instance, people squander more water on lawns than any other part of their yard. Some would no sooner get rid of their bluegrass than they would their children. For those who want to maintain at least a minimum amount of traditional lawn, a new irrigation system may be the answer. One particular system can cut water use by a dramatic twenty percent yet produces grass that is healthier than when it is watered and fertilized the old-fashioned way, with two or three fertilizer doses applied during the season. This relatively new invention attaches to the sprinkler system and automatically fertilizes the lawn as it waters it. A microprocessor determines the amount of fertilizer to inject. Research has shown that a steady, low-level supply of fertilizer is more beneficial to lawns than the sudden jolts administered by periodic applications. This system is made by companies such as FertiGator in Parker, Colorado, and Bio-Green in Santa Fe, New Mexico, and can be installed at a residential site for $350 to $400.

Another approach has been taken by those who relinquish traditional lawns altogether and substitute native plants and grasses; they report that water use drops by half or less. New turfs are the subject of great interest. Among the suggested alternatives to bluegrass are the prolific white yarrow in the West and the Boston ivy in the East; both can be successfully mowed. Drought-resistant blue grama and buffalo grass are already known as dependable substitutes for traditional turf.

It only makes sense to transform some of your property with hard materials such as flagstone, pavers, gravel, or decking to reduce water needs. Introduce shade by planting drought-resistant trees, and erect pergolas and arbors on which quick-growing vines can be grown for shade.

Going small. Does drought mean we can no longer grow exotic plants? One compromise is to use native plants and hard materials in the major part of the landscape while creating a small garden with special-needs plants near the house. Bring it in close, very close—so that leftover water from inside the home can be supplemented to keep these thirstier specimens alive. This is sometimes called an "oasis" garden. But your oasis garden becomes even more practical if you move it onto your porch or patio. Give it a tropical air by including a banana tree, ginger plants, and a tiny pool with lotuses and water lilies. Combined with a few big pots of annuals or houseplants, these features make a splendid setting for outdoor summer living.

Pots are a way to bring color to our little oasis gardens without using lots of water. To increase water retention in flower containers, mix polymers in the potting soil—but only according to directions. Further reduce the need to water by placing adequate saucers under the pots.

No more delay in putting in those emitters. The laggard gardener who has delayed putting in basic irrigation systems must now say to her or himself, *This is the moment.* Soaker hoses make it easy to maintain vegetable beds. Hoses with emitters encircling trees and shrubs will help keep them alive with minimum watering. Root feeders should be used to water trees deeply.

Some canny gardeners are discovering that they can create a variety of microclimates in their backyard, making protected places for tender plants to grow. One method is to change the elevation of the land, for it is a basic truth that hills dry out faster, whereas swales, or little valleys, stay damper. Get a bulldozer in and change the topography of a flat landscape, then place more delicate plants, including vegetables, in the lowlands. Rocks are another means of altering climate. Those experienced with rock gardens know how useful they are in creating small, protected areas for growing plants.

Homesteaders and farmers have done it for centuries—planted hardy rows of trees on the north side of the property. It is a historic way to diffuse the harsh and drying winds of winter. We should never leave our soil showing: if we haven't managed to cover the ground with sturdy plants, groundcovers, or hard materials, then we should sheath the ground with bark mulch or other organic materials to protect it against the sun and wind.

Looking for sturdy survivors in times of drought. It goes without saying that we should obey Mother Nature and plant mostly things that like to grow in our own neighborhoods—regional things, not exotics. "Exotic" means "foreign," and foreign plants won't thrive without those extra touches—profuse water and sometimes fertilizer—that are unneeded and in fact not wanted or desired by our native varieties.

Garden experts are selecting different sorts of plants to write about these days, plants not much in vogue some years ago. They are favorites now that drought is upon us. There are whole lists of xeriscape plants and trees. Two plants recently singled out are grayish varieties, mullein, and eryngium. Both are versatile and look elegant in a formal garden, but jaunty and free-spirited when placed in a wild, or prairie, garden setting.

Mulleins: "not altogether entirely weeds." Lots of people think of mulleins as weeds that pop up and need to be pulled. As the late, great garden writer Henry Mitchell said, "Mulleins are among those glorious plants that are almost but not altogether entirely weeds." Most are biennials, and emerge the first year as a charming clump of fuzzy, oval leaves. The next year they soar into the sky and sprout a column of bright yellow flowers. They're from the genus *Verbascum,* which has 300 species. Some are rose and peach, and smaller than the five-foot or more stature of other varieties, and some attain an unusual "candelabra" silhouette.

Eryngium has spiky gray-green foliage and great clusters of creamy white globular flowers that are long-lasting. This is a changeling-type plant, one that takes on the atmosphere of the garden in which it is placed. Its remarkable grayness cries out for combination with bright colors. One that's a perfect companion is the magenta-colored liatris, another sturdy plant that will survive in days of severe drought.

And when potting up containers for a close-in garden on the patio, consider including two sturdy trailing plants with great character—*Helichrysum petiolare,* or licorice plant, and *Leguminosae berthelotii,* or lotus vine. While other annuals are becoming brown and leggy, these plants only get better as the dry summer progresses. The licorice plant, which comes also in a bigger-leaved variety, "petiolatum," has distinct, rounded, gray leaves on handsomely curved branches. The lotus vine creates a mass of hanging branches with very fine gray leaves and has deep red clawlike flowers that continue all through the growing season. These two, plus the popular sweet-potato vine, can be the backbone for splendid container gardens. Looking at them, no one will ever guess there's a drought. Like xeriscape plants and trees, they can be grown and enjoyed without a guilty conscience.